"Merle Good's literary chops keep getting better and better.

"Riveting. Christine is a college senior, low on self-esteem and vague about her future and romance, as she tries to untangle her challenging past and her overlapping uncertainties.

"Can Christine seize new possibilities of love and meaning? Will purpose emerge in an unconventional musical career, or in taking a stand against a zoning land grab?

"A gripping tapestry of love, roots, and the complexities of family. Brimming with insight, compassion, and an elastic bandwidth that reaches both back into the past and beyond to the future. A lively read with likeable, believable characters.

"I hope they make this story into a movie like they did with Good's first novel."

—WALLY KROEKER, LONGTIME EDITOR (RETIRED),
*THE MARKETPLACE* MAGAZINE

# ADVANCE PRAISE FOR THIS NOVEL

———

"Nursing a crush on a guy she thinks is out of reach, Christine approaches college graduation plagued by questions about what to do with her life. Will she sell herself short? Or will she take the chance to build a life on her own terms?

"Is Christine a talented, fearless writer and performer? Or is she the bottom-rung daughter of a mother crushed by abandonment?

"*Christine's Turn* takes the reader on an endearing journey of self-discovery, demonstrating the power of caring relationships."

—DIANE UMBLE, PROFESSOR OF COMMUNICATION EMERITA, MILLERSVILLE UNIVERSITY

\* \* \*

"A compelling story of longing and belonging.

"As she struggles to define her future, Christine confronts the claims of the past and the expectations of others.

"This engaging novel explores identities both chosen and ascribed. The serenity of the Pennsylvania countryside belies the complicated lives of the characters who populate it."

—STEVEN M. NOLT, AUTHOR AND PROFESSOR, ELIZABETHTOWN COLLEGE

# CHRISTINE'S TURN

## A NOVEL

## MERLE GOOD

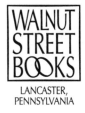

WALNUT STREET BOOKS

LANCASTER,
PENNSYLVANIA

walnutstreetbooks.com

Cover and page design by Cliff Snyder
Cover photograph by Merle Good

Paperback: 9781947597488
PDF, EPUB, and Kindle: 9781947597495

Library of Congress Control Number: Data available.

*Christine's Turn* is published by
Walnut Street Books, Lancaster, Pennsylvania

info@walnutstreetbooks.com

*For Phyllis*

———

# AUTUMN

# One

———

**She should have brought** a sweater. The warmth of the early September day had lured her into forgetting how cool things could be by twilight, walking home from Arlene's place, goosebumps as she passed the banged-up mailbox at the end of the Johnsons' long tree-lined lane, still humming that last haunting madrigal tune.

Her freckles were barely visible in the evening's lingering light. Not that they dominated her face. More like a light cinnamon shaker had sprinkled them there. Sometimes they ruined everything in spite of her decent-looking nose, and other times they perhaps added a touch of attractiveness.

Christine barely heard his car coming, there in his sporty convertible suddenly, window rolled down as he coasted along beside her in the chilly September twilight.

"Taxi?"

"It's not far. I can walk it."

"You're refusing my offer?" Maybe it was his voice that tantalized her, deep and almost songful. "You're a stubborn one, Christine, aren't you? Grandma always said as much." Thomas laughed, a tease stirred into the warmth.

Caught between worry and faint flattery, she paused in her walking. "Is Harriet unhappy with me?" Her tone a bit sharper than she intended.

He laughed again. "Grandma? She loves you, Christine, you must know that. Always talking about you when I'm around, Christine this, Christine that. But stubborn, you gotta admit."

She had heard that Thomas had moved here to teach music at Midstate, but she hadn't seen him until this evening when he led the practice for their little diehard madrigal group. As a favor to Arlene. His upper-class manners and understated elegant style had always stopped her heart. She felt clumsy all of a sudden, her pulse racing. It made her mad but she couldn't help it. Thomas always a throb too far, ever since she made him that sappy valentine when she was eight years old, hoping to hand it to him when he visited his grandparents. But she'd lost her nerve, that sadly sweet message still lying at the bottom of her old jewelry box.

What would it be like to ride with him? She wondered how many Cinderellas had been there beside him through the years. But he's inviting me now, stupid, so why am I holding back? What am I afraid of?

"Come on, Christine, jump in."

Maybe they would overcome gravity, a little girl wish, flying off to where the sun was still shining, where class distinctions didn't matter, peering down on the braids of crops woven and stitched like a natural quilt beneath them, the fields pregnant with unharvested bounty. Would he take her hand, steadying her as they took in the wonder of this native land spread below? *If you'd just see, the true real me, before I blink, before we sink....*

He raced his engine slightly, letting her know her opportunity was about to end. She'd watched him since childhood when he came to visit his grandparents in the big house up the hill, always congenial, three years older, so pleasant with those great eyes his grandmother had given him, such arresting hypnotism that she could barely look away. She knew she should quit this damn infatuation with someone who was clearly out of reach. You're a college senior now, not a high school sophomore with a crush, for God's sake.

"Okay," she said.

And just like that they were up the hill and in front of the little tenant house where she and her mother lived. He pulled off the road, the engine idling.

"I thought our group sounded pretty good tonight," Christine offered. "We really appreciate your taking time out of your busy schedule." Don't give him too much credit.

"I forgot you were part of this group. You've always liked music, haven't you?"

"Your grandpa Ethan got me hooked on madrigals one summer when I was finishing junior high."

"Me, too. I remember several times when I was visiting here — I must have been about 13 — and Grandpa kidnapped me from my video games, put music in my hands, and parked me beside John Jr. I'd always act a little disinterested, but I honestly loved it. Something strangely harmonious about the whole affair. I think that's when I first began to think about music in a serious way."

She remembered now a snowy night long ago, probably right after New Year's, when Arlene insisted they practice in spite of the icy roads. Christine had gone as usual with Harriet and Ethan that night, young Thomas there on the back seat when she crawled in. How awkward. Hard to believe that so much acne could produce the attractive skin she was looking at tonight.

"I don't know a lot of people around here," he said, cutting the engine. "And I don't want to obligate you in any way, but I'd love to go driving sometime. The weather's so great and I've always loved this countryside."

"Oh, sure." Had she really agreed? What was he actually asking her? She saw the silhouette of the big house on the hill, the homeplace of the Turner clan, so close to the old servant quarters where she and her mother lived. So close but miles away.

"Not this weekend though. My girlfriend's coming from Princeton. But maybe next week sometime?"

She should have known better. A guy like Thomas wouldn't be asking someone like her to go out, falling now from those clouds where the sun had disappeared, crashing back to shapeless, heartless earth.

"Her name's Antonia Waldorf. You'll like her."

She couldn't tell if her mother was home from work yet. But if she was, she was definitely planted behind the curtain of that tiny kitchen window of their little house, a pained half-smile on her face. "You only have yourself to blame, chickadee. Will you never learn?"

# Two

———

**Even though she loved** history, she wished some profs had crossed over and become part of the boring past they droned on about. Mr. Shriver looked miserable, sounded distracted, and monotoned about the subject at hand like a dreary funeral director. Christine tried several times to find alternatives but, being a senior and needing certain credits, she coaxed herself into believing she'd find an upside in this truly awful class. No luck so far with that.

Why was she majoring in history, anyhow? A totally unmarketable skill. "Liking it doesn't pay the bills." And going to grad school, if she could get in, would just add more debt and no promise of a job. *Don't worry, girl, about employment, if you can roll with life's enjoyment....*

Why hadn't she majored in music when it always captured her, and she loved being in the little band? Even so, she doubted any future livelihood from music. Deep down, she worried that someone like her would never be a professional anything. She was still surprised she had gotten into college.

Zach and Adam were waiting for her after class, gathering around her as a threesome familiar with each other's presence. "Guys," Adam started, "Skip needs to know."

"Know what?"

"Unless we promise him we'll have at least one new number next Saturday night at the Root Cellar, he's putting that new group on instead of us."

Christine was surprised. "What new group?"

Zach snorted. "You mean those first-year students who call themselves 'The Rejects'?"

"The Scraps." Adam was shorter than Zach but his stocky frame made him seem more substantial. Zach slipped his arm around her playfully now, launching her into a deliberate trot as they headed up past the huge pumpkins someone had positioned on the steps of the Student Center, Adam trying to keep up.

Christine pulled away and faced the two of them. "Are we in trouble with Skip?" She knew her question wasn't a simple one. Skip was the middle-aged owner of The Root Cellar, the most prestigious venue near the campus, a good operator, largely harmless, but occasionally feeling entitled to a little free merchandise. He had always flirted with Christine, though she never gave him an inch. Didn't mean he didn't try. One time backstage he'd taken the liberty of brushing up against her for a long time and she'd slapped him, later regretting it when she realized the sting of her hand only stimulated the bastard more.

Zach's tone was forceful now. "Skip's nothing but a pretentious buffoon. But we have your back, Christine, if he tries anything."

"I know that. I can handle Skip."

"The point is — he wants some fresh material," Adam went on. "If we don't offer some new songs, he'll go with someone else. We can't take The Root Cellar for granted any longer. Some of these younger groups are pretty good."

Zach's common sense kicked in. "When can you get your new lyrics finished, Christine?"

"Soon. Maybe by tomorrow."

"Adam, tell Skip we'll have a wonderful new number next Saturday but we won't go on at The Root Cellar for him in the future if he books those damn Scraps instead of us."

Christine flashed her smile. "Playing hard ball, are we?"

"Hell, yes. Don't mess with The Forerunners." Zach's spikey blond hair bouncing.

Adam wasn't convinced. "We better have some-thing good."

She noticed Zach waving. Turning, she saw Thomas on the other side of the fountain, waving back. "I like Turner," Zach said. "His class rocks."

Christine looked away, wondering when the Princeton princess was arriving in the area. Don't think about it. Don't even glance at him again. The Turners are a different class, a caste out of reach.

"We need to practice soon," Adam was saying. "Otherwise the Scraps could replace us."

She liked that Adam was all business when it came to the band. The three of them had gone to high school together, starting to perform in tenth grade, then con-tinuing when they all decided to go to the local state college since none of them could afford private school.

Adam was already heading for the bus stop to catch the ride to his job at the hardware store. "Wait for me," she called, running after him. She'd grab the bus home and work on her lyrics, remembering that her mother was working day shift at the diner this week. Peace and quiet. And Thomas far away.

# Three

———

**Standing in Harriet's garden,** fading vegetation all around, she raised her arms to the pristine morning air for a fresh cleanse.

"Aren't you the early bird, Christine!" It was Harriet, coming across the lawn with a cup of coffee in her hand, Brownie on her heels, sniffing, sniffing, watching every moving thing.

"Good morning, Harriet. I was just checking for any late tomatoes." Was it sentimental to think that Harriet's 80-year-old face grew more attractive every year? More lines, sure, but still pretty with her perfect nose. And those stunning eyes.

"Are you remembering our quilting group this morning?"

Had she dropped the ball? "I'm sorry, Harriet, did you need my help to set up?"

"No, no, we're fine. Ethan's helping."

"Sorry."

"There's nothing to be sorry about. I only mention it because you had promised to join us this time."

"Oh, no, I can't quilt."

"That's why you're joining us, Christine. To learn. I'm ashamed I never insisted on teaching you before."

Christine loved this woman. Always had. Even as a child, she had come up the hill and worked with Harriet in her garden, pulling weeds, picking peas, silking corn. And then when Harriet insisted on paying her, it became her main way to earn for college, a state school, of course, toiling in Harriet's and Ethan's huge garden, spring to autumn, year after year. *We cannot see the seeds that die, but celebrate what grows so high.* Rhymes were always popping into Christine's brain, always had, even when she was in second grade and Mrs. Wilcox had told her she'd be a poet someday. Lyrics mainly now, for the band.

"We start at nine. You better soon come on in and clean up."

It made her tense. "I'll embarrass you."

"Nonsense. I'm not giving up this time, Christine. A beautiful young woman with your artistic gifts and love of history should know how to quilt. When you get the hang of it, you'll never quit. Besides, it's one of the few truly communal things we still have in this age of endless gadgets."

Christine stood up, a tomato in each dirty hand. "Okay, you win. I'll give it a try."

Harriet let out that irrepressible laugh of hers, and Christine joined in. This was as close to being at home as she ever got.

A door slammed up on the big porch. Must be Betsy, Harriet's bossy daughter-in-law. "Harriet!" Betsy's voice a mix of snarl and condescension. She always refused to call Harriet "Mother," as she knew Harriet would prefer. Always the first name, in a tone like some irritated supervisor.

"Yes, Betsy." Amazing how patient Harriet was with that bitch.

"Tell your quilters to keep their vehicles off my lawn. Last time two of them were on my grass."

Christine could hear the pained sigh escaping Harriet's lips. "Thank you, Betsy. I'll remind them."

"You better!" And the door slammed again.

"They're not allowed to park in the driveway or near the barn," Harriet explained in a low mutter. "They might get in the way of one of Betsy's cars or block one of the tractors or something. Where are my guests supposed to park? Apparently, in an attempt to get off the road so they wouldn't be hit, one or two ended up with a few tires on Betsy's precious lawn."

"But it's your lawn, too."

"Technically, yes. But that's not a distinction Betsy can grasp."

"I'm sorry for you."

"No need." Harriet wanted to change the subject. "I'll be expecting you."

"But you must understand, it's like me persuading you to join our band."

"When can I start?" Harriet deadpanned without a beat. Another hearty laugh.

The big Turner farmhouse had long ago given birth to a small but classic addition, built for Ethan's parents years ago when they retired from farming. A generation later, it became Harriet's home with Ethan when they abandoned the big house in favor of their son Bruce and his brusque Betsy.

Ethan appeared on their small porch. "Harriet," he called. "Georgette is here."

"I'm coming." Harriet turned to go.

"Good morning, Christine."

"Morning, Ethan. You're lookin' tall in the saddle today." It was a saying he often used.

"Backatcha!"

"And don't be nervous," Harriet was saying. "They're a wonderful bunch of women."

"I know, I like them. I've just never tried to stick a needle through my finger in front of such a large crowd before."

But Harriet was halfway to the porch already, striding with a purposefulness that had served her well when she was president of the state Farm Women's Association. Ethan watching with a boyish grin, still in love. And Brownie sniffing everything.

Minutes later Christine was sitting at the frame herself, right next to Harriet.

"But when did Clyde go to the hospital?" Georgette was asking Alice.

"Tuesday. They still don't know what ails him. I just had to come here today to give my mind a break."

"I'm glad you did, Alice," Harriet said.

Margaret started to hum a mellow, supportive tune as others joined, a quiet, communal, prayer-like harmony, drifting through the open window to the fields and skies beyond. "It'll be okay, Alice," Harriet said softly as the music swelled and drifted into silence. "I'm sure of it."

"Thank you, Harriet dear," Alice whispered in a choked-up reply.

"Not to interrupt, but there's coffee and lemonade here," Wanda was saying. "And some of Shellie's incredible cookies." Christine knew Wanda had quilted with the others years ago until Georgette suggested one day that it may not be her natural gift, and Wanda had never again placed another stitch in fabric, so hurt and angry that she threatened to have her Samuel dump a load of fresh cow manure on Georgette's front lawn. It was a tense few months. Harriet had finally broken the ice, managing to get Georgette to apologize for being too honest about something on which the quilters all agreed and helping Wanda to see that quilting may not be her only skill, etc., etc., until Wanda accepted the whole group's invitation to supervise all snacks and beverages going forward. And truth be told, Wanda had a skill at that and felt challenged to perfect her gift, adding a summer picnic and a winter dinner to their annual schedule with such a flair that she was now more important to the group than any of the quilters themselves, except Harriet, of course.

"How are you, Christine?" Barbara asked. She was always showing interest in others and never failed to walk to the garden's edge to say hello when Christine was out there working.

"I'm good. And you?"

"Oh, me, always the same old, you know. Am I remembering that you might be a senior this year at Midstate?"

"Of course, she is," Georgette jumped in. "A history major, even though she plays in that band."

"I know that," Barbara retorted. "I just wanted to hear her talk about it."

"Sorry."

These women knew that Harriet treated her like a daughter, and they always acted as though Christine was one of the family. "Oh, you know, senior year and all," she said. "Lots of good, fun things. But other requirements that I kept putting off are now sorta pinching me, needing to be completed so I can, as they say, 'matriculate.'"

"Oh yes, 'matriculate,'" Barbara said. "There's a word I don't worry about anymore!" Harriet chuckled.

"Is divorce a part of matriculation?" Suzette inquired with a sneaky smile. They all laughed. Suzette had left two husbands behind.

Needles flying the whole time, up and down through the fabric layers and the batting, up and down, down and up, like stitching a sandwich of fine fabric.

Christine could hear the question Barbara wasn't asking, "What are you going to do with your life?" So many people seemed to have high expectations for her. Though she was still amazed to hear herself say out loud that she expected to graduate from college. *Let's get this straight, you're not that great to contemplate that you could rate to graduate — you're nothing, mate.*

Suddenly she noticed Thomas standing in the doorway, hands full of folders and music books, backpack slung over his shoulder. "I'm sorry, Grandma, I forgot about your quilting group."

"Come in, come in," Harriet waved. "Everybody, this is my grandson Thomas who just moved here to teach music at Midstate," her voice full of pride and affection. "We're delighted that he's staying with us." Thomas made his way gingerly around the circle, trying not to trip on anything as he politely smiled at them.

"Hi Thomas," the women all said in their best group voice. It caught Christine by surprise. Why were these older women looking at Thomas with such open admiration? Sure, he was handsome, but really — shouldn't they all have outgrown flirting by now?

Thomas touched her lightly on the shoulder as he went by, but she didn't look up, continuing to stare at her reluctant stitches in the fabric which she now realized were so big that she'd likely be ushered into Wanda's doom. She hoped Thomas didn't notice, assuming he knew about such things. Besides, Harriet would likely rip out her stitches later after everyone was long gone and redo them much more tightly, never telling her.

Only after Thomas opened the door to go upstairs did she look up to find him watching her.

# Four

————

**She came upon her** mother staring at the wall of the kitchen the way she did sometimes, her restaurant uniform still on, her hair in a tussle.

"What is it, Mama?" she asked. "Something more than the allergies?" But she knew before her mother turned her tearful face toward the window that it was more of the same. Just more of the same. Was there no damn way to shake it off? She rebuked herself as she had nine hundred times before. She's my mother, for heaven's sake, stop resenting her all day long. Be positive. Better times will come.

"I'm tired is all, honey."

"Did something go wrong at the diner?"

Another round of silent tears. "Christine, you're such a bright one, but you never remember, do you?"

"Oh, God, I'm sorry, Mama. It's your wedding day."

"My almost-wedding day. Twenty-two years today."

She could live another fifty years and never fully understand it. Yes, it was heartbreaking, she was sure. But to let that moment of being deserted a week before the altar overcloud and poison all the years that Christine had been alive — how could her mother do that? *Why am I not good enough to make her want to live and be happy?*

Was handsome Lenny of the famous Bryer clan really worth all of Mama's secret grief and fretting? A coward, having knocked up her mother before that fucking day of desertion. Family pressure, the story went. Probably so. But her mother blamed herself for having believed she could marry into such an eminent family.

"Totally my stupidity," she said aloud now, as though reading her daughter's mind. "I was young and infatuated. Too big for my boots."

As her mother paused to swat away her tears, Christine knew what was coming next as surely as the liturgy at St. Mark's. Always the same words, the same warning, nagging at her since her breasts had started to take shape, her mother seeming to think attractive womanliness in her daughter a curse. "Remember who you are, chickadee, keep your eyes on the ground, not in the clouds."

But Christine had long ago sworn she would not genuflect to this heresy babbled by her weepy mother. If Karen Ober refused to close the door on that traitor Lenny Bryer, she would.

On her sixteenth birthday she had marched into her mother's bedroom, torn open the bottom drawer, yanked out that old faded high school graduation photo of the man who had held Karen Ober hostage all these years, and put it where her mother would never find it.

But it had made no difference. That goddamn jerk Lenny still had her mother by the throat.

# Five

———

"**You fail to understand** the post-modern woman," Dr. Hutchinson-O'Flannery told her after class. "I can't accept your project and let you continue your provincial pursuits."

Christine was determined to stay calm. The woman was not only a card-carrying bitch, but one of those liberals who used "tolerant" language to disguise her own narrow-minded views. "I don't understand what's wrong with the subject."

Hutchinson-O'Flannery looked impatiently at her watch. "I really have to go."

"I'm curious—" Christine began. She had never had a professor treat her like shit before. What the hell was wrong with this woman?

"Yes?"

Christine stared directly at the teacher, waiting until she looked up from her papers. She's going to look me in the eye through those properly feminist glasses of hers, even if it means I get the first damn failing grade I've ever had.

Finally the pudgy prof laid down her papers impatiently and looked up. Christine paused a second longer, daring "Hutchery," as the students called her, to disrespect her again. "Do you see me as a woman?" Christine asked in a firm, take-no-prisoners voice.

Hutchinson-O'Flannery actually emitted an abbreviated sputter. "A woman?"

"Yes, our course is about the history and identity of women, right?"

Hutchery grunted with a touch of disgust. "Is this a come-on?"

"Pardon?"

"If you think flirting with me will improve your grade, it won't work. That's been tried a thousand times."

Christine almost laughed aloud at the ridiculous image, a long line of blonds and brunettes stringing out the door, stretching on around the quad, each eager for a moment to seduce the unattractive Hutchery. Weird.

"What I'm asking is — are all women equal, in your view?"

"I don't have time for this."

"I think you do. Do you give failing grades to those women who disagree with you?" Christine knew she was in danger.

"Ms. Ober, women professors deserve the same respect as male ones do."

"I agree. What about female students?"

"I don't understand the question."

"I'll ask it again. Do you give failing grades to those female students who disagree with your point of view?"

"Okay, we're done, Ober. If you can't grasp the concepts and do the work, you can't get the grades. It's that simple."

"In other words, I should rewrite my paper to make it sound as though you had written it?"

"Absolutely not!" her teacher exploded. "Your work needs to be your own original work. But it can't be stuck in the damn Middle Ages and expect a passing grade."

Christine was able to make herself suddenly very calm. "Thank you for your time," she said. "Let me give it another try." Hutchery looked puzzled, Christine's response unexpected. And before the professor could muster another demeaning comment, Christine was out the door. Furious but calm.

Am I like that, she wondered as she headed for the library. Am I so hellbent on my narrow agenda that I bully those who disagree with me? Would I use the threat of bad grades to get a student to ape my opinion? *Shut up, grow up, be more like me, because I'm open-minded, babe, and not a stupid narrow thug like you, be more like me, although I sorta hate myself, you see ....*

She was still furious when she bumped into Adam on the way to the library. "Not sure what the hell happened to you, Christine, but you look—I don't know—damn pissed," he said.

Christine thought she had masked her fury. Angry words had always been her weakness. A nagging warning light was blinking inside her brain. Go easy now. You don't need to upset Adam, spouting off when you're upset.

"Didn't know it showed," she murmured.

"You can't hide from me," Adam replied, slipped his arm around her protectively. "You can tell me about it, you know."

She gave him a peck on his cheek and pulled away. "Maybe another time." Starting toward the library again, she turned and called back to Adam. "Thanks, man." He simply waved, watching her go. A minute later, coming around the fountain, Christine was startled to see Uncle Jimmy standing in front of her. At least it looked like Jimmy. It had been a while.

"Hello, Christine."

"Uncle Jimmy?"

"Sorry to surprise you." He was wearing clean bib overalls over a plaid shirt. His mustache was new.

"What brings you to campus?"

"Don't worry. I'm not trying to go to college!" he said, laughing with that sucking sound he'd always had, his teeth worse than she remembered.

"You'd make a good student, Uncle Jimmy. Really."

"Thanks, Christine. You've always been kind to me. But we both know better."

They turned and walked a few steps. "What's up?" she asked.

"I know your mother doesn't want me to be talking with you. So I couldn't call the house — in case she answered."

"Where are you staying these days?" She remembered hearing that Jimmy had been back in prison and didn't know he was out until this moment.

"I'm crashing over near Quarry Corners," he said. "Working part-time at the poultry plant."

Christine wasn't sure what to say. "I want to talk, but today's not good. Late for a meeting."

"I apologize. I knew it was a risk." He started to walk away.

Christine reached out and grabbed his elbow. "Is tomorrow afternoon a possibility? We could meet at the café in the Student Center over there. My treat."

A sorrowful cast swept across Uncle Jimmy's face. "All I want is to talk with you once in a while, unless that upsets you or your mother."

He was such a sincere guy, really. But why was he always in trouble? "Shall we say tomorrow at the same time?"

"I'll be here. Thank you so much."

And as suddenly as he had appeared, Uncle Jimmy was gone.

# Six

———

The whole community was consumed by the spectacular fire at the old Wissler place, the massive conflagration lighting up the night sky for miles around, destroying the historic barn and sheds. Without help from eight different fire companies laying hose for a quarter of a mile from that huge pond on the neighboring Ritchey farm, the beautiful Wissler house would have been gone by morning, too.

Christine was tempted to call Zach or Adam and see if they wanted to drive out to the site to survey the damage, but she knew they'd likely ask if she had finished her lyrics yet. For a moment, she fantasized about calling Thomas to see if he wanted to go, but she knew she had to harness that new song. So she knuckled down and, in a spurt of inspiration, finished it in less than an hour, aided in no small part by thinking of Thomas.

She was just emailing the new lyrics to Zach when Harriet called to ask if she could possibly come up and do a weeding in the garden before the end of the afternoon. Apparently Thomas had invited his girlfriend for a visit, Harriet said. Christine acted as though it was news to her. Harriet then went on at length about the tragedy at the Wissler estate. "I just hope it wasn't foul play," she said.

Sometimes on a clear day in Harriet's garden, Christine could see the whole way to the river, even the outline of Turners Rise. The first Europeans to the region had initially settled there, she knew, centuries ago, living side by side with the Lenapes whose numerous longhouses had dominated the slope below Turners Rise, then known as the Mount of the Great Spirit.

Ethan came walking across the lawn, a promising piece of wood in his hand, the color in his face encouraging in spite of the tentativeness of his gait. "Nice of you to come on short notice." Brownie sniffing her legs now.

"No problem."

He watched her as she spruced up the edges, first with her fingers, then with her hoe. "Apparently Thomas wants to impress this woman," he offered with a chuckle.

"Anything to please."

"Terrible thing about that Wissler fire last night," he added. "They say it was so massive and so hot that it singed the hair on the arms of some of the firemen. What a loss."

"It sounds heartbreaking."

"You included their barn in that project you did in high school, didn't you? Was it called 'Forebays and Gables'?"

"You have a good memory, Ethan."

"You did a really good job, I remember that."

"Thanks." She hoed around the end of the row. Ethan was the closest thing to a father she had ever known. "Harriet said something about foul play, is that right?"

Ethan took a long pause. "I certainly hope not. That's a wretched thing when someone starts lighting barns." He paused, lost in a reverie.

"You've certainly observed a lot of this sort of thing, Ethan. Why would someone light a barn on fire?"

Ethan just looked at her steadily for a moment, almost as though he hadn't heard her. She waited. "I remember when I was a boy that an ex-con named Butterwood was arrested for lighting four different barns. They said he did it just to watch them burn. A sort of sickness, I guess."

"That's scary."

Ethan nodded solemnly. "Other times I think it's been a prank that's gotten out of hand. Plain stupidity."

She wondered how much sleep Ethan had lost over the years, worried that their beautiful historic barn might end up in flames. But he gave no indication. Then his hand came up to his face, his voice lowered. "I think that more than not, unfortunately, it's about revenge."

"Revenge?"

"Yeah, you know, jealousy or a grudge. Getting even."

"You think the Wissler fire was that?"

"Who knows? I'm sure the police are checking it out." He rubbed his face again. "Well, I better get to work." He turned to go, then looked back at her, changing the subject. "What are we going to do without you next year, Weeny Christeeny?" he asked, using the name he had sometimes called her for as long as she could remember. "You'll graduate and get a job on the other end of the country and we'll never see you again. You're going to break my heart, aren't you?" His voice filled with the cloudy affection that never failed to pain and thrill her simultaneously.

"Oh, no, not going to happen. I'd turn down an offer if I knew it meant I couldn't still see you and Harriet regularly." She wondered what sort of job he thought she could get.

"Glad to hear it." He sneezed. "Well, I'll leave you to your work. Heading down to my shop for a while."

"What are you going to create this time?" she asked, pointing at the piece of wood in his hand.

He laughed. "You know I never tell," he said, taking a few more steps toward the house as she hoed around the radish plants. Then he stopped again and turned. "Christine," he said, all serious now. "You won't go off and get married without talking it over with your Ethan, will you?"

She wondered if he could see that her eyes were misting up. This man had always believed in her, always protected her, so unlike her mother who wanted her to lower her hopes and horizons.

"I promise you will be the first person I check with."

He nodded. "I'll hold you to it."

"Don't worry, Ethan. It ain't gonna happen," she added, lightly brushing off an emotional moment.

"I agree there aren't many men good enough. But I pray there's a special one for you, Christine, so you may be as fortunate as I've been."

And with that benediction he was off to his precious shop to find just the right knife to tame and carve that block of wood. She'd always loved to watch him work. "Negative creativity," he called it. Whereas most creative processes birthed something new and original by adding words or notes or paint strokes,

Ethan's hands created something novel and interesting by cutting away, by subtracting.

The morning passed. She heard the whistle at the factory in the distance, signaling the middle of the day. She'd need to hurry more if she hoped to finish the garden before the late-afternoon arrival of Princess Antonia.

She heard loud voices over at the big house and looked up to see Betsy's teenage Travis chasing his younger brother Leopold around the corner, catching him halfway across the lawn and throwing him roughly to the ground. "I never told anyone," Leopold was pleading as Travis held him down and pummeled him with his fists.

Betsy was not far behind. "Boys," she bellowed. "Get back in the house this minute." They ignored her as they continued to tangle and roll across the lawn. She strode toward them, her fists coiled for emphasis. "Unless you two listen to me right now, you're not going along to the State Fairgrounds events next week." Betsy glanced toward Harriet's porch to make sure she wasn't being overheard. She pulled the boys up by their collars and marched them toward the house. "Now get changed. We want to leave in five minutes." Leopold followed Travis across the porch. "I never told anyone," Leopold was insisting as they disappeared into the big house.

Christine bent as far down into the garden as she could, but out of the corner of her eye she could see Betsy striding toward her across the lawn. "I shouldn't have to tell you, Christine, to mind your own business," Betsy snapped.

"Didn't know I wasn't."

"We really won't be needing you to hang out here in the garden anymore," Betsy added pointedly.

Christine stood up tall now. "I work for Harriet, not for you."

"It's my land and I'm saying you're fired."

Christine could feel her face getting red. "You have no say over me, Betsy," she said, her voice rising. "I've worked for Harriet since before you ever married into the Turner clan."

"I said you're fired."

Christine knew she might regret it later but she couldn't stop herself. "Oh, shut up, Betsy. No one's impressed, especially not Harriet or Ethan!"

"We'll see about that," Betsy sputtered, marching back to her porch, slamming the door as she went in.

*Betsy can't really fire me, can she?* It took a half hour of rapid weeding and hoeing for Christine to begin to cool down. She hoped Ethan and Harriet didn't hear the exchange.

Betsy was Bruce's second wife, and Christine knew she had never gained the full respect and affection of the Turner clan. They had loved Nancy so much, a perfect wife for Bruce, until a rare heart condition took her from him and their two little sons, Bruce a broken man for several years until he somehow found Betsy's assertiveness comforting.

The sun was warmer now and she rolled up her sleeves, wiping her sweat with the old farmer's kerchief she'd used for years. Another hour passed. Her eyes fixed on the shining pathways of the river far away and she wished she could be there on that ridge above the mighty waters, safe from her struggles and failings.

Her dustup with Betsy forced her to think about questions she was trying to avoid these days. Was she just going to end up working in Harriet's garden the rest of her life? Of course not. She knew she would need to get a full-time job before long. So, fired or not, she'd have to face the future. But it still felt arrogant to her to assume that she, the lowly daughter of bottom-rung and troubled Karen Ober, was good enough to take a gigantic step out of her mother's heavy shadow into a professional future.

"Big garden." A female voice.

Startled, she turned to see a lovely young woman at the garden's edge, hands on hips as though familiar with addressing servants, decked out in a young privileged woman's best imitation of country clothes.

"Yes, Harriet always manages a beautiful, bountiful garden."

"You mean Mrs. Turner? Thomas's grandmother?" The visitor's tone had an unmistakable tone of rebuke and disappointment that the help would presume to use first-name familiarity.

It had to be the princess, she realized. She was early. And different than Christine had expected. Thomas liked this package of pretention? Really? Gorgeous, yes, but lacking all of Harriet's grace. Oh, shut up, there you go again, always tearing down blue-blooded women. Remember who you are.

"You must be the girlfriend," she responded lamely, avoiding first names. Here was Antonia, perfect and as spotless as the sunlight itself, and she all sweaty, dirty, tongue-tied, and definitely out of place.

The princess turned and hurried toward the little porch. "Smells funny around here," she muttered, sniffing, leaving Christine behind, wilted and furious in the Turner weeds.

# Seven

———

"**I had no idea it** was such a big deal," her new friend
Emily was saying as they tried to find a better spot
on the sidewalk. A helicopter reverberated overhead
with the TV station's logo on its side.

"Sure, for the local news. Two thousand runners
is pretty huge."

"I've never been to one before," Emily said, slipping
on her stylish sunglasses and flipping her long black
hair.

"Really? You don't have marathons in Philly?"

"I grew up in the suburbs."

"I think someone set that Wissler fire," Christine
overheard the grey-haired man behind them specu-
lating to his friend. "I hear they say it was suspicious."

Just then there was a roar from the spectators up the street and they strained to see what caused the stir.

"Must be the first wave of runners!" a woman behind them yelled. They stretched again and still could see no one. Then in a streak the first sleek athlete came rushing by, so fast, she thought, so muscular and toned as though he'd been bred to inhabit the front of the line. Maybe runners were noble after all, as Zach sometimes fancied himself. Then two more. And suddenly, there was Zach, sweating and smiling, running almost effortlessly, the way he lived, the way he sang.

"My God," she said aloud, "there's Zach."

Before Emily could reply, Christine had dropped to the back edge of the sidewalk, starting to run at full speed to keep Zach in view, running so fast she surprised herself, her hair streaming behind her, Emily clutching to keep up, sweeping around the corner where they could see the finish line. Would Zach win? There were four ahead of him, but amazingly he was flying toward the tape. In the micro-interludes between her steps as she ran, Christine was remembering some of the fun moments she and Zach had had over the years. This might top them all. She could go all fantasy about flying off beyond the horizon, but here was her friend and band bud actually flying. She couldn't believe it.

By the time she and Emily reached him, Zach had flopped onto the embankment beyond the finish line, stretching out on his back, his body gasping for oxygen. "Zach!" she yelled, and he rolled over and waved to her. "Let me give you a big hug."

"I'm sweaty."

"I don't care. That was great. You were freakin' terrific!"

Zach jumped up and swept her into his arms.

She laughed. "Hey, don't break my ribs!" She was all wet as he let her go. He wasn't lying about the sweat.

"Oh, Zach, this is my friend Emily."

"Congratulations, Zach," Emily smiled, extending her hand.

"I think I came in fifth," he said. "That's by far my best. Forty-seventh was my previous best."

"Are your parents here?" Christine asked.

"I think so. Oh, there they are. See them waving?" She followed his gesture and saw them further up the embankment. She waved and they waved back.

Later, as she and Emily walked back toward the Student Center, they paused on a bench to take in the fine day, watching the brilliant sunburnt leaves. "So are you and Zach an item?" Emily asked.

"Zach and me? Oh, no. We're just friends. Have been since high school. We both like history, and we sing in a little band together. The Forerunners."

"You're at The Root Cellar tonight, aren't you? I'm planning to come because kids told me you guys are good."

"I write the lyrics and Zach writes the music. The two of us and Adam have been together for more than five years. But don't expect much. Strictly amateur. We do it for fun."

"If he can sing as well as he can run, I'm in for a treat." Sounded like Emily, as so many before her, was charmed by Zach's charismatic self-confidence.

They fell silent then, the way new friends can, listening to the autumn air shifting the branches, students calling to each other, a young child crying, the helicopter far in the distance. One of those perfect days, she thought, hoping that she and Emily would still be friends at Christmastime.

# Eight

_____

**She knew she always** enjoyed performing more if she got there early. Adam would be there already, fussing over the details, with Zach not expected for another half hour, swearing off early arrivals as a "damper" on his confidence and boisterous freedom. Tonight he could be excused, of course, having run the marathon with such energy and discipline.

She liked to just sit in a corner backstage for ten or fifteen minutes, talking to no one, gathering her inner calm, though here at the Root Cellar she always had to keep her eye out for Skip who, though basically on good behavior, was one of those men who felt his position entitled him to sneak around and take a few liberties on his own turf.

She hoped she and Zach wouldn't stumble too much on their new number, having found so little time to practice, Zach being consumed by the marathon and other stuff.

Both times when she looked up just now, Adam's eyes were on her. And when he quickly looked away, she realized it was more admiration than preparation. She had never had the heart to discourage his infatuation, if that's what it was, Adam being such a solid friend and a totally reliable buddy. She liked him as a friend but had no romantic feelings toward him. She was sure she had astutely avoided anything that might lead him on. Except, of course, that solitary time last year when, during her backstage costume change midpoint in their performance, she changed her bra without pulling the privacy curtain, knowing Adam was watching and treating him to the full show. She even took longer than usual, never meeting his eyes, her bare breasts not even three feet from his hungry face.

Why would I do such a thing, she'd asked herself a dozen times. It was mean. I'm not an exhibitionist like Zach. I like my privacy. Was it a little thank-you for all of Adam's attentiveness? Or was it some warped indulgence on my part to prove that my bare essentials can leave boys as smitten as more aggressive girls' can? No wonder Adam keeps watching me backstage.

Zach showed up with a drink in his hand, full of optimism and energy. "I've made some more changes to our new song," he said.

"You can't keep making revisions, Zach," she countered before a period could attach itself to the end of his statement. "Adam and I haven't even heard them yet."

"That's why I fuckin' came a few minutes early," he answered cheerfully. And as soon as he started to play and sing, she knew it was one of those moments. Zach could write a song in ten minutes sometimes, with a genius touch of sorts. Not always, not even often. But this was one of those epiphanies, and she had to fight back tears as he reached the refrain. *Why can't you feel my eyes on you, why can't you turn and see how much I long to be with you, if you could only see.*

Zach's music had captured the intimacy of her lyric. Everyone knows that feeling, right, that longing, waiting to be known, hoping to be seen? She knew she dared not think of Thomas.

Later when Zach introduced the new song and sang it with her in their final set, the crowd was on its feet, applauding long before they had finished. It was perfect for their voices, Zach singing the lead and Christine harmonizing about desires that clearly filled the room, the applause continuing long after the number ended. Was this who she was, a confident performer in front of supportive crowds? Or was she still that reluctant introvert Zach had taken under his wing in high school, persuading her to try to sing with him?

Jenn, her friend since first grade, was the first to step up on the little stage afterwards, her eyes shining as she hugged Christine. "My God, you killed it this time," she gushed. "That song could make it to the big time. But who's the guy? There has to be someone new to spark such a hot lyric!"

Christine noticed Emily standing near the back of the club. She waved to her and Emily gave her a thumbs-up. "Oh, no, Jenn, there's no guy," she lied. "It's just about proverbial wistfulness, I guess."

Skip was waiting for her as she came off the stage. He put up his hands when he saw her stiffen. "Christine darling, I promise I'm on good behavior."

"You better not be drunk."

Skip grimaced broadly. "I just wanted to shake your hand. You guys were the best I've ever heard you."

"Thanks," she said, extending her hand with a smile.

# Nine

———

**E**ven though he was living with his grandparents in the big house up the hill, and while he and she must have been in the same vicinity on campus from time to time, she could go many days without spotting Thomas. Apparently Antonia was back in Princeton now. At least Christine hadn't seen her around since that awful garden encounter.

She knew subconsciously that she circled through the Campus Café more these days than she used to, but she wouldn't admit the real reason to herself. In fact, she would deny any purpose other than the need for caffeine.

Why did a Thomas sighting brighten her day so? When exactly was the expiration date for nursing crushes, she wondered. The guy was out of reach.

"Are we still on for Saturday?" That voice. She turned slowly. His eyes could be so friendly, but this time she raised a steel-like barrier in response.

"I thought Antonia—" she mumbled, feeling bad for pretending ignorance.

"Oh, no, she's back at school."

"I see."

"Look, I didn't mean for this to be awkward, Christine. I just thought who better than you, as an old friend, to show me some of the back roads and sweeping countryside?"

Old friend, was it?

Christine seldom felt like her mother but, standing there, she wondered if this is how it had gone with Karen Ober and that Lenny jerk. Was she, like her mother, so hungry for a handsome young man many degrees her social better that she was ignoring the signals? But wait a goddamn minute! I am not Karen Ober.

"Sorry, it's not going to work this weekend," she said, wondering whether he could tell she wasn't being truthful. "Maybe some other time. I'd love to help you out."

"Oh." Clearly disappointed.

Maybe she was good at this. Nice touch, that feigned sadness that she couldn't help him out. But what had she just done? She'd never dreamed of saying no to Thomas before.

She took distinct pleasure in the disappointed look on his face. Did he know her feelings and her deception? Or was she giving him too much credit? Maybe he wasn't as smart as Harriet? After all, he was dating that highhanded snob from Ivy League Town.

"Another time then." He smiled as he turned. And as mysteriously as he had appeared, he was gone.

Holy shit! She had just turned down Thomas Turner. What adrenaline! He probably didn't know that she didn't actually have other plans. But she knew it.

What was that exaggerated pulse in her neck? Satisfaction? Or the nagging tartness of regret? Why did she do it? Goddamn though, what a feeling. Followed by a flood of nervous shaking through her extremities.

In her cunning little tangle with Sir Thomas, she had totally forgotten why she had come to the Campus Café in the first place until she abruptly bumped into Uncle Jimmy near the blue doors. He could see she was surprised.

"Hey, Christine, if it doesn't suit you, that's okay."

"No, I was counting on it. Nice to see you. Let's sit over here." She led him to an out-of-the-way booth where there was less noise. They ordered coffee and sat back to politely wait for the other. She was still a bit shaky inside, glancing around to make sure Thomas hadn't come back.

"Tell me about yourself, Uncle Jimmy."

"Oh, you know me, nothing much."

Christine sensed the best way she could be a friend to the only uncle she knew was to encourage honesty. That's what Jimmy wanted, deep down.

"How long were you in prison this time?" It came out a bit more pointed than she had intended. A flush of color reddened his neck.

"Two years, Christine."

"Sorry, I don't know why I asked that."

"It's fine. You have every right to ask. I'm way past denying it. I'm the no-good son in the family, third time in prison. About as banished from the family as your mother is."

Christine winced. Her mother's transgression had been getting pregnant, kicked out by the strait-laced Obers. But Karen Ober was an outcast, not a criminal. Jimmy was a different case, a charming fella who never seemed to have the common sense required to survive in today's world. A heart too kind, perhaps. Many fond memories of Uncle Jimmy reaching out to her when she was younger, against his family's advice and wishes.

"It's not right," he would always say. "That Bryer jackass ruined your lives. I'd love to beat him up for you sometime." But her mother, still fantasizing that she was secretly in love with Lenny though she hadn't laid her eyes on him since he had deserted her years ago, would sound alarmed. "Oh, no, Jimmy. Don't do that. You could go to jail again. Don't hurt Lenny."

She sipped her coffee. "What can I do for you?"

"Oh, nothing, really. I just needed to talk to someone like you, someone who's special and intelligent, full of prospects. Instead of a bunch of foul-mouthed convicts."

"Prospects, huh? You make my life sound hopeful."

"Well, isn't it?"

Jimmy's eyes were most unusual with a sort of speckled quality, tiny red dots left behind here and there. Otherwise he seemed ten or twelve years older than he was.

She smiled at him. "Why have you always been so kind to me, Uncle Jimmy? For as long as I can remember."

"Everyone deserves a favorite uncle." That sucking sound of a laugh again.

"You're the only uncle I've ever met."

"Even so."

"Well, thanks." She patted his hand. Is this how most young people feel about their favorite uncle?

"I haven't been a reliable person. And I know your mother doesn't approve of me anymore. But in prison, when I tried to think of the few good things I still have left, I always thought of you." She could see a blush of warmth in his face. "You're a light in my life, Christine. Always have been."

She was caught between caution and tears. Why couldn't he get his life together? He had such a mellow center and his "crimes" were only petty thefts and pointless fights. He drank too much and got embroiled in small-time thieving and questionable conspiracies.

"Karen was always my favorite sibling," he said. "When we were growing up, our three older brothers ruled the roost and were really mean to both Karen and me. But she was such a sweet young woman. And pretty. I was so proud of your mother when she became the lead cheerleader. If only she'd never met that Lenny prick from across the river."

They talked for over an hour. She became convinced that Jimmy wasn't after anything, wasn't trying to win her over to some scheme or plan. All he wanted was a little nonjudgmental human conversation. And a pinch of love.

Was that too much for an uncle to hope for?

# Ten

—

**H**arriet **called to ask** if she could go along to buy some fabric. They followed a narrow road that ran up along the top edge of the Jagged Valley, nearly falling off the ridge before diving straight down to Threshers Creek. Christine didn't remember having ever traveled the road before.

Harriet seemed more excitable than usual, she thought, and Christine wasn't sure it was all about fabric shopping. "I can't get that Wissler fire out of my mind," Harriet said as they followed Threshers Creek toward a wooded area. "They think someone may have set it deliberately. What sort of person does such a thing?" Her voice had an angry edge. Christine thought of all the farm families worrying about their barns. Had to be a helpless feeling.

They emerged from the wooded area and followed a dirt lane that wound up to a sleepy little country shop tucked under the joyous trees, a lonely car and a grey-topped Amish buggy parked in front. Three women came out onto the porch, carrying bags of purchases and talking loudly about notions, thread variations, and batting. "I didn't know they had such good selection," the tall one said, twisting at her home-made vest and trying not to drop her bags before she made it to the car.

"I really thought you should experience this," Harriet said. "Ten different women can choose the same quilt pattern, you know, and only one of them has the talent to choose the right fabrics to maximize that pattern into something truly beautiful."

Christine had never seen so many bolts of fabric. Every color, endless shades, stripes and dots, circles and triangles, flowers, animals, and birds. "How do you know where to begin?" she asked Harriet.

After Harriet had bought stacks of the lovely fabrics, she insisted that Christine choose several pieces. "It's my treat, buy any 15 yards you want."

"Oh, no, that's too much."

But Harriet insisted and stood by her as she laid bolt after bolt next to each other to make her selections. Christine found it exhilarating. "I'm wasting your money, Harriet."

"Hey, if you decide not to use any of these fabrics, I can always work them into one of my projects."

As they left the colorful shop and settled back into the car, Harriet sighed deeply. "Have you seen men around the neighborhood with blue helmets?"

"Blue helmets?"

Thomas' grandmother turned, face troubled, eyes snappy now. "They have surveying equipment."

"No, I don't think I've seen them. What's up?"

"It's Betsy's scheme, I'm sure."

Later, as they left Threshers Creek behind and climbed the hill above the Jagged Valley, heading home, Harriet pulled off the road and suddenly started to sob. Christine was startled.

"The farm has been in Ethan's family for eight generations. All Turner blood since the original four thousand acres deeded from William Penn after Benjamin Turner the First landed at the ridge above the river. Eight generations. Bruce is the ninth. But Betsy, not a Turner and not a farmer, not a cultivator and not a sustainer, wants to turn our rich soil into cold hard cash and populate our farm with houses for the well-to-do. 'Great view,' she says, but what she really means is 'Great financial windfall.' Cashing in the hard work of the earlier eight generations and acting like a genius. It's a scandal."

"How long—?"

"Just yesterday afternoon. Both Ethan and I have been suspicious that something was afoot. But when these men with the blue helmets showed up and started surveying for the streets, we knew the end had come. I'm disappointed in Bruce. He still hasn't told us what the plans are. All I know is what Betsy said to Ethan about the great view." Harriet's face had reddened so dangerously that Christine feared she would burst into pieces like an eighty-year-old tomato in the hot sun.

"I'm so sorry, Harriet," she said, reaching out to touch the arm of Thomas' grandmother. "I'm really sorry. Ethan must be heartbroken."

"It's not over," Harriet snorted. "This time Betsy went too far."

# Eleven

———

Sharon came out of her office at the Historical Society and walked over to the table where Christine was sitting. "Morning."

"Hi Sharon. You're looking all chipper today." They had known each other for years, ever since Christine had done her first Lenape project in fifth grade. Sharon's dimples still dominated her pretty face.

"Underground Railroad?"

"Yeah, not sure I'll find anything new that's not already been published in one of your periodicals."

"That's why we research. Never know." Sharon paused, then continued. "May I ask you something?" It was early in the day, with no one else in the library.

"Please."

"Mind if I sit?"

"That seat's reserved. Sorry." Their easy banter was one thing she liked about coming here. Unlike some librarians and archivists, Sharon enjoyed people who were alive as much as people who were dead.

Sharon sat and studied her for a moment.

"What is it?" Christine asked.

"I know you're busy. But I didn't know if you might consider working here part-time. Sue Mae is leaving."

"That'll be a loss."

"Yeah, she and Rodney are expecting another baby and she's decided it's too much. She gave me notice last Monday."

"Wow, that'll be different. She's been here a long time."

"Eight years."

"So you're asking—?"

"I need someone to help me until we can hire someone to replace Sue Mae."

"As a volunteer?"

"No, we would pay you. Not big bucks, but decent wages."

Christine was surprised. "How many hours?"

"As many as you can give me. And I'll be glad to tailor it around your school schedule."

The Historical Society building sat on the edge of a knoll overlooking Orchard Valley. The small new wing had been added five years earlier and featured large windows on the south side, bringing in lots of light and great views of the valley.

"I might be able to help. The garden work's pretty well finished for the year."

"That would be wonderful. But I don't want to upset Harriet," Sharon said, raising her eyebrows in that emphatic manner of hers. "She and Ethan have been some of our best supporters. Hopefully, by the time the garden operation starts up again, I'll have hired a replacement for Sue Mae."

Christine stared out the window, down across the valley toward the hills beyond. She had volunteered here for years, especially when they needed extra help with their festivals. But she'd never really thought about working here. However, if Betsy's plans were moving forward and her job in Harriet's garden was over, she would need to look for some work. She needed to be more focused on her career, whatever it might be.

Before Sharon even stood up and went back to her office, Christine knew she would say yes. This could be fun. Maybe this was what she was searching for. But was the pay enough?

The next day, Emily agreed to go with Christine down to the river. "It's amazing how the Underground Railroad was so active in these parts," Emily said.

"We're close to Maryland," Christine explained. "Pennsylvania wasn't safe-safe, but it was at least partway to freedom for those enslaved fugitives."

They were crawling along an old moss-covered, broken wall just above the river's edge in what appeared to have been an entrance to a hideaway tucked into the embankment, part brick and part sod, now nothing more than a tangle of wild weeds and broken bricks.

"The madrigal practice was fun last night," Emily said. "Thanks for inviting me. I love the blend of the group."

"We were lucky to have you," Christine said. "I hope you can come again."

They crawled a bit further along the embankment.

"I hope this helps you with your paper," Emily said. "You think this is it?"

Christine couldn't be sure. Was it big enough for a human to crawl into? Had it really connected to a tunnel leading to the cellar of the old dilapidated house a hundred yards up the ridge?

"When I stand here in the afternoon sun," Christine said, "I can't imagine the terror they felt, swimming across this endless river in the dark, knowing vicious dogs and bounty hunters were not far behind, their prospects scarred over with hopelessness and welts, families violently ripped apart with barely a flicker of hope."

The thoughts seemed to overwhelm the stylish patrician inside Emily as she sank into the weeds, her slender wrist to her forehead, her long hair covering half her face. Christine couldn't tell if she was in tears, Emily's eyes turned away as though the troubles that this place had witnessed were too grievous to think about. Had some enslaved Africans perished at this very spot many years before?

"*Swing low, sweet chariot,*" Christine whispered. "*Swing low.*" They were silent for a long moment, listening to the sounds of the river. "I've come to understand that prayer more in recent years," she said quietly to Emily. "I know it's sacrilegious to compare my troubles to those of the fugitives who tried to hide here. But I do sometimes understand the wish to be rescued, to be swept up into the sky away from everything that strains and pains. *Swing low, sweet chariot, scoop me up and take me home.*"

Emily reached out and took her hand gently. "It's hard for me to believe that we Americans could have done such awful things."

"Do you identify with the slave owners more than with the abolitionists?"

"My grandfather's family was from Virginia with lots of land holdings. I'm sure there are many stories my family doesn't tell."

They climbed the embankment and rattled around the forsaken house, trying to find the reported cellar to see if they could spot the tunnel but, if it had ever been there, it had long since fallen in on itself.

"Thanks for bringing me along," Emily said. "I never thought I liked history very much, but I do when I hear you talk about stuff like this."

Christine laughed. "I've just always been interested in how things are connected, I guess."

They spent another hour trudging along the river embankment. Christine could hear the dogs growling and barking across the river on a little barge now, gliding across the treacherous water, *help!*, snarling all the way, the bounty hunters pointing their guns at her hideaway, forcing her into chains to take her "home." No chariots in view. Forsaken.

It started to rain all of a sudden and they ran up the bank to the car, shielding themselves against the driving storm with their jackets.

On their way back to the university, following the river road and climbing the ridge, they saw a gorgeous rainbow unifying the evening skies. "Wow, there's a promise," she said to Emily.

But as they approached the Five Points intersection, they came upon a serious accident, the ambulance just arriving, police lights flashing the news, a woman's body motionless on the road. The rain stopped and the sun came out as the emergency staff gently lifted her body onto the stretcher and put her into the ambulance. Two teenage girls, bloodied and nearly hysterical, were standing by the mangled car, restrained by an officer as they watched the woman taken away.

*"Swing low, sweet chariot,"* Emily said softly as a cop waved them on by. Then she started to sing the ancient ballad in that wonderful voice of hers, Christine joining in as their wistful duet of incredulity and distress rose toward the heavens, now dark and otherwise preoccupied.

# Twelve

———

**C**hristine was suddenly awake. Was someone in the house? Maybe it had been an early morning truck backfiring on the road outside. Or had her mother called out in her sleep as she sometimes did?

The dim grayness of her room told her that it wasn't the middle of the night, nor was it yet dawn. Just pre-dawn. So what had wakened her?

She climbed out and checked the hallway, the shadows forming silhouettes like crouching robbers or arsonists waiting to pounce. Shadows, Christine, shadows.

Then she knew. Something inside her head had snapped her into consciousness, not something in the hallway or from the road.

As she slipped back under the sheets, a shiver passed through her body, a sensation she had felt only once or twice before, the warmth of her organs wrung by a frosty tremor.

Their house would go, that was guaranteed. If Harriet was right and Betsy had her way, their little tenant house would be bulldozed to make room for upscale homes. Soon. She lay there, eyes peeled open, staring at the picture of her mother holding her when she was two or three, realizing that the only home she'd ever known, humble, cozy, was one step from the landfill.

How is it that our minds temporarily protect us from the threats we face, she wondered. She should have thought of this the moment Harriet mentioned Betsy's scheme. Maybe that was one of the reasons Harriet had sobbed so much when she told her what was coming there on the ridge above Jagged Valley.

But what's the big deal, really? She was probably moving on after graduation, God knows where. But still the memories, the familiar sounds and smells.

She thought of her mother then, who barely coped as it was, who had known no other home since her parents kicked her out as a pregnant unmarried teen, left to dangle until big-hearted Harriet learned of the situation and took Karen in, offering her the little tenant house as a home for herself and her baby.

Life can be flowing along, the worries pushed back to relatively low decibels. But breaking up the home she had shared with her mother her whole lifetime — that was an earthquake. All so Betsy could pocket more money. Devastating the land, blacktopping the rich soil, bulldozing the heritage.

Before Christine had even snapped on the lamp by her bed, wide awake now, she was working on a plan.

This had to be stopped.

That evening after practice she sat on the stairs in Adam's back basement, next to the keyboard and drum set, and spilled out the news of Betsy's plan to destroy the Turner farmstead. Zach got really fired up, his voice rising louder as he paced back and forth in quick, deliberate steps.

"Leave it to me," Zach said.

"Oh, no," she said. "I don't mean to involve you. I just needed to tell someone. Not many people know about it yet."

"Your problems are our problems, darling," Zach continued. "It's always been that way. We love you. Right, Adam?"

Adam was about to answer when Zach amended his thought.

"We love Christine like a sister, right?"

She saw the flicker pass through Adam's eyes in the mini-moment he paused before gushing in a voice unnaturally loud for Adam, "Absolutely!"

"I don't want us to cause any trouble for Harriet and Ethan," she said.

"Of course not. But let's not kid around. Someone's gotta take on that damn Betsy fraud," Zach went on, louder yet. "I have nothing to lose. I'd love to stop that bitch."

Christine tried not to wince, but suddenly it sounded oversimplified, like some superhero comic book. "We gotta be careful," she said.

"Leave it to me, darling" was all Zach said as he rushed out with his guitar, Adam suddenly nervous and a bit aroused to be all alone with her in his back basement.

Something about the moment reminded her of that cold winter day when she had gone to find Adam after he had run away from home. Seniors in high school then, she knew Adam's dad could be rough, but she really had no idea how abusive until she found Adam in a motel, halfway to Philadelphia, his face bruised and dark.

"Adam, Adam, Adam" was all she could say as she hugged him. That was the first she had realized the measure of his crush on her, when she felt the firm bulge in his pants pressing against her as they hugged. It was all very confusing. Adam had called her and made her promise to tell no one, to come alone, to make sure she wasn't followed. And when she found him, knocking three times before he would open the room door, she was shocked to learn how nasty Adam's father was. And equally shocked and confused that something about the situation apparently aroused Adam sexually.

Adam begged her to stay with him. "I can't go home tonight, although I am worried about my mother and sister alone with him," he said. "I hope they go to Aunt Esther's until he sobers up. And I don't want kids at school to know. Not even Zach. If my father has a day to cool off, things will be better. Since tomorrow's Saturday, you won't have to cut school."

They sat a long time, talking while she pondered what to do. "You're the best friend I have, Christine," he said. "I totally trust you. Please stay with me."

"Trust is a two-way street, Adam."

"Meaning?"

"I'd need to let my mother know what's happening. Confidentially, of course. And I'd need to know I can trust you."

Adam looked alarmed. "What do you mean, Christine?"

"Why did you call me and not Zach? Do you have an ulterior motive?"

"Like what? I trust you, that's why."

"Look, Adam, I'm here for you. As a friend. I want to help. I'm willing to comfort you, hug, even cuddle if that helps you at this difficult time. But if you're asking me to make love, I'm not ready for that. It seems like a bad idea, in any case. You're angry and traumatized. Mixing sex with all that is probably not smart."

She could see he was disappointed. He probably hadn't premeditated it, but now that he was alone with her and she was staying the night, he suddenly had a vision of his wildest dreams coming true, an unforeseen consequence of the worst beating he'd ever taken from his dad as he defended his mom. And the sudden promise of Christine's warm bare skin sliding gently against his was almost more than he could bear.

In the end, trust won out. She and Adam did not make love that night. Or any night since then. She had decided it was one of the uneasy mysteries of being true friends and bandmates.

# Thirteen

---

She was caught off guard when Bruce called to see if she would drive tractor because his hired man Little Pete was sick. He offered her the usual low wages and she agreed, knowing she would need to cut only one seminar. It was a lovely day. She'd always been good on the tractor, thanks to Ethan's careful tutorship years ago. She didn't get many chances anymore because Travis and Leopold helped a lot, in addition to Little Pete. The boys were in school today, of course, and Little Pete was sick, Bruce said, so he could use her help.

Why does beauty hurt so much—the greens, golds, and blues so vivid in mid-morning cheerfulness, unaware of coming destruction. Must these fertile fields, which burst with harvests for hundreds of years, providing for generations of Turners, now be destroyed by concrete, asphalt, ostentatious structures, and fake little fields domesticated as "lawns"?

From the upper field she could see the whole way to the flamboyant mountains beyond Jagged Valley and, turning, the entire vista to the river and the river hills, including Turners Rise. Must be a sweep of ten or fifteen miles, gorgeous as a brilliant autumn quilt with vivid rainbow extravagance.

She would ask Bruce about the rumors if she had the chance. What's the worst that could happen? It would be much easier with Betsy not around.

Just before they broke for lunch, she lingered for a moment while Bruce was unhitching the wagon. "What are the guys in the blue helmets up to?" she asked.

She could see Bruce stiffen as though he couldn't believe her ballsy nerve, weighing how to answer this old family friend appropriately. In some ways he looked like his father and, in other ways, Bruce didn't resemble Ethan a bit.

"I think they're doing some surveying," he said as though that was all he knew. She kept her gaze steady on him, refusing to pull the tractor away while she waited for a clearer explanation. Bruce fidgeted and waved for her to drive the tractor away, but she waited. Finally he looked at her, a quick glance, and then back to the field. "Nothing's definite yet," he said.

As she pulled the tractor away, she could see he knew she wasn't satisfied with his skimpy explanation, but she knew that a better answer wouldn't be forthcoming.

Later when the equipment had a problem and she had the chance to catch her breath, she lay on her back and watched the clouds. Her mother used to get her to name the clouds when she was young. They'd lie side by side in their back yard, watching King Alfred chase Big Leonard and Silly Susie across the sky.

*I used to have fun with Mama. What's happened? Why are we at each other so much? If I finish here on time, I'll run home and make that Mexican dish she loves so much and have it waiting for her, with the pineapple cobbler she can never get enough of. If our little house is going to be sacrificed to the wrecking ball of "progress," might as well enjoy a few good times before it's forever too late.*

A friendly face squeezed in between King Alfred and Big Leonard.

"Would you like a cookie?" Ethan asked.

She sat up, surprised. He was holding a small plate with two chocolate chip cookies in one hand and a cup of lemonade in the other.

"You always know what a girl needs, don't you?"

Ethan carefully lowered himself and sat beside her. "Enjoying yourself?"

"Truth?"

"Truth," he nodded.

"I feel caught between being bittersweet and full of rage," she said softly.

He touched her arm in his fatherly way. "Yeah, me, too."

Bruce yelled for her to come, the equipment problem now fixed. Ethan touched her arm again. "If I had known you wanted to farm, I would have held the place for you."

Bruce yelled again.

She patted Ethan's hand gently. "You're a little late," she smiled.

She jumped up and ran toward the tractor. As she stepped up to start the engine, Bruce approached. "We'll need to work into the evening," he said flatly. "Gotta get this work done."

"But I have plans."

"They'll have to wait. The boys have a sports event at school and Little Pete is still throwing up. We need you here." Bruce's voice could get a firm tone.

For a long moment she weighed whether she should tell Bruce to go screw himself. What gave him the right to boss her around like a hired hand? But Ethan was still watching and she thought better of it. So much for that Mexican dish and a special evening with Mama.

# Fourteen

---

**Z**ach **seldom dropped by** her house unannounced. He clearly was quite animated. She wondered if there had been an incident with Betsy.

"I think I may have tracked down your father," he said.

She thought he was joking. "Good to hear. When do we meet?"

"I'm serious."

Christine jerked around to scrutinize Zach. "Hell you talking about?"

He raised his hand. "I realize it's touchy. I don't want to upset you."

"Out with it." She knew her face was getting red.

"Somehow my parents and I got to talking about your dad the other evening. Can't remember what started it. And I realized you and I have hardly ever discussed it. Who has he turned out to be? Where is he? Is he even alive anymore?"

Christine could feel her knees going limp and sat down on the nearest chair. What the fuck? She felt totally ambushed and confused. "What gives you the right?"

"Nothing does. It just made me sad. And I thought maybe I could help."

"Did I ask for your help?" Her voice was angry now.

"No, you did not. I'm sorry if I misstepped."

"You have no idea what my life is like. You and your parents are great together. So why would you interfere with my life?"

"Sorry."

"No shit. Is that your apology for ruining my day?"

Zach reached out to hug her, but she swatted his hands away. "Keep your arrogant paws off me!" The pitch of her voice startled her. What was happening?

There was a wisdom about Zach sometimes, part of why she liked him so much. He walked around the table and sat quietly watching her, then dropped his gaze. Time passed. Later she had no idea if it was a few minutes or an hour. Zach just sat there quietly, staring out the window.

She finally broke the silence. "So?"

"I *am* sorry."

"Okay, okay. Sorry I got mad. But you must admit it came out of nowhere."

"I admit that. Sorry."

She studied him. Clearly he meant to do a nice thing. "What did you learn?"

"We can talk about it another time."

"Don't be annoying."

Zach cleared his throat, stood up, and walked to the window. "I was just exploring the first steps."

"And?"

"I discovered a Dallas Bryer who has a business across the river. I think he may be Lenny's brother. But I wanted to discuss it with you before checking further."

Christine could not hold back the tears as the reality of the whole thing swept over her. *Are we talking about my father?* She realized she had nourished a fatherless identity, wiping that Lenny guy from her mind. True, there were times when she was young she'd sneak a peek at that old faded photo Mama kept in her bottom drawer and fantasize about being a normal family. Strange idea, really, especially with Karen Ober as a mother. Sometime around fourth grade she decided to secretly adopt Harriet and Ethan as her guardians, as a step-family of sorts. So the idea of having a real father had long been scrubbed from her sensibility.

Zach had tears in his eyes now as he watched her crying. "I should have known better," he said in a hoarse whisper. "It's unfair to you, Christine. I am sorry."

# Fifteen

———

She noticed **Thomas slip** into the back of the club part way through their first set. Nice crowd. Their earlier gig here must have sparked some word of mouth because tonight was the biggest crowd they'd ever had at The Root Cellar.

They were saving "If You Could Only See" for the final set. She hoped Thomas wouldn't leave before that.

During their break, Jenn came back to ask if she could talk with her sometime. "I know you're busy now. But can we set a time to meet another day that's convenient?" Although she hadn't gone to college, Jenn had remained good friends with Christine, was their band's biggest fan, seldom missing a show.

"Sure, Jenn," she said. "May I ask what it's about?"

Jenn looked around sheepishly, pulling her off to the side.

"I wanted to ask you about Adam," Jenn whispered.

"What about him?"

"Not now. You have to go back on stage soon."

Christine smiled knowingly and squeezed Jenn's arm. "Is that a crush I'm sensing?"

Jenn blushed as she pulled away. "I never make fun of you."

"Oh, Jenn, I'm sorry. I didn't mean to be unfair."

"I know I'm not as smart as you guys. But you used to be one of my best friends and I thought I could trust you."

"You can." She paused and watched her friend's expression. "What do you want to know?"

"Is he — you know — is Adam seeing...." her voice trailed off.

"Not that I know of."

"You think maybe — ?"

"Go for it. Can I do anything to help?"

"Could you invite me to a party maybe when he's gonna be there?"

"I'll set it up, Jenn. But don't worry. Just relax. He's easy to get to know."

"Thanks, Christine. You're the best."

Later, when the performance was over and the crowd was still applauding their new hit, Thomas was suddenly beside her. She wasn't sure she dared to look at him. *Why can't you turn and see, how much I long to be with you?*

"Really superb," he said. "You and Zach are excellent together." She could tell he was actually quite impressed.

"Thanks."

"No, I mean it. That last number could go places."

"You think?" She noticed Jenn across the stage, talking and laughing with Adam. You go, girl.

"Christine, I do. I have a friend in the industry. Would you mind if I sent my friend that song?"

"I'll have to ask Zach and Adam. But I think we'd be fine with that."

He hesitated and looked across the big room, then back to her. "You ever going to be free to take that drive you promised me?"

"You still want to?"

"Only if you don't feel obligated."

"How about tomorrow then? It's supposed to be a beautiful day."

She could see him relaxing, as though approaching her had made him tense.

"That's great," he smiled. "How about if I pick you up at 10:30? And maybe you can think of some nice spot where I could treat you to a bite?" Then Thomas turned and walked out of The Root Cellar, moving with an elegance learned in Connecticut. Christine watched, her heart in her throat, sensing pleasure, fearing danger.

The next day was colder than she expected, October's touch of November sweeping over the countryside. Thomas put up the roof of the convertible and even turned on the heat a bit. She wore the new sweater she had bought discounted online. Red was one of her favorites.

I'm not the date, she kept telling herself so often that she worried she may have actually said it out loud. I'm the tour guide, not the date.

"How's teaching different than you expected?" she asked him as they meandered the narrow back roads near Orchard Valley. The corn was picked in some places by now, and they could see for miles on the higher ridges.

"Hey, it's not the Ivy League," he chuckled.

She waited. "Not sure I understand."

They came through a covered bridge and climbed the hill toward a stand of trees which had dropped most of their leaves already. The chilly breeze whipped the branches and cartwheeled a thousand gold brown leaves across the road in front of them, spinning on point.

"It's magnificent," he said in a hushed tone, easing the car off the road along the ridge where they could see the hills beyond the river, the whole way to the capitol bridge.

"I haven't been up here for years," she said, suddenly relaxed.

"You know how it is," he continued.

"Actually, I don't."

"It's different teaching a bunch who feel entitled, whose parents think they run the world. Teaching at Midstate has another feel."

"Tell me how."

He looked at her and smiled as he steered the car back on the road. "Take you."

"Me?"

"Yeah, Christine, you. I never get the feeling that you think you deserve the best, the first, and always the most."

"Sounds like a weighty fault." Was it a subtle put-down?

"It tells me who you really are. Or take your friend Zach. He'll go places in life and run circles around the entitled gang."

"Zach—you think?"

"I came here to be close to my grandparents because they've always been so authentic. I like that. And they won't be here forever, of course. But you asked and I'm answering—my biggest surprise has been to discover others here, even some young students, who are amazingly genuine, too."

She wasn't expecting that. He turned and looked at her, full face, with a quiet smile. The rest of her life she would hold this moment in her mind's sweet vault, a brisk but spotless day on top of Pheasant Ridge, Thomas relaxed, earnest, handsome as ever in a gingham shirt and navy sweater. And to her surprise, she wasn't nervous anymore. It doesn't matter if a romance never happens between us. I like this guy, and maybe that's better than nursing my old crush. Maybe he's more like Harriet than I realized.

"For as long as I've known you, Christine, even when we were kids, I've been fascinated with your two faces."

"Did you just call me two-faced?"

"No, no. Hasn't anyone ever told you that?"

"Lots of people don't like my face." She was puzzled.

"You have a beautiful face. I've always thought so."

"A lot of ugly freckles."

"Your freckles are attractive. They're like —" he paused, sensing errant possibilities.

"Yeah?"

"Like a delicate seasoning — on a distinguished face."

"What a crock."

"No, I mean it."

"So what were you —?"

"Many times, when you're not smiling, your face looks sober, almost sad, maybe irritated."

"Sorry."

"No, it's fine. But then when you smile, your entire face lights up, your eyes — the whole world, really. It's a terrific smile. Until you smile though, I think I might be in trouble. Two different faces. That's all I meant." He coughed. "Sorry I brought it up."

"No, it's okay. You wish I'd smile more."

"No, I like you just the way you are, Christine. Sorry I started talking about this." She could feel her heart pause as she tried to figure out what was happening.

They crossed the middle branch of Threshers Creek and slowly entered a little hamlet. A big house sporting many additions and a large barn had Amish buggies parked all around it. He looked at her, a question in his eyes.

"I almost forgot it's Sunday," she said. "They're having church. They rotate between their homes." Little children were running around and the adults were standing in line by the food table. "Lunch time after church." The wind whipped off the hat of a young boy, and he and his friend took chase as it rolled toward the road. Thomas braked and waved them onto the road to rescue the hat. The young owner of the hat waved, grabbed his hat, and ran back to the yard, the fathers watching and warning the boys to be careful.

Later at a little country restaurant built on the ledge of a sloping hill, they sat and surveyed the spectacular scene from their table as they splurged on meat loaf, barbecued chicken, mashed potatoes, good-as-fresh limas, and gravy. And cherry pie.

"How's Antonia?" she finally asked.

His face brightened. "She's good. Thanks for asking."

"What's she studying?"

"She's finishing an MBA in international business."

"Really? That's interesting."

"You think so?"

"You don't?"

"Well, I'm here at a state school teaching music and she's being interviewed by Fortune 500 companies." They watched a group of bikers zoom by on the road. "I had a few offers from what people would call top schools," he said.

"And—?"

"Midstate's a good school, Christine, don't you think?"

Was it a trick question? He rubbed his face, looking very vulnerable, as she watched him finish his cherry pie.

"My grandparents are just about the steadiest thing in my life. As I'm sure they've told you, my folks split up years ago. But bless them, they still can't stop having long-distance spats. Always about money. They have enough money to burn, really, they do. But it's never enough. I just hate that. Whereas for Grandma and Grandpa, even though they have considerable resource, it's not the center of their lives. People are. And creativity and words. And a sense of community. I've always been attracted to that."

"You're one lucky grandson, I'll say that for you, Thomas."

"Yes, I am." He smiled again, his eyes settling on hers. "I'm lucky to have you as a friend, too, Christine. Thank you for today." Then he took her hand and lifted her fingers to his lips, kissing them exquisitely like some European royalty.

"Thank you, too," she said, an unexpected thrill sweeping through her center.

# Sixteen

———

The moment she came down to the kitchen the next Saturday morning, she knew something was wrong. Her mother was leaning against the refrigerator the way she often did when her admonition pressure tank was about to blow.

"Were you ever going to tell me?" Her tone was unusually sharp.

Christine had slept in late because of their concert the night before. "Sorry, Mama, tell you what?"

"About this place being demolished for development."

"You heard?"

"There isn't a lot happening that someone doesn't tell us at the diner. 'Karen, did you hear your place is gonna to be torn down?' And my own daughter knew and couldn't be bothered to tell me herself!"

"I think it's still at the proposal stage, Mama. I wanted to tell you, but I've been trying to learn more details before I worried you."

"That's what you think of me—a poor soul who'd be overwhelmed to learn she's losing the place she's rented ever since you were born? Why do you treat me like a weakling?"

"Mama, let's not fight about it."

"I'm not fighting. You still live under my roof and, as long as you do, I demand the respect a mother should get."

"Sorry."

Then Karen Ober nearly lost it, her voice rising and her still attractive face twisting in outrage. "You think you're smarter than me, don't you? You think because you're in college you know everything. You think you can stand by while they evict me from this place because you're planning to fly the coop and it won't affect you. Where am I supposed to live?"

The assault caught Christine by surprise, barely awake without her first cup of coffee. "That's not fair, Mama."

"You just wait. You'll have your comeuppance one of these days and we'll see how grand little Christine Ober is then. You'll never marry Thomas Turner. You're no better than I am, no matter how much you try to convince yourself. I want you out of this house. By this weekend. Find another place to live your hoity-toity life. Be a big shot someplace else. I've had it with you. Out."

With that, her mother stormed out of their tiny kitchen, slamming the door so hard it rattled the collection of ceramic candleholders her mother kept on the top shelf above the sink. Christine could hear her start the car and spin her way out of their drive onto the road as a truck blared a loud warning horn.

And before she had her first coffee or even washed her face, Christine collapsed in a chair by the table. As much as she fought against it, a stream of hot, bitter tears pushed their way down her face. *Sometimes I feel like a motherless child.* And a homeless one, too, apparently.

# Seventeen

---

**M**inutes later, the call from Arlene's Becca caught her by surprise. "My mom and I need to meet with you, but it must be kept secret."

"Is this a joke?"

"No, I'm dead serious. Sooner the better."

Becca was Arlene's oldest daughter, a gangly 19-year-old, unapologetically at peace with the farm girl she was. And a lovely soul, just like her mother. Arlene had lost her husband Nathan in a farm accident nearly ten years ago, and Christine always admired how Becca and her two sisters pitched in and supported their mother, a close family determined to make the farm a success without the man they loved.

"Tell no one," Becca instructed.

Christine realized it was serious, cut class, and walked down past the end of the Turners' lower field, through the standing corn, over the old fence, through the wooded area along Whisper Run to the rail footbridge they used sometimes, up through Arlene's field of towering corn, past the old smokehouse with its intricate roofline adornments, and slipped into the far end of the large implement shed through the small door farthest from the road. The shed was midnight dark compared to the bright light of the forenoon, and for a moment she thought she was alone.

"Thanks for coming," Arlene said, coming out of the shadows. Becca stepped out, too.

"I'm still not sure if this is a prank," Christine said.

"It's very serious, I'm afraid. But I need you to keep this absolutely confidential."

"Wow, what's up, Arlene?" Christine couldn't hide her surprise.

"I love you, Christine, you know that," Arlene responded, reaching out in the shadows to take her arm. "But I need you to swear."

"Okay, I swear. Gosh, it sounds top secret."

"It is." Arlene handed her an envelope with a few dirty smudges on it. Inside was a sheet of paper with a message of pasted letters which had been cut out of magazines. In the dim light, Christine could barely make out its message — "UR Barn B 3. U call police, URs next. We R watch."

Christine was stunned. "My God, Arlene! How did you get this?"

"Someone put it in our mailbox. It was there this morning when I went to mail a letter."

Christine felt lightheaded, looking around in the shadows. "I think I need to sit down."

Becca took her elbow. "Sit here on these bags of fertilizer."

"I trust you, Christine," Arlene was saying. "I didn't know who to tell without being seen from the road or from the south ridge."

"You think they're watching from the south ridge?"

Becca puckered her brow and spit on the floor of the shed, a farmer gesture her father had used a lot. "I think we should call the cops."

Christine turned to look at Arlene. "But?"

Arlene was near tears. "We can't afford to lose our barn. We have insurance, but if we lose the livestock and don't have a place to store our crops, we may have to sell the place." She wiped her eyes. "You have a lot of common sense. Can you help me think this through?"

Damn. What the hell's going on? Is this a threat or a prank? Christine got up and hugged Arlene. Poor woman. They had been friends for years as neighbors, as households without fathers, as madrigal buddies. "Do Ellen and Susie know?"

"I let them go to school without telling them. I didn't know what to say. Becca and I were going to dig up sweet potatoes today, but she could tell I was upset, so I told her."

Christine's eyes were adjusting now, and she could see deeper into the long shed, the disc parked there, the wagons, and the large tractor with big lights like eyes staring at her. "Do you have any idea who would make such a threat, Arlene?"

"No, I don't. I've been beating my brain."

"Is there someone who's upset with you?"

"Honestly, I'm not perfect, but I can't think of anyone." It was hard for Christine to imagine anyone being even mildly upset with Arlene, let alone furious enough to strike a match.

Becca had her hands on her hips. "I still think we should call the police. They know how to handle these things, don't they?"

Arlene was unpersuaded. "What do you think, Christine?"

Christine walked over and stared out through a crack in the doorframe. What the devil was happening? Had Arlene gotten herself into severe trouble she didn't want to fess up to? Was there more to the story than she was telling? Why didn't she want to call the police?

"And they didn't demand money?"

"You have the letter in your hand." Arlene was so stressed that she was kicking the bags of baler twine sitting near the disc, as though they'd squeal out an answer. Christine studied the letter more carefully. From the fonts, the different paper stocks, and the varied ink colors, she could tell the letters had been cut from at least four different magazines before they were pasted into the message. "UR Barn B 3."

What was this about? If not revenge or extortion, was it simply pure terror? But who would terrorize a struggling widow and her wonderful daughters? Think, dummy, think. There must be an answer staring you in the face.

Becca paced, sighed, and chewed her lips. "We gotta do something," she kept saying.

"I have a question, Becca," Christine finally interrupted.

"Shoot."

"What if someone is upset and, instead of demanding money, they simply want to send a scare through your family? Maybe to get even. Can you think of anyone?"

"I don't think so. Some guy from across the river offered to buy the farm and we turned him down, but he seemed to take it just fine. I can't believe he'd be this stupid."

Christine walked over and looked Becca directly in the face. "Maybe it's not related to the farm or to your mother. Is there anyone who wants to get even with one of you three girls?"

She could see the surprise of her question smack Becca hard, but then a question rose in her eyes. "Ellen's been dating a sorta weird guy, but they broke up."

"How recently?"

Arlene jumped in. "Two weeks ago, but I can't believe Floyd would threaten us like this."

"Okay, I just thought it might be a copycat prank by someone who knows people are really frightened and decided to use that fear to scare the hell out of your family?"

Arlene moved closer to her now and whispered, "But what if it is real, what if it's actually the guy who set the Wissler fire?"

"So let's call the cops. I don't want you blaming me." Christine wished she could ask someone like Ethan. He would have some wise counsel.

"But they say we can't. Are we ready to risk them burning our barn? If we call the police, they'll have to come out here and, if someone's watching, they'll see the cop cars." Arlene had more lines in her face than Christine remembered, and the stress she was feeling brought out every one of them. Becca went to sit on the disc now, more perplexed than before.

"I'm so sorry, guys," Christine responded softly. "But I agree that calling the cops may be a mistake until you find out more. On the other hand, maybe the police are the best option."

"You're a big help," Becca groaned.

Christine grimaced. "I agree, I'm not worth much."

Arlene started to pace again and sneaked a peek through some of the cracks. "I'm worried we're staying out here too long in case someone is watching. For right now, I say we don't call the police. But we want to talk with you again soon. Okay if I have Becca call you in a few hours?"

"Absolutely. I want to help any way I can. Or how about if I come back the normal way to help you to dig up the sweet potatoes? Then it won't seem strange if we're talking with each other?"

Arlene hugged her. "Thanks so much, Christine. Sorry to drag you into this. I still can't believe it's real. You better go now and keep out of sight as you go home the back way. We'll wait a few minutes before we go to the tool shop again and get the stuff for digging up the sweet potatoes."

As Christine made her way carefully back through the tall corn, along the little stream, she tried to sort her thoughts. Was there a serial arsonist on the loose? Was even the Turner barn at risk? Or was the Wissler fire an isolated incident which some loony jerk was using to frighten Arlene and her girls? I know I said I would tell no one. But I think Ethan might be able to help.

# Eighteen

---

**B**ecca **called back later** that afternoon with a cryptic message. "Mom wants to take another day or two to think and pray about it. Please don't tell anyone."

"You tell your mother she can trust me."

"We do trust you, Christine."

Caught between melodrama and actual jeopardy, she pitied Arlene and her girls. What if it was real? Christine was still preoccupied as she arrived a bit late for the meeting in Thomas' office.

"I can't promise anything," Thomas was saying. "It's a crazy business, and I only know what Sam tells me about it occasionally. Sam's the expert."

"We genuinely appreciate your time, Professor Turner," Zach beamed. He could lay on the charm when he felt like it. "Does Sam have his office in Nashville or L.A.?"

"Sorry, I should have explained. Sam is short for Samantha. We were in a little band of sorts at Princeton. Never went anywhere. But Sam knows her stuff. She's the real thing. I think she works out of her home in Maryland."

"I see." Zach sounded a little deflated.

"Hey, you can work with anyone you wish. I just mentioned Sam because I know she's always had a way of making things happen."

Adam sounded skeptical. "How would this work? Do we have to pay anything? Who owns the rights?"

Thomas smiled. "Look, like I said, I'm not the expert. My simple offer was to put you in touch with Sam if you three want that." He looked at Christine, clearly unsure of her thoughts. It was her first time in his office. She liked the posters and paintings on his walls.

"What's the downside of talking with her?" she asked. "Will she charge us just to have the initial conversation?"

"Oh, I don't think she would. But let me ask her." Those eyes of his swept over the three of them but ended on her face. "So I'm asking again. Do I have permission from all three of you to contact Sam, assuming there's no expense involved?"

Zach didn't hesitate. "I'm in."

Christine looked at Adam. He had really served as their manager all these years, though they didn't call him that officially. She could see him struggling with whether he wanted their little project to be taken over by someone else. "I'm not opposed," he said finally.

"What can it hurt to have a simple conversation with Sam, so she can answer some of our questions?" she asked.

"Okay, let's do it." Adam frowned as though it pained him to say it. "I trust you guys, really."

"So thanks for your kind offer, Professor Turner," she said, careful not to act too familiar with Thomas. "I doubt anything will come of it, but I don't see how it can hurt to find out."

"I'll email her today."

Later as they were leaving the music building, Zach caught up with her. "Do you have a minute?"

She stopped and reached out to touch his hand. "Sorry I got so upset about the Bryer thing."

"No, I was out of line. I hope it doesn't upset our relationship."

"Oh no, Zach, it won't. It just caught me by surprise."

"I understand. If you want me to pursue it further anytime, let me know. Of course, you're an expert yourself on tracing family trees for people."

She smiled. "Talk about irony." Then she frowned. "Maybe it's not so urgent at the moment. Okay?"

"That's all I need to hear." Zach smiled in his charming way and then headed toward the library.

# Nineteen

———

The surprise overnight snow created a lovely landscape in the morning. The sunlight glistened on the wet snow clinging to the still unfallen leaves like so much burnt orange canonized in white. An amazing number of the quilters arrived at Harriet's place on time. Christine had promised Harriet that she would attend several more times.

"The back roads are really slick," Georgette was saying. "But it takes more than a little premature snow to shut down this quilting group."

"You got that right," Suzanne chimed in. "We've got grit."

The phone rang and Harriet hurried to answer it. "How serious is it, Samuel?" Everyone came to a motionless state, sensing danger. "Uh-huh. Well, let me know as soon as you know. I'll tell the others."

As Harriet hung up and turned to the rest of them, Christine realized again why she loved her so much. Harriet was a natural leader, feeling the pain of others more deeply than her own, shunning sensation, quick to reduce a situation to something she and others could act on rather than ventilate about. Never a need to exaggerate or to make herself the hero of the situation.

"That was Samuel. Wanda's car slid off Beaver Road at that wicked curve, close to where it crosses the creek. "

"How bad is it?" Georgette asked.

"The good news is that she hit a tree instead of rolling into the creek. But the bad news is—"

"She hit a tree," Alice finished her sentence.

"Samuel called from the hospital. Wanda's in the emergency room right now. She was insistent that he call to tell us that there won't be any snacks. I guess they got sorta wrecked."

"Oh, my," Barbara said. "I hope Wanda's not hurt too much."

"Car's demolished, according to Samuel," Harriet added. "Must have been really scary."

They all fell silent then, their needles flying faster than usual as they thought about Wanda, hoping she wasn't injured beyond repair.

"I'll go get some cookies out of the freezer," Harriet said, retreating to the kitchen.

"We don't need any snacks today," Suzette insisted.

"Let me see what I have so they can start to thaw a while." They could hear Harriet talking with Ethan in the kitchen.

"Beautiful things like the first snow can bring so much pain with them. Why is life like that?" Barbara asked. Someone started humming an old hymn and others joined in, a prayer for Wanda, stitched to the eternal question, rising above the quilting frame like so much misery blended with comfort.

But Christine's mind had jumped to concerns for Arlene and her three daughters and the threat hanging over them. Twice in the past day her mind had started composing lyrics about the sabotaging terror of their situation, but she knew she didn't dare to put the words on paper.

Her mother was waiting for her when she got home. It looked like she'd been crying. "Hi, Mama," she said as warmly as she could. She decided to sit at the table and just wait to see how her mother would respond.

"What are we going to do?"

"How do you mean?"

Karen Ober twisted her head around, her face more forlorn than usual. "I've never had to move," she said. "I wouldn't know where to start."

"Mama, if it comes to that, I promise I will help you pack and settle in at a new place."

"Where?" A mix of exhaustion and near terror filled her voice.

"Come and sit, Mama. Let's talk."

Her mother pulled out a chair and released her weight into its contours.

"Betsy and Bruce may not get approval for their plans, Mama. I'm going to a township meeting next week to learn more."

"You are?"

"Yes, Zach thinks there may be a way to stop this."

"Zach? Your music friend? What's he got to do with the township?"

"Nothing, really. We're just going to educate ourselves."

"You can do that? Don't you need to be a powerful person to have influence?"

"I think that's part of what we're trying to find out."

"But if it can't be stopped, where will we live?"

"There are a lot of nice places, Mama. I know it's a big change, but I'm sure we can find something you'll like. It may even be closer to the diner."

"But it'll cost a lot more per month, won't it? Harriet has been so kind all these years, keeping the rent really low. I don't think I make enough at the diner to swing a rent that might double or triple what we pay here."

Christine reached out and laid her hand on her mother's. "One step at a time." Her mother actually smiled, the storms consuming her face at bay for a moment. "I've taken a part-time job helping Sharon at the Historical Society, so I can maybe help you with the rent."

"You did? When?"

"I start tomorrow. She wants me to work as many hours as I can give, but I don't want to skimp on my school work. It's very tempting to take your foot off the pedal during your last year."

Her mother leaned front. "I'm sorry for yelling at you. Of course, you can live here. I'm sorry for what I said, Christine."

"No, I understand. The news was a shock. And I probably should have told you what I knew, even if I wanted to check it out first."

Her mother smiled, almost peaceful. "We should have more talks like this."

# Twenty

———

She was surprised to receive an urgent text from Uncle Jimmy. They met at the same booth in the Campus Café. He seemed anxious.

"What is it, Uncle Jimmy?"

"I'm worried about your mother."

"What about her?"

He handed her an envelope. It was unopened, addressed to her mother. Across the angle in big red letters, clearly her mother's script, were three words. Return to Sender. She saw Jimmy's address in the upper left.

"So?"

"Your mother won't open my letters."

"I see."

They sat in silence for a moment, Christine examining the envelope as though there was more to discover while Uncle Jimmy fidgeted.

"What's the letter say?"

"This is for you and Christine."

"What is?"

"That's what the letter says."

She looked at him. "That's all?"

"It's a short letter."

"It feels thicker than that. Is there something else in here?"

"One hundred dollars. Cash. Ten 10s."

"Why?"

"It's a gift for the two of you."

She still didn't get it. "But why?"

"I want to help. I'm sure she can use it."

She looked at him sharply. "Are you trying to get Mama in trouble? Is this some kind of scam, Jimmy?"

"No, no. It's on the up and up."

"How do I know that?"

He paused and rubbed his face. "I guess you'll have to take my word for it. It's clean money. No strings attached. I swear."

"But why would you do this? How can Mama know this money isn't stolen?"

"It's not. I earned it at the poultry plant."

What the hell was going on here? Why was Uncle Jimmy acting nervous? What was he trying to get her involved in?

He cleared his throat. "I asked her not to tell you."

"What?"

"Years ago."

"Tell me what?"

He rubbed his face again and took the envelope back from her. "Sorry to have bothered you, Christine."

"That's it? What the fuck are you up to, Jimmy."

"Sorry, honey, you'll have to ask your mother. I thought maybe you knew." And with that he stood up, started toward the blue doors, then turned and came back, looking at her with those strangely speckled eyes. "Please don't give up on me, Christine," he said, pausing, waiting as though she would answer. And when she didn't, he turned and was gone.

# Twenty-One

---

"**There were several issues** at the school," Emily was saying. "But the real blow was that my father's business failed and suddenly the funds dried up. At the same time, my mother asked Dad for a divorce." They were on the train to New York for a music event, talking about Emily's time at Columbia and the reasons she had transferred at the last minute to Midstate U.

"Oh, my God," Christine said. "You poor thing."

"No pity needed. My problems aren't as bad as some other people's."

They rode for a while in silence as Christine watched the drab New Jersey swampscape go by. A train going south on the next track created a noisy impact of air pressure, rattling the windows as it thundered past.

"How did you ever survive?"

"I tried to reassure my dad that I was fine, that the disruptions in my life were minor." She swept her long hair back in an elegant motion.

"And he bought that?"

"He probably knew better, but he didn't have any energy to think about it. Not only was his fortune lost, and his marriage. He had always valued his reputation as a respected businessperson and community leader." She bit her lip. "Couldn't face the world anymore. Just sat at home hiding from creditors."

They had found seats that faced each other, and Christine could see the fissures in Emily's strong and well-controlled features. Might she break into tears right here?

"Couldn't Columbia give you a scholarship or something so you could stay there and graduate?"

"It was complicated." Emily fell silent, her lip quivering now as she stared out the window. A tear perched prominently on the precipice of her cheekbone, waiting, waiting, then crawled down to her chin and fell onto her linen shirt. Again, a long silence. "Turned out my father raided the college funds he had set aside for me and Tammy. None of us realized how desperate he was. I don't think Mother had any idea. He was distant and irritable with her, I guess, and she got fed up, not really knowing what he was dealing with. She split when he needed her most."

"Does she have money of her own?"

"Yeah, she had money when they got married, I guess, money he couldn't get his hands on. She was old money, he was new money. Now she's off with Theodore, and Dad's alone and penniless. Theodore's old money, too."

"Holy shit."

"To be honest, what keeps me awake sometimes is worrying about Dad's mental health. I don't know how to help him. Tammy's been giving him an endless tirade of blame and shame. And hanging out with Mother and Theodore."

When they came to the Newark stop, a pair of twins got on, men who looked to be in their seventies, dressed in the same purple sweaters and identical charcoal overcoats. They walked down the aisle and sat several rows behind them.

"My mother's a twin," Emily said.

"Really?"

"Yeah, fraternal. Not identical, like those two suave gentlemen." A trace of a smile crossed her face. "Identical twins have always fascinated me."

"Yeah, me, too."

"I keep wondering if their brains are linked telepathically in a way none of the rest of us ever experience. Wouldn't that be something?"

"Twins tend to run in families, don't they? Maybe you'll have twins."

Emily's response was quick and tart. "I'm not having kids."

Again a long silence.

Christine cleared her throat. "Not to be intrusive —"

"It's okay."

"Well, if your mother has access to money, couldn't she have helped you stay at Columbia?"

"That's not the way she thinks. My mother's always had a gift for letting the ball drop in a way that made my dad look bad, even if catching the ball would have helped Tammy and me. Well, especially me. She somehow sensed a special connection between Dad and me and was always attacking that connection. She'd rather make the mess bigger instead of preventing it, so Dad would look like a ginormous moron."

"My God, was it always that way?"

"I'm sure not. I think it got worse as we got older."

As they got off the train and headed out of Penn Station onto Eighth Avenue, Christine caught a glimpse of the Empire State Building's iconic tower, so close it seemed touchable. Walking up Eighth Avenue, they came to 42nd Street and continued toward Broadway, noticing the shows and artificial glitter. Christine had never walked the famous block. She felt her senses being bombarded, so far from Harriet's garden. Suddenly she picked up the pace and Emily had to hurry to catch up.

"It's sorta crass, isn't it," Emily said.

Christine caught herself. "Not sure what happened. Something inside me was...I don't know...shows what a naïve country girl I am."

"Christine naïve? No way. I think the authentic part of you is uneasy with all this sensation and pretense, right?"

They stopped a few blocks later at 46th and Broadway and looked at the theater marquees. "Did you ever try out for a Broadway musical when you lived here?"

"Me? No. I was too much in the classical vein at Columbia. Not that I would turn it down if the opportunity came along. I just never thought I had a chance. It's very competitive. And I'm probably a better singer than I am an actor or dancer."

"When I was much younger, I used to dream of making it in New York. But I got over that a long time ago." They watched a screaming police car nudging through the traffic.

"You have such a lovely voice, Christine."

"No, I don't."

"But you do. You have a great voice for madrigals — and a whole different voice in your band. I know you'll go places."

"I seriously doubt that."

"Damn," Emily almost spit, "why do you always put yourself down? How can you succeed with that attitude?"

"I'm realistic, that's all. Hard knocks will do that to you."

They continued up Broadway toward Lincoln Center. Christine tried to change the subject. "Where do you get your love of the classical?"

"My father loves music. Never had the native ability, but he took Tammy and me to lots of events and concerts when we were growing up. Was your dad like that?"

Christine paused. "I've never met my dad." No point in mincing it.

"Really?" Emily looked shocked, almost scandalized.

"He backed out of marrying my mom a week before the wedding and returned to his proper upper-class family. I've never even seen him."

"Wow." Pause. "Do you know who he is?"

"They met at a basketball game, my mother the cheerleader, he the star of the opposing team. Storybook gone sour."

"So you know—?"

"He lives on the West Coast or someplace. I have no idea, really. But his family still rules the other side of the river."

"Your mother remarried?"

"No, it wrecked her life. Literally. She's never recovered."

"Damn, we both had tough family situations the way it sounds."

"Like you said, many others have had it worse."

They got a bite to eat at a deli near Lincoln Center before the concert. It was a gorgeous November day, the fresh air sweeping away some of the soiled weariness of the sprawling city. "Hey, do you want to go up to Columbia afterwards and show me around?"

Emily's brow puckered, her eyes turning frosty. "Not today," she said. "I don't have the energy to go back there."

The six-member a cappella group was the best Christine had ever heard. Not only did their vocals float out over the audience in perfect key and harmony, their own instrumental inventions accented their voices in a mini-opus unlike anything she had ever heard before. The six used their lips, tongues, and mouths to create a myriad of sounds, an organic orchestra accompanying their own cultivated voices. Christine was swept away.

The train was well past Downingtown on the way home when Emily roused from her nap next to Christine and said softly, "I used to get much more wasted in those days. Somehow I woke up in the bed of my voice coach one morning near Columbia and realized I hadn't consented to everything that had transpired." Then Emily slipped back into sleep, riding along beside Christine without another word.

# Twenty–Two

---

The meeting room at the township building would best be described as small and spartan. Plain and unadorned, lacking any warmth except the township's insignia hung in a frame on the wall behind the table with the seven chairs.

The Chair of the Planning Commission was Fredrick Stevens. "Fat Freddy," as he was known. He called the meeting to order and followed the agenda, point by point. He kept his voice so low that Zach and Christine had to strain to hear him from the back row. There were only six other people beside the Commission members. "Turner Request" was the last item on the agenda.

The Fricke family wanted to subdivide their three acres into three one-acre lots. An Amish farmer wanted zoning permission to build lawn furniture in his barn during the winter months. Albert Scooter wanted to re-zone a little sliver of land next to their manufacturing plant from ag to industrial. On and on, voices so subdued it was hard to tell if some of the Commission members in the big chairs up front were asleep or just spending a long time looking down at the engineer's drawings.

Zach was fidgety. Christine reached out and laid her hand gently on his leg, her eyes straight ahead, trying to calm his nerves. Easy does it, Zach. We have to stay calm.

Then suddenly Betsy and Bruce were up front, discussing their request. Where had they come from? Had they been waiting in the corridor outside, entering with their lawyer only when their request came up on the agenda?

Again the voices were low, as though subdued by ordinance or maybe simply bored by another mundane discussion.

But then Deb Brewster's voice kicked in on the loud side, a bit agitated. "We can't rezone to residential so many prime acres that are zoned agricultural. That does not fit the ten-year zoning master plan we adopted last year."

Fat Freddy stared at Brewster. "I hear you, Deborah," he said softly. "Maybe we should listen to their lawyer's comments first."

"We know what Mr. Peters is going to say," Deb Brewster responded, even louder now. "Same old story. 'Tired of growing crops. Let's grow some houses.' There's no great mystery to this."

"Mr. Chairman," Eli Gibbons jumped in, but in a low voice as though he and others had sworn an oath to speak at half the volume of that Brewster hothead. "I'd like to hear the petitioner's representative's comments."

"Me, too," Fat Freddy responded, louder now. "Mr. Peters?"

Peters looked a little out of place with his mustache and suspenders. But his voice was calm and engaging. "I think it's all covered in our petition. My clients and I are open to questions."

"Yes, I have a question," Deb Brewster cut in quickly. "Is there a compelling reason for us to consider rezoning this, other than the owners wanting to get even more wealthy?"

Everyone in the relatively small room could hear Betsy Turner sigh. Loudly. Christine remembered how her mother used to talk about the epic fights between these two women over the years, the 'Betsy and Deb Catfights,' she called them. Deb repaid Betsy's audible sigh with a heated glare.

No decision was reached. "Please come back next month with more information about the stormwater plans in your sketch plan," Freddy was saying. "Thanks for coming in."

And then it was over. The six persons in the audience besides Zach and Christine got up and wandered out with little show of emotion. Betsy and Bruce sat on the front row, conferring with their attorney. Several of the Commission members had already slipped on their jackets and left by the side door. All in all, a rather tame affair.

"Well, I guess that was educational," Zach said. "Looks like there's at least one of the group not sold on Betsy's plan."

Before she could answer, Christine sensed someone standing beside her. She turned to see Betsy.

"What are you doing here?" Betsy demanded.

"Just observing."

Betsy wasn't pleased. "I'm warning you, Christine. I don't know what you're up to, but if you get in my way, you and your mother will be sorry. Very sorry."

Christine wasn't sure why she said it, but she did. "Sounds like a threat, Mrs. Turner."

"Don't mess with me, little girl." With that, Betsy spun on her heel and marched over to Bruce, waiting for her by the door. Betsy gave Christine one last scowl and pulled Bruce along with her out the door.

"Holy crap!" Zach exclaimed. "She's a first-class bitch."

"You see now what we're up against, Zach. She'll eat us alive if we don't know what we're doing."

# Twenty–Three

———

For four years running, Thanksgiving Day was her mother's single biggest day of the year for tips. Christine couldn't remember when the two of them had celebrated the holiday together, apart from the late-night assortment of leftovers her mother would bring home from the diner, always counting her money while eating a plateful of turkey, mashed potatoes, gravy, cranberry salad, and whatever else she had been able to fit into one of the boxes Danny provided as she left the restaurant. And then, money counted, falling asleep while Christine ate alone and put the food away. Not your normal celebration, but a happy one when the gratuities had been counted and recounted.

So Christine usually had nowhere to go on Thanksgiving Day itself unless Harriet invited her. Which she often did. Christine had never known her mother's family, cut off as her mother had been since before Christine was born. Except for Uncle Jimmy, of course.

She had run into Thomas the day before as she was leaving the library. "Thought you'd be in Princeton or Connecticut."

"Oh, no, it's only a long weekend, and I'm drowning in papers and grading."

"Too bad."

"What are you doing tomorrow?"

"For Thanksgiving? Not sure. I'll probably work on my research paper. You?"

"I thought you often went to my grandparents for Thanksgiving, Christine."

"Sometimes I did. Haven't heard anything this year."

"Aunt Betsy invited me two weeks ago, and I assume Grandma and Grandpa are going, too. Why not join us? Grandma probably just forgot to say something. You've always been next thing to family."

"Oh, I don't know."

"I'll clear it with Betsy. I'll see you there tomorrow at twelve noon sharp. And" — he hesitated, then continued, reaching out to touch her on the elbow — "maybe we could go driving again in the afternoon. I need to do something other than read another thirty mediocre first-year papers."

She'd barely said goodbye to him when Harriet called her, all apologetic. "I don't know how it slipped my mind, Christine. Ethan just reminded me. Can you join us for Thanksgiving tomorrow?"

"Oh, don't apologize, Harriet. You don't need to worry yourself about me."

"We always include you for Thanksgiving. I simply forgot. Betsy's hosting this year. I'll tell her that you're coming, too. Can we count on you?"

"Sure, that would be lovely, Harriet. Thank you."

On Thanksgiving morning the landscape was coated with a light appetizer of snow, not so much that it would interfere with travel but perfect for a storybook holiday vista. Christine was working on the first draft of her paper, trying to decide whether to start at the beginning or in the middle, when her phone rang. It was Betsy.

"Good morning, Christine." Well, she could be pleasant sometimes.

"Good morning, Betsy. Happy Thanksgiving."

"Yes, about that, I don't recall inviting you to our Turner family meal today. Am I forgetting?"

Awkward. "No, Betsy, you're not forgetting."

"Yet I'm told that you're expecting me to set a place for you."

"Both Harriet and Thomas invited me."

"They're not hosting, are they?"

"Listen, Betsy, if you insist—"

"So glad you understand." Betsy replied quickly. "After all, you are an adult now, and you definitely need to learn to take care of yourself rather than relying on charity."

It was a moment she'd probably never forget, standing beside the table by the kitchen window as Betsy disinvited her, her paper about fugitives spread out in front of her, the snow masking the imperfections of the landscape before her. "It'll probably be your last time to celebrate the holiday there in that place you rent from us at that ridiculously low price Harriet insists on. Enjoy it while you can."

After Betsy hung up, Christine tried to subdue the emotions cooking inside her. Clearly Betsy was worried about Zach and her. Why else would she go to such extraordinary lengths to reverse two invitations she had received to the Thanksgiving meal? Or was she simply mean-spirited to the core? Just when Christine had been scolding herself for not being more receptive to Betsy's possible good traits, Betsy had demonstrated her true center once again.

Christine's appetite had disappeared. She put together a small plate of leftover apple cranberry salad she had made on Sunday, along with leftover sweet potato casserole. She sat at the table trying to write, picking at her food, thinking about her mother at the diner, giving every last bit of energy to serving her customers, wishing them a happy holiday, and keeping a mental tab on her tips. Meanwhile, up the snow-coated hill, the tense Turner clan would be gathering around Betsy's Thanksgiving feast. Thomas had probably forgotten about his proposed little excursion.

She was just about to text Emily when her cell jangled. A text from Uncle Jimmy. "Forgive me, pleas. I ment to help, not offendd. I really need to see u from time 2 time. Sorry if I skrewed up."

She finished the apple cranberry, watching a long V-shape of geese far across the sky flying south. Lucky things. A predictable life, accepted by and surrounded by their community. With neither matriculation nor love to fret about.

That night there was another barn fire, this time on the Miller farm a mile north of town, a huge fire which soon became known as "The Thanksgiving Fire."

# WINTER

# Twenty–Four

**From where she sat** in the café, Christine could see Thomas coming up the walk, talking and laughing with a rather good-looking giant of a woman. Must be Sam. Watching Thomas in friendly interaction with another female stirred a rush of emotion in her. But he's mine, she wanted to protest. Which was not quite true, of course. Okay, totally not true.

Zach and Adam came through the blue doors just as Thomas and the giant walked up. Introductions all around. Coffee orders with the café's special peanut-butter-and-chocolate biscuits.

For some reason, Christine felt the urge to assert herself. Why should Zach always go ahead? No wonder Thomas thinks Zach has promise.

"Tell us what you do," she asked rather abruptly. Sam gulped a swallow of coffee and got up to remove her stylish jacket. She stood at least six feet tall, maybe more, with grey green eyes, broad shoulders, and rather severe features. Less attractive close up than she had appeared from a distance, more rough-hewn than refined.

"I think your song has promise."

"We know that, but what can you do for us?" Christine realized too late that her tone was pretty snappy.

Zach gave her a quick look and Thomas jumped in. "Maybe we should slow down a bit," he said, glancing at Christine with perplexed surprise. "Sam is doing you guys a favor by coming here."

Normally Christine would respond to such a signal but this afternoon she wasn't in the mood. So she forged ahead. "I understand, Professor Turner," she replied as though he were someone she had just met for the first time. "But my question for Sam is still the same — what can she do for us?" Adam reached over and laid his hand on hers, saying nothing but letting her know he was a bit startled by her brusque tone. She pulled her hand away.

Sam seemed unfazed. "The music industry is very tough," she said, wrapping her tall frame around her chair. "Look, I can't promise you anything. But I wouldn't have driven the whole way up here to meet you if I didn't think your music has some potential."

Christine could see Thomas staring at her with puzzlement.

"We really appreciate your coming," Zach said quickly, turning on his natural charm, rubbing his blond spikes. "Let's just take a moment to hear what your thoughts are, Sam."

Sam was impressive, really. She sketched out a series of options for The Forerunners, and Zach and Adam asked good questions. But Christine remained silent, lost in the fog of a funk she couldn't quite pinpoint.

In the end, she heard very little of what Sam said. Her inner agitation spread like a scratchy numbness through her upper arms. Why did she feel so alone, so unappreciated, so clueless about her future? Why didn't she have at least one true friend she could be totally herself around? Why didn't she have a clearer sense of direction about what she wanted to do with her life? And why did Thomas toy with her, acting half-romantic one moment and treating her like a half-sister the next? She was a senior in college, for fuck's sake. But after sixteen years of school, it now seemed as though her life was almost over, not just beginning. She and her mother were being evicted by Thomas' aunt, and neither Harriet nor Thomas could stop it. So why are we sitting here with this techie genius dreaming about the big time when everyone knows it'll never happen? Her mother was right after all.

Going out through the blue doors, Thomas paused. "Are you okay?"

"Sure," Christine snapped. "Why wouldn't I be?" She spun and walked away.

# Twenty–Five

———

**Several times since the** Thanksgiving Fire, Christine found herself in the run-down Ford she had bought to get to and from work, driving along the upper ridge south of Arlene's farm to see if anyone was watching Arlene's place. Was their barn really going to be next as threatened by that message weeks ago?

A retirement rancher squatted next to the lane going into the old Swedeson farm. She had known Sue and Milford Swedeson for years, an elderly couple as genuine and friendly as could be. Impossible to imagine them involved in something so cruel. The only other structure along that road from which one could surveil Arlene's place was the old house where Marcy Young lived with her little brother and their parents. Hard to suspect them.

So who could it be? Maybe someone parked along the ridge to watch Arlene's place—but wouldn't the neighbors notice their car?

She wondered suddenly why Becca and Arlene thought they were being watched from the upper ridge south of their farm. And why hadn't they contacted her since the second fire?

As she arrived at Zach's place, she was confused to see Mr. Sickman in his trademark bowtie and slouchy mustache sitting beside Zach at their dining room table. Sickman had a way of getting his photo in the newspaper. Zach's mother Shirley waved to her from their kitchen where she was stirring energetically at the stove. Shirley had new glasses. Pretty classy, really.

"Christine," Zach said, standing politely. "I think you may know my uncle, Toby Sickman." The attorney managed a sort of rumpled unfolding into an erect position, one hand full of papers as he extended the other to her. "Nice to meet you, Christine." She shook his hand, still puzzled.

"I invited Uncle Toby because I thought his experience as a lawyer might be helpful to our cause."

"I see" was all she could manage as they sat down. She noticed Shirley was listening carefully from the stove, holiday music playing in the background. *Sweet little Jesus boy.* Christine felt a bit ambushed. Zach had invited her over, she thought, to work on a plan to stop Betsy from converting the Turner homeplace into upscale housing. And while he had mentioned that his parents were sympathetic to their cause, he hadn't said a thing about Toby Sickman being there.

Did they need a lawyer? She hadn't thought so. Who was going to pay him? And furthermore, if they engaged an attorney, Toby Sickman was at the bottom of any list she could imagine. A gadfly, known for losing the big cases and winning suits for causes not many people supported. What was Zach thinking?

"Ethan is my mother's first cousin," Toby said, clearing his throat in that peculiar manner of his, his left eye twitching as he looked at her through his smudgy glasses. "I've always really liked Ethan and Harriet. But when Bruce lost his first wife and married that ferocious Betsy, I knew we were in trouble."

She wasn't sure what to say. Zach could sense her unease. "It all sorta came together over Thanksgiving. Uncle Toby and Aunt Sally were here for the meal, and we were discussing our concerns about the Turner Estates proposal. Uncle Toby offered to help out, if we wished."

"Pro bono," Shirley clarified, having drifted in from the kitchen. "My brother's pretty knowledgeable about real estate development deals and the ins and outs of zoning procedures."

It wasn't what she expected. "The last thing I want to do is offend Harriet and Ethan," Christine said softly.

Shirley came to sit beside her. Christine could see why Zach and his mother were close. Shirley had a dignifying manner. "You have a lot at stake," she said now. "We understand that. Bob and I don't want to upset you. I think what came to us during our Thanksgiving discussion was that time is pretty short. If we have any chance of stopping this, we have to get organized quickly and file a motion for the January zoning meeting. Or it may be too late."

Sickman's eye was twitching again. He shuffled his papers noisily as though the sound would give them privacy from him.

She needed space. She got up and walked over to the antique corner cupboard, staring at the dishes and china so beautifully arranged there. What should she say? How to not hurt any feelings but be honest? "I had drawn up a list of things I thought we were going to discuss. I guess I didn't realize we needed a lawyer involved yet." There, she had said it.

Zach came over. "Let's just stop right here and give you the time you need to feel comfortable with this."

"Hey, it's not about me."

"But it is," Shirley insisted. "It affects you and your mother very directly."

Zach nodded. "Betsy clearly would like to kick you out."

"But what's most important to me is that I don't alienate Harriet and Ethan. They've done so much for me."

Toby Sickman was on his feet now, too. "I don't want to offend Ethan and Harriet, either. But I think I know where they are on this. We have to stop Betsy."

That alarmed her. "Have you discussed this with Harriet and Ethan?"

"No, I have not." Seeing Christine's skepticism, Sickman raised his right hand.

"I swear."

Christine turned to Zach. "I'm worried that this thing is getting out of control."

"I'm sorry." And she knew he meant it. Zach looked chastened. He hadn't intended to get ahead of her.

The meeting ended more abruptly than any of them expected. Christine hoped no one was upset with her, but she didn't regret mentioning her unease. Sickman was a wild card.

# Twenty–Six

---

**S**he knuckled down, still half-incensed about life, and rewrote her paper for Dr. Hutchinson-O'Flannery in a style she figured Hutchery would accept. She felt too old and tired to try to be original anymore. Her school days were nearly over and they sure as hell didn't add up to much. How had she deceived herself so badly? Just like Mama had warned. She'd let herself be swept away with fanciful mirages of wishful prospects. *The dusk moves in and welcomes night, my hope is thin, I see no light, no warmth or glow to slow my plight.*

When she got home she sat at the little desk in her bedroom, staring out at the brownish drab farmscape of the Turner fields, brooding despondently about the shorter days, the flight of color, and the creeping cold of winter. "Who the hell do I think I am?" she said aloud, hearing only a soft moan in the December drafts whipping around the house. "Even if I make it through college, that won't change a thing. I'll still be timid Christine Ober with that weird mother. And I'll never be able to stop Bruce and his cunning Betsy. I'm a nobody."

Later her mother found her asleep at her desk and wakened her, looking more worried than usual. "What's the matter, chickadee? You aren't often so low."

It touched her to see her mother concerned, even if it was for a short moment. Mama sat on Christine's bed then and took her hands in her own, searching her face. "I know we're not close, Christine, but I do want to be here for you. Can you tell me what's wrong? I don't often see you down like this."

"You'll just say 'I told you so.'"

"No, I won't, honey. I promise I won't." She didn't bother to argue with her mother. What was the point? The wheel of inevitability was beginning its slow turn. "You've been a really good daughter to me," Mama said. "Sorry I don't say that more often."

They sat there holding hands as they watched the darkness envelop the fields and the tree line, running along the edge of the woods up to the Turner home-place on the ridge. *My hope is thin, I see no light.*

# Twenty–Seven

———

The sun came up the next day. That was a relief. She had just settled into her work area at the front desk when Sharon stopped by. "I got a call from a lawyer in Arizona who claims he's a descendant of the Johannes Gerbach who settled here in the 1740s, and he'd like us to trace it for him. For the usual fee. Is that something you'd enjoy, Christine?"

"If you think I'm up to it."

"You did a good job on the Shapiro request we got last week from Georgia."

"Okay, give me the details."

She looked up to see Uncle Jimmy standing by the front entrance, appearing shabby and cold in his thin coat. He gave her a tentative smile, and she waved for him to come to the desk, wondering what was afoot.

She knew she'd need to be careful since Sharon could watch.

"Good morning, Uncle Jimmy."

"Hi, Christine. Sorry to drop in like this."

"Something wrong?"

"Oh, no. I just wanted to connect with you, and I heard you were working here."

She picked up the phone and called Sharon's office. "May I have five minutes to talk with my Uncle Jimmy?"

"Sure, I got you covered."

They sat in the back room near the reference section. She could see he was nervous about whatever he wanted to discuss. "How are you, Uncle Jimmy?"

He beamed. "Oh, I'm good. Sure am. And you?"

"I'm good, too. Thanks." She paused. "You seem a little uneasy. May I ask why?"

"I don't want to upset you or your mother."

"Don't worry. Just tell me what's on your mind."

"I miss family." He stated it simply, three short words, but the ring of it could have filled a dozen pages with scripted tenderness, the way he said it.

"I'm sorry, Uncle Jimmy. I should have been in touch with you again before Thanksgiving."

He stared at the high shelves of old books, his lips puckered in reluctance. "We all hate to be excluded, don't we?" he said with that sucking sound he made. "Well, not you, Christine. I'm sure you don't know what that's like."

"Don't be silly. I know as well as anyone."

"Really—you?" His countenance got a clouded look as he thought of Christine suffering rejection. "Makes me mad that anyone would treat you like that."

She reached over and touched his hand. "Can you tell me what you're getting at?"

"Oh, I'm taking too much time, I guess. You're working. Should I leave?"

"Uncle Jimmy."

"Yes?"

"Just say it."

"Oh, okay." He coughed. "I wish you and your mom and I could get together sometime over Christmas. I'd be glad to take you two out for a meal, if it would suit."

She was braced for something worse. "Oh," she said. "I'd like that. Let me check with Mama."

Uncle Jimmy raised his hand. "I know this is a big deal for Karen. She said she never wanted to hear from me or see me again the last time I went away. So please understand, I don't want to make things worse."

She looked at him directly. "I'll try to make it happen."

"Really?"

"I'll try."

And before he could stop it, his eyes filled with tears, spilling down his cheeks, a deep whimper escaping from within him.

Years of isolation, regret, and pain came surging out of Uncle Jimmy in little swells and sobs until she too was in tears, the long years of her uncle's life and those of his sister, her mother, etched in the tapestry of her mind, so much energy wasted on worry, estrangement, and frustrated wishes.

# Twenty-Eight

—

**H**arriet invited Christine to come bake Christmas cookies again, along with Barbara and Wanda from the quilting group. This year most of the cookies would be refreshments for their madrigal Christmas program at the Community Center.

Ethan was sitting in his chair in the corner watching, mostly without comment, his bout with a bad cold having weakened him in recent weeks. Brownie snuggled in his lap, one eye open. Christine pulled up a chair and visited with Ethan when she first got there, alarmed and saddened to see how exhausted he was. Ethan had even felt compelled, she learned, to cancel this year's annual carol sing which he had hosted the week before Christmas for as long as she could remember.

Harriet's energy level hadn't flagged a bit, however. She buzzed around the kitchen, assigning tasks to Barbara, Wanda, and Christine, making and rolling the different doughs, designating the cookie cutter designs, and making sure the baking times were perfect. The place smelled like heaven.

Wanda tried to ask Harriet about Betsy's development project, but Harriet refused to engage. Barbara entertained them with stories of her grandson's acting in his middle-school drama. All the while, Harriet hummed Christmas carols and sneaked little bites of the various cookies to assure the quality she wanted. Christine could tell she was concerned about Ethan simply by the way she tried harder than ever to include him in the conversation, though he was mainly silent.

"I remember my first Christmas with the Turner clan," Harriet chuckled. "I worried I wasn't first class enough. My family came from up the river. We had some nice things. But Ethan's parents were a stylish bunch, and I was nervous that first Christmas. So nervous, in fact, that when I was helping to dry the dishes after lunch, I twisted off the handle of a coffee cup from their fine china set. I was mortified. But Ethan's mother was a peach, acting as though it was her fault, which it wasn't, of course."

Ethan chuckled from his corner.

"The Turners have always had that touch of class," Barbara added. "I remember my mother used to talk about Ethan's parents and what fine people they were."

The side door opened and there was Thomas, his face red from the cold. "It smells fantastic in here," he announced. Christine hadn't expected to see him there and wasn't sure how to act.

"We're making most of them for your madrigal program," Harriet said.

He walked around and surveyed the variety. "May I have one now, Grandma?" he asked with the pleading tone of the little boy he once was.

Ethan raised his hand as though to flag a violation. Harriet laughed. "One and only one," she said cheerfully.

Thomas picked up one of the iced gingerbreads and took a big bite. "Wow, that's amazing!" he exclaimed.

Ethan found his voice. "Praising the bakers doesn't get you more cookies. One and only one." They all laughed. It was the playful family atmosphere Christine loved about this kitchen.

"Your grandma was just telling us about her first Christmas with the Turners," Wanda told Thomas. "Sounded pretty scary."

Thomas laughed again. "Yeah, we Turners have always been a scary lot, wouldn't you agree, Christine?"

She blushed slightly and tossed it right back. "I'm shaking in my boots even now," she said. Ethan let out a chuckle.

"Well, thanks for the cookie, Grandma, even though it was only one." As he turned to go, Thomas paused beside Christine, lowering his voice. "We missed you at the last madrigal practice."

She wasn't sure what to say. She hadn't meant to skip, but after getting so mad at Thomas during that meeting with Sam, she seriously considered dropping out. It would be the first madrigal program she had missed since she was a junior in high school. After all, she couldn't do everything, could she? "Sorry, Sharon needed me at the Historical Society for their Christmas craft bazaar." Which was technically true, though Sharon would have excused her for the madrigal practice. "I'm working there about twenty hours a week now."

"So I heard."

"If I forfeited being in the program, that's fine. I'm not expecting any favors."

He looked at her directly then, as though trying to figure her out. "Christine, may I speak with you a second?"

"Now?"

"If that's okay with you." He started walking into the living room. She grabbed a towel to wipe her hands as she followed him. He motioned for her to sit. She waited. "Have I done something to offend you, Christine?" He was really a thoughtful guy, she realized anew. Very considerate and caring.

For a moment she was torn between melting under his spell and stiffening her spine, weary of not knowing what he thought of her. So she played the middle. "Why would you say that?"

"I think you know."

"Can you please explain?" She wasn't letting him off the hook this time.

"I feel like you treat me very differently than you used to."

"Really?"

He paused. "It feels like you're playing games with me. Which is your privilege. I just wanted to apologize if I did something to antagonize you."

What to say? I love you, dummy, can't you see that? Why am I not good enough for you? What does haughty Antonia have that I don't? Christine caught herself. This was childish. Grow up. Get over it. He's out of your league. "I'm sorry if I offended you, Thomas," she said meekly. "I guess I'm going through a tough stretch right now."

"Sorry to hear that."

"It's no big deal."

"Seriously, if I can help in some way, please let me know."

Oh, God, those eyes, those strong shoulders.

"No, I'm fine. And I realize I missed a practice without letting you know. So if you think I shouldn't sing in the program, that's not a problem."

"Of course not, Christine. It's not the same group without you."

He turned then and went upstairs to his room while she sauntered back to the kitchen and the cookie-making operation. Harriet met her eyes, checking if she was okay, and Christine replied with a smile.

"It's not the same group without you." What did he mean by that? Maybe he was more observant than she gave him credit for. Oh, stop dreaming, Christine. Get your feet on the ground.

# Twenty–Nine

—

"**A**re you home alone?"

It was Becca, calling to ask if she and her mother could drop by to talk with her briefly. They could be there in five minutes.

"Sure. My mother's at work."

Becca and Arlene stayed standing when they got there, even though Christine invited them to sit down and offered them coffee. The sky was overcast with flurries in the air, and both women had on the heavy coats they wore around the cow barn on cold days. The accompanying aroma confirmed that.

"Sorry we haven't been in touch," Arlene said.

"No problem. It's really none of my business."

"But we brought you into it and then rudely never followed up."

Christine raised her hand to indicate that no apology was expected. "If I may ask, did the fire at the Miller place affect your thinking?"

From their reactions, it appeared the two of them still did not agree about the whole matter. "It was a terrible thing," Arlene's voice broke as she looked away, the thought apparently too weighty. "I know the neighbors and the Amish helped the Millers clean up and built them a new barn. But the trauma of it all, and the loss of so much that was in that huge barn...." her voice trailed off.

Becca's face took on a fierce quality now. "We still have not taken that pasted-up note to the police."

"The one you showed me?"

"Becca kept saying we should, but I wasn't at peace about it."

Christine walked over and hugged Arlene. "I'm really sorry for you."

Becca grunted. "I still think it's either mischief or revenge."

"Revenge for what?"

Arlene nodded. "That's what I always say."

The three of them fell silent, a feeling of skittish jeopardy pregnant in the air.

Arlene's body started to silently shake with sobs then. "I have never felt so terrified, so completely helpless." Becca had no tears, though. Just a determined look and a set jaw.

As the two were leaving, Christine had a thought. "Would it be okay if I dropped around occasionally to play games with you and the girls, to get your minds off things?"

Arlene beamed. "Please feel no obligation. But that would be nice."

"I'll text you later today to set a game night for next week." This time even Becca smiled and reached back to hug Christine.

# Thirty

———

**fter class, Dr. Shriver** asked if she could stay a moment. The professor spoke briefly with several students, gathered up his lecture notes, and motioned for Christine to come and sit. "I hear you're working at the Historical Society."

"Oh, yes, I am. Part-time."

"You like it?"

She was puzzled. "Sharon's great. And yes, I've always enjoyed seeing how people and events are connected." Pause. "Did I do something wrong?"

Dr. Shriver chuckled a sort of high-pitched screech. "Wrong? Oh, no, Sharon told me you're doing a terrific job. I'm on her board, you know."

Christine was tempted to say that lowered her opinion of the Society's board, but she simply waited while the professor fussed with some of the papers on his desk.

"Here at Midstate we normally can't afford assistants, but I've gotten permission from the department for next semester."

Christine decided to wait rather than trying to fill in the blanks. How did any of this relate to her?

"What do you think?" Shriver asked.

Again, Christine paused. "Not sure I follow."

"I'm asking if you're interested."

"In what, exactly?"

"In assisting me next semester with the one class."

"Me?"

"You're surprised?"

"You're serious?" He better not be trying one of his lame jokes.

"Only if you're interested."

"But why me?"

The teacher vibrated with that high-pitched screech again. "You're a modest one. I like that."

"Look, you'll have to explain more before I know what you're asking."

"This assistant will help with my American history class next semester. Some tutoring, some research paper responding, and perhaps a bit of teaching. I got approval for an outstanding senior history major to help with this. You'd get an extra course credit and a small honorarium."

Christine was astounded. Totally unexpected. "I really enjoy having you in class," Shriver continued. "And I've been watching you."

She had no idea. You mean some good things can come along in life that you did nothing to instigate? Unless Shriver was being creepy.

"It would be a good step toward your being able to teach history in the future."

On her way out of the building, she ran into Emily who was stretching as though she had a cramp from taking an exam. "Hey, would you come visit me in Philly for a day or two over break?"

"Sure, if I can fit it into my work schedule at the Historical Society. I'm trying to stash away a little extra cash over break."

Emily smiled and slipped her arm around her. "It would mean a lot to me." They darted out of the cold wind into the alcove below the library's west windows. Christine told Emily about her conversation with Dr. Shriver and the prof's invitation to assist him. Emily acted impressed.

"I probably made a mistake by not taking education courses," Christine shrugged.

Later as she drove down to the Historical Society to finish the genealogical chart for that high-flying Arizona attorney, Christine surveyed the December late afternoon sky, pondering how a request from a boring, slightly strange professor could brighten a cold day. Hot damn, she might even discover that she had the chops to become a teacher. Life wasn't over after all.

That evening Zach called her to say he had inadvertently learned one more detail about Lenny Bryer. "He lives in California and owns a real estate business."

"And you're telling me this, Zach, because of—?"

"I stumbled onto it. I debated if I should tell you. In the end, I decided you'd feel more betrayed if I didn't pass along the info."

She expected to be angry and was surprised that the news somehow picked her up. She was silent for a long time.

"You still there?" Zach asked finally.

"I am."

"I apologize if I upset you again. But here's my question to you—do you want to live the rest of your life and not try to reach out to your dad?"

"I don't have a dad," she snapped.

"Okay, Christine. Sorry I misjudged."

# Thirty-One

---

Thomas' car was in the shop, which meant that Thomas and Christine were thrust together with Arlene on the back seat of John Jr.'s old Buick on the way to the Community Center for the madrigal concert. It was so snug with the three of them together that Thomas put his arm up behind her on the seat back, and she leaned into him unexpectedly as John Jr. took several sharp corners on the back roads.

"John Jr., you should slow down a bit," his wife warned.

"Yes, Bertie, I'll try."

"There are five of us in here. There won't be a concert program if you kill the director on the way there." Ordinarily they would have all laughed at her comment, but John Jr.'s foot was pressed to the pedal so firmly they were all a bit worried.

On the next sharp corner, Christine, in the middle, had nothing to grab hold of when the car's momentum threw her body tight against Thomas, her chest against his side and her face against his cheek. Thomas' hand slipped onto her shoulder then, landing for a sweet eternal moment on top of her breast, his lips against her forehead as John Jr. pulled them out of the long wicked curve.

"Whoa, whoa!" Thomas laughed nervously. "That was one sharp corner."

But he held her snug for a moment longer than he needed to as the car came out of the turn. God, he felt great!

"John Jr., shall I drive?" Bertie demanded.

"Sorry, everybody," John Jr. called out. "I'll slow down. Five people in the car makes it swerve more than usual."

"You want us to walk?" Arlene piped up. They all laughed in relief as they came over the ridge toward the straightaway on the edge of town.

"You smell wonderful," Thomas whispered in her ear as he pulled her tight for one more instant before placing his arm back on the seat behind her, the dark of the countryside replaced now by the town's street lights and colorful Christmas decorations on some of the homes. Christine said nothing, glancing quickly at his face, searching for a clue to his real intentions, seeing in those eyes what seemed like definite pleasure. And maybe a touch of heat.

Neither one mentioned their unintended caress as they piled out of the car at the Community Center, snow flurries adding to the romantic atmosphere. A moment later they were backstage with the other singers, warming up. Emily looked smashing in her elegant red dress.

It wasn't until they filed out and began their first number for the large crowd that Christine noticed Antonia Waldorf seated in the front row, her perfect face aglow as she watched Thomas lead the group in its otherworldly music. Did he know Antonia was coming? Or was she a surprise?

Afterward, as people ate cookies and showered them with compliments, Christine reached out and took Emily's arm. "Your solo was terrific," she said to her friend. And she really meant it. Emily had a great voice.

"Oh, thanks, Christine. But he should have given you a solo, too. Your voice has such cultivation."

Before she could thank Emily, Christine became aware of someone standing beside her. Antonia. Christine started to smile politely until she saw the hot darts in her eyes. "Stay away from Thomas," the Princeton duchess hissed at her.

Christine was shocked, but her resolve hardened. "I'm just one of the singers."

The eye embers only burned more brightly, intensifying the highhanded young woman's bewitching face. "I know you have a crush on him. But I'm warning you to remember your place. Stay away." She spun on her fashionable heels and marched away toward Thomas.

Goddamn, if Thomas marries that bitch, then he deserves her. Stay cool, Christine.

John Jr. walked up. "We're ready when you are. They say the snow's really coming down."

"Let's go then," she answered, trying to keep her fuming emotions from showing in her voice.

John Jr. stopped for a moment. "I apologize for my driving manners on the way here. Sometimes I forget to slow down when others are in the car."

"No problem."

"Thomas won't be riding back with us. Apparently his girlfriend showed up and is taking him home."

People weren't kidding about the snow. As they stepped out of the Community Center, the landscape lay plastered with several inches, cars skidding around and spinning out of the parking lot. Christine reached out to catch and steady Arlene as she started to fall on the way to John Jr.'s car, Arlene laughing with giddy fright. "You're always looking out for me," the older woman said as they crawled into the back seat, brushing the snow off their coats and shaking it out of their hair. Arlene lowered her voice. "Thanks for listening last week and for coming to play games. It meant so much to the girls. And to me, especially."

Christine nodded, then leaned front to address John Jr. "Could you wait a second while I call my mother to see if she might need a ride home? She was working at the diner tonight, but I assume Danny let her go early when he saw this snow."

"By all means," Bertie said. "We can all sit here and let the car warm up while you call your mom."

Turned out her mother was already safely home. So John Jr. lunged out of the parking lot like a somewhat cautious wild man, charging down the back roads in the silent snow while she and Arlene held on for dear life in the back seat.

Mama actually hugged Christine when she pushed through the door, snow-covered and cold. "Welcome home, honey. I was getting a little worried."

"Oh, thanks. John Jr. got me here." She peeled off her scarf and coat.

Her mother clearly wanted to say more. "It meant a lot that you thought of me and called," she said. "It feels like you're watching out for me." There were tears in Mama's eyes. "It really made me glad, like old times." Her mother reached out and hugged her again.

"You're not alone, Mama. Always remember that."

Later as she lay in bed, unwinding the many emotions of the day, she touched her breast, the nipple rising, as she relived that exhilarating moment with Thomas on the back seat, his big beautiful hand slipping over her. What would it be like to really be with him? She couldn't block it out, much as she tried. The most slender of hopes, true. But she wasn't ready to sever Thomas from her dreams. Not yet.

# Thirty–Two

---

She was just getting ready to leave work the next day for the meeting at Sickman's office when Sharon asked to see her. "I won't keep you long. But I wanted to put something into your brain."

"Okay. Getting into my brain may not be as easy as you think," Christine said with a sly smile, following Sharon into her office.

Sharon laughed. "I have a long needle here in my cupboard I use for that very sort of thing. It reaches right into your innermost thoughts."

Christine pretended to be scandalized. "Did one of the original settlers bring it from Europe?"

"Yes, from Transylvania." The library was empty at that moment, and Sharon gave her best imitation of a wolf's ravenous howl.

Christine was impressed. "Sharon, you should do stand-up."

When they stopped laughing, Sharon turned serious. "You know we're in the middle of our year-end fund drive, right?"

"Ah, yes, I'm aware. But I honestly haven't focused on it. Sorry I don't have a few thousand to kick in." Sitting across from Sharon, Christine kept wondering what secret but historic torture tools might be hidden in the cupboard in the corner.

"It's a bit slow this year," the Society director confided. "I shouldn't be worried, but I am. Look, I'm not soliciting you personally, but if you think of anyone who may be willing and able to donate, I welcome suggestions."

Christine was surprised. She hadn't paid any attention to the fund appeal. "I'll try, but I'm not sure I know anyone you don't already have on your list."

"Don't let it worry you. But if you think of anyone, let me know."

"I'm sure Harriet and Ethan are on your list."

"Oh, yes. They've been our most faithful donors for decades. Amazing people."

"And Bruce and Betsy?"

Sharon paused, choosing her words carefully. "Being blunt—Betsy's not yet caught on to the concept of generosity."

Christine smiled. "I noticed." A thought struck her. "What about Toby Sickman, the lawyer? Maybe he'd make a donation."

Sharon took her pen and made a note. "See, I knew you'd come up with a good idea. I'll contact Toby."

"But you won't mention my name, right?"

"No. Lips are sealed," Sharon winked.

As Christine was leaving, she paused by the door. "Is my job in danger?"

"Oh, no, I don't think it will come to that. I always go half-crazy between Thanksgiving and New Year's, waiting to see how much we'll get in donations during this very important time. This year's a bit on the slow side, so I'm jumpy."

Christine paused again, unsure if she wanted to share her next thought. "Maybe our band could do a benefit concert for the Historical Society," she said.

Sharon literally flew out of her chair. "Would you? That would be so great!"

"Let me check with the guys. It would take some quick planning with time so short."

Sharon took her arm. "It's my problem, not yours, Christine. But if a concert could happen, I would be forever indebted."

"Forever? That sounds like a good bargain." They chuckled as Christine headed out the door for Toby Sickman's office. She was running late now.

Sickman's demeanor during the meeting did little to reassure her. Maybe because Zach and his parents had known the lawyer as a family member, they could overlook his eccentricities. She found his throat-clearing and eye-twitching disconcerting, not to mention the multiple high stacks of documents and other papers spread out across two large, rickety-looking tables next to his desk. True, she had been in very few attorney offices, but this seemed a little yesteryear to Christine. At the Historical Society she worked with old documents and papers all the time, but Sharon had a clear system. Sickman probably had a system, too; she just found it a bit unnerving.

Bob Collins, Zach's dad, led out with his questions. He was a manager at the local Roger's Supermarket and said he needed to head right back there for a meeting. "Is there enough water on the Turner farm to support the proposed housing development? What about traffic — was a proper traffic study executed? And how about environmental studies and stormwater?"

Sickman nodded. "Those are all good questions. Even if our goal is only to slow them down for six or eight months."

Christine's response was immediate. "I'm only interested if we can actually stop the project."

Shirley nodded. "My sense, Toby, has always been that the supervisors and the zoning people respond to public sentiment. Right? So shouldn't we be trying to pack that Township room at the January hearing with concerned citizens?"

Zach tapped his fingers on the big desk. "Christine, if we really worked at it, I bet we could easily get enough students to cram that Township room."

She nodded. "Yeah, by mid-January everyone will be back from the holidays."

Mr. Collins had other thoughts. "Most students don't vote in local elections. What we really have to do is make the officials worry that they may not be re-elected if they side against popular opinion on this big issue."

"Votes mean more than noise," Sickman grunted.

"So we need to jam the room full with voters," Shirley said.

"How do we do that?" Christine asked.

Zach wasn't fully convinced. "I still think we can mobilize students to make Betsy sweat."

In the end, Sickman agreed to file the petitions related to the traffic, water, and zoning issues, Zach's parents agreed to take the lead in recruiting other local voters to attend and raise concerns and objections, and Zach said he would work with Christine and other friends to figure out a way to harness student power against the mighty Betsy.

"It's not going to be easy," Sickman intoned, pulling on his droopy mustache.

# Thirty-Three

---

The night before **The Forerunners** benefit concert, Christine and Emily met at Leo's for an early bite. Darkness already wrapped the landscape. Christine could hardly wait until the days stopped getting shorter.

Emily was having a hard time deciding what to do after graduation. "My voice is not good enough to go professional. I'm not sure I want to teach music either in high school or privately. I don't even know where I want to live."

"Grad school seems a good place to delay decisions," Christine smiled. "Why not hang out there for a year or two?"

Emily didn't smile back. "If I had the money, that's where I'd go. But—you know about my sweet mother."

They returned to their salads for a moment.

"What's up with you?" Emily asked.

Christine pursed her lips and debated how much she should say. "I hadn't really thought seriously about being a teacher until Dr. Shriver offered me the assistant position. I suppose him being such a bad teacher gives me an advantage — by comparison, I mean. But even if I do well, that doesn't guarantee anything. History jobs are very hard to find, not to mention that I didn't major in education. So it's probably a dead end." She paused. "I know this may sound weird to you, but with my background and my mother's constantly badgering me not to try to be 'somebody,' I've never assumed I could be a 'professional' anything. I felt lucky to even be in college."

Emily shook her head in protest. "You are so talented and wicked smart."

"I may seem confident, but deep down I'm always braced for failure and ridicule. It's been such a thick cloud over much of my life — you can't just shake it. And now as a senior, creeping self-doubt sorta paralyzes me. I know I'm gonna just fall on my face. I like history, but there's likely no future there, no job. I love music, but our band probably won't even exist a year from now."

Emily's face brightened, and Christine turned to see Thomas striding toward their table. She braced herself. She'd never seen him at Leo's before.

"Hi, you two," he smiled.

"Hey, Thomas," Emily beamed. "Where's Antonia?"

"Oh, she's visiting a friend near Philly today."

"You want to join us?" Emily offered. The whole thing flustered Christine.

"Actually, Christine, I was wondering if I could speak with you a minute."

"Oh."

Thomas Turner was unfailingly considerate, she realized again. "Why don't I let you guys finish your conversation. I'll just sit over at that end and you can join me, Christine, when you're ready. Unless, Emily, that messes up—"

Emily jumped right in. "I have a final tomorrow and need to study. No problem."

Later, Christine was sipping a cup of coffee while Thomas fussed with a piece of carrot cake. What could he have on his mind? Was he going to add to Antonia's reprimand somehow? Did he want her to stay away? But he had asked to talk, right? She was confused.

He cleared his throat. "The reason I wanted to speak with you before going back to Connecticut for the holidays...." He paused, choosing his words.

"May I say something first?" she blurted abruptly.

"Sure."

"I don't know if you're aware of it or not, but a lot of people are upset about Betsy's plan to convert the home farm into upscale housing."

"I gathered that. I know Grandma's been very unhappy."

"I just wanted to say that I've been to a few meetings with people who want to stop Betsy's petition."

He nodded. "I wasn't sure. But Grandma thought you might be involved."

"Is she upset with me? I haven't discussed it with her."

"Oh, no, she and Grandpa are quietly cheering for the opposition. They can't go public, of course."

"So my involvement won't jeopardize my relationship with them?"

A faint smile passed across his handsome features. "The other day Grandpa said to Grandma and me, 'I never thought I'd see Betsy meet her better, but I believe our Christine might be up to the task.'"

"Dear God!"

"Word for word."

"Ethan's always been so gracious to me in spite of my faults."

He laughed. "Oh, come on, Christine."

"Are we here to make a list?"

He chuckled again, reaching up to push his hair back. "Let's not spoil things."

"But I interrupted you."

"Yes, you did. One of your dreadful faults!" He laughed softly, then fell silent. She waited. Finally he cleared his throat again.

"I understand that Antonia was pretty rude to you after the madrigal concert." She bit her tongue as he continued. "I want to apologize. She can be very possessive about things. She should never have treated you that way."

"What do you see in her, Thomas?" She had blurted it out before she could retrieve the words.

His gaze was steady, his face thoughtful. "Maybe less than I once did."

"Oh." She could feel her pulse quicken.

"When I come back from the holidays, I'd like to have some time to sit and talk with you, if you're willing." She waited. He smiled. "Is that a possibility?'

"I'll have to check my schedule," she frowned, sounding skeptical. Then she flashed her smile. "Time for you is always possible."

"Glad to hear it," he responded, taking the last bite of his cake.

"Have a good Christmas," she said, getting up to go. Why was she cutting the conversation short? "I'll see you in the new year."

For a moment he seemed a bit astounded by how abruptly things were ending, looking almost worried that he was losing her, his eyes a bit anxious. Then his great smile. "You, too," he said, reaching out to shake her hand.

# Thirty–Four

---

Sharon came backstage at The Root Cellar the next night to wish her luck. "I can't tell you how grateful I am that you guys are doing this," she enthused, looking good, dimples, smiles, and all dressed up.

"I hope we raise enough," Christine said.

"Anything is more than nothing. Just relax and do your thing." Christine felt especially close to Sharon these days, ever since the evening recently when they both stayed late to finish a grant proposal and Sharon confided about the years of anxiety that she and Bradley had endured as they tried to conceive. "I guess it's not to be," she had shrugged, her face wet with tears.

Jenn was over with Adam as he prepped for the show. On her way out, she stopped by Christine's little corner behind the stage.

"What's up, Jenn?"

"Hey, would you have a minute sometime?"

"For you, always."

"Thanks."

"A problem?"

"Not here. Not now."

"Got it. Let me know when." Christine saw Adam watching them.

"I'll be in touch, Christine."

Zach could raise his performance to a whole new caliber sometimes. Tonight was one of those moments as he played his guitar with inspired energy, his voice filled with contagious emotion. The Root Cellar was packed with an unusual medley of older patrons of the Historical Society mixed with the Cellar's typical younger crowd. Zach did his own funky version of "Silent Night" and the place went crazy. Then she and Adam joined Zach in a simple version of "Jingle Bells," and they soon had the audience singing along.

"We have no future without understanding our past," she told the crowd during one of the breaks. "Memory is important. So please be generous in helping our Historical Society."

They ended the concert as they knew they must with "If You Could Only See." It connected with the crowd as it always did. *Why can't you turn and see how much I long to be with you....*

She had just finished changing when she heard someone knocking on the side stage door. She grabbed her things and went to check.

"Sorry to intrude." It was Gordon Masterson, lighting up his dark, handsome features with that confident smile. "I loved the show. You're getting better all the time, Christine."

"Gordon! What brings you here?"

"I wanted to hear you sing. You know I've always loved your voice," he purred, reaching out to touch her arm.

"How's Wendi?" she asked, pulling her arm away. Gordon as smooth as ever. She literally hadn't seen him since he married Wendi two years ago.

"We're getting divorced. I thought you probably knew."

"So soon?"

Her bluntness made him wince like he always had when he knew she didn't approve. Gordon and she had dated in high school off and on. And then pretty constantly the summer after graduation. Gordon was a nice enough guy. The Mastersons had a construction company, and Gordon had stepped right into major responsibility after high school. Never one for books, but president of their senior class. Marsha and Wendi had jousted for his attention, but Christine normally won if she decided to compete.

For some of the cool girls, high school was all about flirting, making out, and snagging a man. But Christine had the band, her work in Harriet's garden, and her interest in college and history. Getting a man was not uppermost, apart from Harriet's grandson from Connecticut, a dream more than anything else. Gordon probably had sensed her self-sufficiency, and that only made him pursue her more.

It had come to a head during her first year of college. Gordon would take her for long drives in his new pickup truck to show her different houses their company had built. He kept asking her which her favorite was, and even talked about starting a family. It was too much too fast. And when he presented her with a beautiful diamond one evening, asking her to marry him, she panicked. "No, no, no," she had said. "I'm not ready."

Within two months, Gordon had announced his engagement to Wendi.

"May I drive you home?" he asked now, standing there by the side door of The Root Cellar.

She was shocked. Did he still like her? Was he trying to get back together?

"Oh, no, I'm fine," she said.

He was disappointed but unfazed, never one to lack confidence. "Maybe another time then?"

"I'm not interested in having Wendi slash my throat, Gordon," she said, pushing past him to the sidewalk.

"I'll call you," he replied.

Her reply was immediate. "Gordon, please don't." She kept walking, right by the big, shiny pickup parked along the snowy street with "Masterson & Son Construction" painted on the side door, never looking back.

# Thirty-Five

---

She was helping Anita, the volunteer coordinator at the Society, when Sharon rushed in, her face full of concern. "Arlene called and wanted you to know they just took Ethan to the hospital by ambulance. Sounds pretty serious."

"What's the problem?"

"Arlene wasn't sure."

"May I go?"

Sharon understood that Ethan was the closest thing to a father Christine had. "Go, go, I got you covered."

She tried to gain control of her emotions as she headed to the parking lot, climbing into her beat-up Ford. The snow had stopped but the road was slick. Coming around the curve on Double Lantern Road above the forge, her car went into a fast skid, and she nearly slid over the edge into the deep ravine below. "Slow down, you imbecile," she said very loudly, almost shouting, as though to frighten herself. "You can't help Harriet if you're in the fuckin' hospital yourself."

When she found Harriet in the waiting area, Thomas' grandmother rushed to hug her, fighting tears. Bruce was there, too.

"How is he?"

"We're still waiting to see. They're still checking him."

There wasn't much to say. Bruce went in and out to make some phone calls.

"I thought Ethan and I had more time," Harriet confided to her when Bruce was out.

Christine put her arm around her shoulders, now drooping uncharacteristically. "You'll have time, Harriet. I'm sure of it."

"You don't know."

"I'm gonna believe that until the doctor says otherwise."

Harriet gave her a worried smile. "I don't know what I'd do without Ethan."

"Fortunately for you, you don't have to worry about that just yet. Let's try to be positive."

Bruce came back. "Drew wants to know if he should drive down here?"

"Oh, no, tell him to stay put until we know more. Christine thinks it won't be too bad."

"How do you know that?" Bruce demanded, looking at her sharply.

"I was only trying to be optimistic."

"Then keep it buttoned," Bruce snapped. He turned to Harriet. "So I'll tell Drew to just wait until we call back with more information."

Drew was Thomas' dad. Wealthy hedge fund guy, quarrelsome, and arrogant. At least three unhappy marriages. Christine hadn't seen Drew for years. Thomas always seemed the opposite of his dad.

No one ever mentioned the third son in the family, Oliver, who had long ago cut off communication with his parents. Christine had never figured out why. And she never felt free to ask Harriet or Ethan what had strained their family.

The doctor turned out to be a young woman, pleasant and reassuring. "We did a number of tests. I think it's nothing more serious than a pretty heavy case of pneumonia. But that is serious enough."

"When can he go home?" Harriet asked.

"He'll need to stay here for now. Then—it all depends," the doctor answered.

"Can we see him?"

"He needs rest. So keep the visits short."

Ethan Turner looked like a phantom of the strong farmer he used to be, sunken into his pillow, his face white and barren without his glasses. Harriet's hand instinctively went to her mouth when she saw her husband shriveled beneath the hospital sheets, but she quickly recovered, taking his hand in hers, his eyes flickering open. He smiled sleepily.

"Ethan, they say you'll be fine," Harriet sang out. She leaned in to kiss his forehead.

"Be careful," Ethan warned in a weary voice. "Don't get what I have."

"Oh, don't fuss at me, old man," she scolded cheerfully. "I've survived pretty well for 80 years."

"A horse is what you...." Ethan said quietly, his voice trailing off as the medications pulled him back into sleep.

Harriet beamed, clearly relieved. "Any time he compares me to a strong horse, I know he's not dead yet." She reached out and hugged Christine. "He'll be okay, honey," she whispered, trying to fight back tears. "My Ethan's coming home soon."

Christine kissed her on the cheek. "He's lucky to have you, Harriet."

The nurse suggested there was nothing more they could do. But Harriet wanted to hang around a while longer. Bruce came back and said he needed to go. Christine said she'd see that Harriet got home.

After sitting in his room for another half hour while Ethan slept peacefully, Harriet admitted she was hungry. So the two of them went down to the expansive hospital cafeteria, a huge Christmas tree adding cheer, its colorful lights glittering.

They found a corner where they could watch people coming and going from the main entrance. "Look at them," Harriet mused, more relaxed now. "Every emotion known to humans right there on those faces. Grief because some loved one got a terrible diagnosis. Pure joy because a new baby was born. For others, boredom with endless waiting. Both ends of life and everything in between." It was true. Just then a teenage girl on crutches, dressed warmly against the cold, came by on the street outside their cafeteria window, laughing with her mother.

Christine knew the best gift she could give Harriet was just to listen as she struggled to reassure herself that Ethan would be okay. "The other time he really scared me was years ago, long before you were born. Our kids were young. We were going to an event at church, I think, and he had come in from the barn chores and was washing up quickly in the upstairs bathroom when I heard this loud crash. I couldn't figure it out, and Ethan didn't answer when I called him. I tried to open the bathroom door to see what had happened, but I couldn't budge the door. It opened inwards. I pushed and pushed, really scared as I realized I was pushing the dead weight of my husband. He had fainted for some reason and had fallen against the inside of the door. But I was scared he was dead. Our three little boys helped me push, and we finally got the door open wide enough for me to crawl in." Christine could see the tears in Harriet's eyes now.

"We called an ambulance that time, too. We never found out what caused it. The doctor thought maybe a kidney stone, I believe. But it was scary with three little boys at home."

Harriet paused, looking a little exhausted. "And forty or fifty years later, here we are. Relatively healthy. And basically sound in the head."

Christine reached over to take her hand. "And in love, too. You guys have lived the greatest lives."

Harriet brightened, still holding Christine's hand. "Love's coming your way, too. I know you'll find it soon."

"Wish that were true."

When they got back upstairs, Ethan was still sleeping, so they decided to head home. The sun reflected brightly off the fields of snow, almost blinding her as she drove. The wind had dropped off, and it felt a bit warmer.

"I can walk you to your house, Harriet."

"No, no, the walks are cleared. I'll be fine." But before she got out, Harriet leaned over and hugged her as Christine suspected only sweet old women can, pulling her unusually close. "You're the only daughter I've ever had, Christine. Ethan often says as much. And we both pray that you'll find a great love like we have."

Then Harriet darted in the walk and disappeared into the house, leaving Christine behind, sitting there in her dilapidated Ford in a glowing cloud of checkered hope.

# Thirty-Six

——

The next day Christine took a big step, doing an extensive search online to see what she could learn about the man who supposedly was her biological father. She found seven different Lenny Bryers but eliminated six of them by age and birthplace. After several hours of probing, she decided Zach was probably right. Mama's old boyfriend apparently now lived in San Jose, California, head of Bryer Real Estate, a sizable firm according to their website. Lenny's email address and phone number were plainly listed.

Christine closed it as soon as she saw it. Holy crap. Would it be that easy to make contact with the mythological Lenny of her childhood? Just dial? What would she say? What made her think he would take her call?

She tried to forget it, but it haunted her all day. Was this one of those Pandora things where curiosity sets off a curse? What good could possibly come from pursuing this further?

Living with a sense of fatherlessness for so many years had deprived her of many emotions she figured "normal" daughters had. She'd come to accept her hollowed-out center. Somehow her lack of threads stretching into the past created an impotence about her future. Not a daughter, not an orphan.

She had no one to talk with about it. Zach would encourage her to contact Lenny Bryer. She didn't know Emily well enough to discuss it. She realized she couldn't guess what Harriet and Ethan would counsel — how would being two generations older influence their answer? Mama would go nuts if she breathed a word of this to her. And she couldn't afford a therapist.

By the time she left work and headed home, she had made peace with doing nothing. What possible good outcome could result from contacting the man who apparently was technically her father?

# Thirty–Seven

———

**J**enn was waiting for her when she got home. It was one of the shortest days of the year, so it was already dark. "Gosh, I used to come here all the time when we were in high school," she said, looking around Christine's little bedroom. "Remember when you were hanging out with Stanley Neale and I was thick with Bobby Sassman?" she laughed. "Shit, those were the days."

Christine sat on her bed and offered Jenn the chair. "Whatever happened to Bobby Sassman?"

"He joined the Marines and never came back."

"Oh, sorry, I forgot."

"I never liked him anyway." Jenn tossed her head, jostling her crop of cute blond hair. She sat on the edge of Christine's desk now, flipping through some of the old photos Christine kept in the little box in the corner. "Wow, here's a shot of us at the prom. I didn't know you had this. May I have a copy?"

"Sure, I'll get you one."

Jenn kept looking through the photos, but she clearly had something else on her mind. Christine paged through a magazine she'd picked up. Sorta like old times, sitting around, half-talking, half-dreaming, half-lonely.

"Adam says you guys are recording some music early next year."

"Yeah, it sounds that way.

"Your heart isn't in it anymore, is it?"

"No, that's not true."

"Adam says you seem distracted."

Christine frowned. "Maybe since I got my job at the Society. And with all of the turmoil about my mom and me being evicted from this house. And Ethan in the hospital. I'm busier than I had been, true."

"I just hope you don't drop out, Christine. I've always loved your voice, going back as far as I can remember. And your lyrics only keep getting better."

"Thanks, Jenn. But we're seniors, you know. Nothing lasts forever." Christine laid down her magazine. "I figured you were coming here to tell me that you and Adam are getting hitched. Is it true?"

Jenn acted incredulous. "Where'd you get that crazy idea?"

"You gotta admit you two are together a lot."

"That's true."

"Is it good?"

"That's what I wanted to talk with you about."

"Uh-oh."

"No, it's good. I really like Adam a lot. He's a great guy, don't you think?"

"I've always loved Adam, you know that. Not as a romantic thing, but as a comrade in arms, let's-go-conquer-the-world sort of thing."

"He's one of the most stand-up guys I've ever met. He's gotten me to enroll part-time at Midstate next semester."

"That's great, Jenn! I didn't know."

"Yeah, I'm tired of being around so many smart people and not knowing anything."

"Hey, I always said you were intelligent, Jenn. I think you can be anything you want to be. I really do."

"Thanks, Christine."

They sat quietly for a few moments. Christine waited. Finally she slid across the bed and sat on the edge next to her old friend. "Do I hear a 'but' hanging in the air?"

Jenn's eyes welled up. "I don't know what to think."

"About what?"

"You need to swear you won't tell anyone."

"Okay—about what?"

"Not Adam. Not Zach. You can't tell your mother or Harriet. No one." Jenn's face became intense.

"You're scaring me, Jenn."

"That's because I'm sorta scared."

"Oh, God — what?"

Jenn got up and moved toward the door. "May I use your bathroom?"

"Sure."

When Jenn returned, she pulled Christine's door shut, though they were alone in the house. She sat on the desk chair now and stared out the window. "I don't want to betray Adam," she said quietly.

"I don't want you to either. There's no pressure from me."

"Did you know about Adam's dad?"

"Uh — not sure what you mean, Jenn."

"He gets drunk sometimes."

"Yes, I know that."

"And violent. He beats Adam's mother sometimes, apparently. And Adam, too, if he can. But never Adam's sister Ashley."

"Yes, I've sorta known that for a while."

Jenn turned on her, angry now. "Why didn't you tell me?"

"I didn't think it was my business."

"I thought you were my friend."

"Hey, that's not fair. It's not like *Adam* gets violent, right?"

Jenn wrapped her arms around herself as if she was suddenly very cold, though the temperature in the room had not changed.

Christine reached out and laid her hand on Jenn's arm. "What aren't you telling me?"

"I accidentally saw Adam's mother the other day when I was upstairs at their place, looking for Adam. It felt like she was trying to stay out of sight. The side of her face looked bad — all black and blue. Clearly someone had hit her."

"What did Adam say?"

Jenn tightened her mouth. "I didn't mention it to him. But I'll be honest, it really frightened me." She walked to the little window again. "That could be me."

Christine stood up and went to Jenn, hugging her as she started to sob. "Jenn, my friend, I'm here for you."

Jenn pulled away, wiping her face with her sleeve. "What if Adam turns out like his dad? I had an uncle Dennis who had the same problem. I couldn't live like Aunt Dottie did."

At that moment, the doorbell rang downstairs. Christine was hesitant to go and leave Jenn in such a state. But Jenn was insistent. "Go see who it is. I'm fine."

It was Gordon Masterson, all dressed up. The situation left Christine perplexed and a touch angry.

"Hi Gordon," she said, sounding annoyed.

"May I come in?"

"Probably not. What's up?"

"How would you like to make your boss happy?"

"Meaning?"

"I have a proposal for you. But it's cold out here."

"The sooner you spit it out, the less likely that you'll freeze, Gordon." She started to slam the door.

"Wait," Gordon insisted, sticking his foot in the door. "I got permission from my dad for our company to make a $10,000 donation to the Historical Society's fund drive. It should help Sharon reach her goal."

Christine was wary but impressed. "That's generous, Gordon. Thank your dad for me. But I think you should go to the Society personally and hand your check to Sharon. She'll be very happy."

Gordon still had his foot in the door, his large frame partly blocking the cold air from coming in. "There's a condition."

"A condition?"

"Yeah, the donation can't be made unless that condition is satisfied."

"Oh, I'm sure Sharon will do some research on your dad's ancestors, if that's what he wants."

"I'm the one setting the stipulation."

Christine was getting really cold, but she didn't want to let him into the house. "Spit it out or leave, Gordon."

"It's you."

"Me?"

"For Sharon to get that $10,000 donation, you need to go out to dinner with me. Before the end of the year."

She was angry now. "Get your foot out of the door, Gordon, or I'll call the police. And I'm not kidding," she snapped.

Gordon removed his foot but didn't budge otherwise, pulling up the collar of his overcoat and putting on some warm gloves. She pushed the door closed, glanced out at him, and turned away, reaching for her sweater on the kitchen chair and pulling it on. Then she jerked open the door. "Sharon's just going to have to get by without your bribe. No way in hell I'm going out in public with you."

"You mean you're willing to do it privately? All the better!"

"Oh, shut the fuck up, Masterson. I'm not going out with you, period."

"I promise I won't try to get you into bed."

"I'm going to call the police."

"No, no, I promise to be a gentleman. I just want to catch up. No hanky-panky. Just a little gift from you to thank me for the generous donation to your boss. I already made reservations for the day after Christmas at Quincey's."

"Will you have a permission slip from Wendi?"

"Wendi? I haven't seen her in months. I told you we're getting divorced."

Everything inside her was protesting, and yet she could see Sharon's big smile if she brought her $10,000.

"I need you to swear there will be nothing physical. No touching or rubbing or anything." She wasn't sure why she included "rubbing."

"See, you're just trying to turn me on."

"Okay, forget it." Christine slammed the door and locked it, leaving Gordon standing there with a half-happy smile on his face. She snapped off the kitchen light so he couldn't see her in the dark. After a moment, she heard him start his truck and drive away.

Upstairs, Jenn was standing with her hands on her hips as she came back into the bedroom. Clearly she had heard. "Damn, Christine, aren't you the flirt!"

"I am not. I told him 'No' ten different ways."

"But that Gordon still thinks he has a date with you."

"I can't be bought. And I don't trust that son-ovabitch for a second."

"All I'm saying is that Gordon thinks he's going to persuade you. You watch."

Later, after they talked further about Adam and his dad and the vicious cycles they each had observed in families, she turned to Jenn. "If you really like Adam, I'd give it a chance. I have never seen anything in him for you to worry about. It's not fair to Adam or to yourself if you permit his dad's terrible shortcomings to torpedo the happiness you can have together."

A look of huge relief came over Jenn and she gave Christine a happy hug.

# Thirty–Eight

—

When **Karen took the** time and made the effort, her cooking could be nearly as good as Harriet's. But most of the time she was too tired. Or Christine wasn't home and "cooking for one isn't much fun."

But on Christmas morning, Karen Ober buzzed around her kitchen as though she loved nothing better than preparing turkey cutlets, baked corn, and the wonderful oyster filling she had learned from Harriet years ago. Coupled with fresh potato rolls, gravy, the cranberry salad she had brought home from the diner, and a cherry pie Christine had made the night before. A feast. And Mama was actually singing under her breath. *Away in a manger.*

The night before, Christine and Mama had taken time to do something which they hadn't done for many years. When Mama said she didn't have to work on Christmas Eve after all and suggested it, Christine changed her plans and accompanied her to the 9:00 p.m. candlelight service at St. Mark's Lutheran. The church was packed. The choir was actually better than she remembered. And amazingly, there was eighty-year-old Harriet in the front row of the choir, beaming down at Ethan who was perched in the third pew where he and Harriet always sat, looking a little tuckered out but smiling. *All is calm, all is bright.*

Christine had ordered a new blouse and skirt for her mother. When Mama opened the two packages on Christmas morning, she even took time to go and try them on, parading down the steps like the cheerleader she used to be. The smart new outfit fit her perfectly. "Thank you, chickadee. I love it. But all I got for you is a gift certificate to Amazon."

"Oh, Mama, that's plenty. I really do appreciate it."

Later, Uncle Jimmy showed up ten minutes early and fell all over himself fussing and reminiscing. Mama had agreed to the idea more readily than Christine had feared. Maybe it was the growing realization that this would likely be their last Christmas in this modest house. Why not make it special.

"May I say grace?" Jimmy asked his sister as they took their places at the table. Karen paused. They hadn't said grace in years. Then she smiled. "That would be great, Jimmy. Thanks for offering."

Uncle Jimmy hesitated. "Would it be going too far to ask if we could hold hands like we did when Christine was a young girl?"

"I'd love that," Christine answered before her mother could respond.

So the three of them joined hands around their table brimming with festive foods as Jimmy intoned his best "Look, I'm doing the prayer" voice. Christine could feel Uncle Jimmy's hand trembling. She gave it a reassuring squeeze.

"Dear God, who gives all good gifts, accept our thanks on this the day of your son's birth, for the peace and joy, and now for this abundant meal prepared by my loving sister and my very special niece."

Christine wondered if it was a prayer adapted from something the chaplain in the prison may have used. Or maybe Jimmy had written it out days ago and memorized it. In any case, he delivered it with grace and a clear voice without a single sucking sound, in spite of the little tremor in his hand and voice.

They spent two hours eating and talking, topping it off with coffee and cherry pie. "Remember when Christine pushed you into the little creek below the forge?" Karen was laughing at Jimmy. "You must have been younger than ten, honey, and your uncle was pestering you, all in good fun, and you just jumped up and gave him a big shove, and he fell smack into the water!" Mama laughed so hard she started to cry.

"I still haven't paid you back for that, Christine," Uncle Jimmy warned. "One of these times, out of the blue, you'll find yourself falling into a creek. When you least expect it. And you'll look around, but you won't even see me!"

It was the most happy laughter that house had witnessed in many years. Christine could hardly absorb it. She kept waiting for it to take an ugly turn, but, as the afternoon wore on, she began to relax and decided it would be a Christmas to remember.

# Thirty–Nine

———

**C**hristine had never seen Sharon's face light up with such spontaneous joy as when she handed her the $10,000 check from Masterson & Son Construction. Sharon came around her desk and hugged her so intensely that Christine could actually feel the air being pressed out of her lungs.

Sharon was crying when she released Christine, sitting down abruptly. "Excuse me, I'm feeling light-headed. I've been so worried. And suddenly, like some majestic bird diving out of the heavens, you walk in here with a check that puts us over the top."

"I'm glad if it helps," Christine murmured.

"Help? It saves us. I didn't want to scare you, but I knew next year's budget would be trimmed if we fell short of our appeal's goal. Our board members were quite concerned. And besides, the Masterson folks are new donors. That's good news, too."

Christine watched as Sharon slowly regained her composure, the news growing on her. "I've gotta get you more involved in fundraising," Sharon said.

"No thanks. Not my thing."

"Christine, honey, you brought me a lot of tea in the last week, between your benefit concert and now this check."

"Like I said, not my thing." Christine decided not to tell Sharon about the stipulation Gordon had attached to the check.

Later, Zach and Adam were already seated at the table in the café's far corner when she came through the blue doors. They could barely contain their excitement. "Sam has gotten us an offer from Toyota to use our song in a commercial," Zach blurted out.

"Toyota?" She looked at them in disbelief. "Our song in a car commercial?"

"They're offering us $20,000 for the option. Much more if they move ahead. Could be big."

Christine was flabbergasted. "$20,000?"

Zach put his arm around her. "We're going to be rich, darling!" And he kissed her on the cheek and then kissed Adam on his cheek.

"Hey, man, stop kissing me," Adam complained. But he was clearly delighted with the turn of events.

The recording session in Baltimore was now set for early January to meet the contract schedule. "They need a state-of-the-art recording before exercising the option and paying the $20,000," Zach explained. "Then, if Toyota picks it up for their commercial, we'll get more payments. Sam says it could easily be $100,000 or more."

"I would have tried to go to a better university if I had known I could afford it," Adam sighed.

"You still can for grad school," Zach replied.

Christine's head was spinning. "Hey, let's wait a goddamn minute. If I understand this, we have to practice and prepare, then go to Baltimore for the recording session, and then wait. It's possible we will get no money at all, right?"

Zach kissed her on the cheek again. "Are you pissing on the best parade we've ever had?"

"I'm not trying to be negative. But let's keep our feet on the ground and not be heartbroken when it all falls apart."

Zach smiled. "Christine, darling, would you indulge me for a minute?"

"Okay."

"Sam said our chances of getting the $20,000 are nine out of ten. And fifty-fifty that we'll get more."

"We have to pay for the studio recording, right?"

"No, Sam's covering that."

"Well, then, Zach, what is Sam's cut?"

"She gets 80% of the first $5,000, 50% of the next $5,000, 30% of the next $10,000, and 15% from there on."

Christine couldn't help laughing. "Sounds like the music business! Nothing for the artists."

Zach was on the edge of being upset. "The Forerunners will get more than $10,000 of that $20,000 option money, Christine. That's $10,000 we don't have now."

Adam's voice became more robust. "How do we split up whatever we get?"

Zach didn't hesitate. "Equally, three ways, right?"

Adam seemed surprised. "But Christine wrote the hot lyrics and you wrote the inspired tune. Why would you give me an equal share?"

"Because we've been a team since high school," Christine said. "We all inspire each other."

"I think we should discuss it more," Adam declared. "I don't want you guys mad at me later."

"OK, we can discuss it, if that makes you feel better. But I won't change my opinion," Zach said, kissing Adam lightly on the cheek again.

Adam smacked Zach across the head. "Stop kissing me or I'll quit the group!"

Christine laughed. "You guys are still so juvenile."

"Sam thinks we should consider changing our group's name," Adam said, trying to wipe away the smooch from Zach.

"Really?"

"Yeah, it's not mandatory. But she wants to discuss it."

Zach laughed. "Oh, the pains of show business!"

Christine frowned. "May I request that we keep all of this confidential until we see if it materializes. We don't know if Toyota will definitely pick this up. We could make zero bucks. So let's keep it quiet, OK?"

Adam nodded. "I agree. It could be embarrassing if we act like big shots and nothing happens."

"Zach?" Christine turned her gaze on him.

"We can tell our parents, right?"

"I'm not telling mine," Adam said quickly. "My dad will try to grab the money and change it into liquid in a bottle."

Christine agreed. "It would blow my mother's mind — and then if things don't pan out, she'd say, 'I told you so.' But Zach, I have no problem if you tell your folks. And Adam, you can tell Jenn. As long as everyone understands it's confidential until we actually have a check in our hands."

As they walked out of the café, she thought they all had a new swagger. Was the future there to be grabbed, or was the future luring them into public failure?

Then she abruptly remembered the promised appointment with Gordon at Quincey's that night. "Oh God, help me!" she muttered under her breath.

Zach stopped and turned. "Did you say something?"

"No, not me."

Gordon arrived five minutes early to pick her up in his shiny pickup. That was one thing about Gordon — he was always punctual. Which didn't do anything to lessen her dread of the evening to come. "In a few hours it will be over," she murmured as she heard the truck's engine quiet and the driver's door open. "Anything for Sharon." She stepped out onto the porch so he wouldn't have to come in. "Good evening, Gordon," she said as cheerily as she could manage.

Under the glow of the porch light, she was struck anew with how handsome he was, all cleaned up and smiling. Even the little scar on his forehead from a motorcycle accident in high school somehow added to the attractiveness of his features.

She was sure he would take liberties at every opportunity, but as he opened the pickup door for her and gave her a gentle assist with his hand on her elbow, he couldn't have been more of a gentleman. "Thanks for agreeing to do this, Christine," he said sincerely. "I know it's a sacrifice on your part. My goal is that you'll have an enjoyable evening."

They were clearly expected. She hadn't been in Qunicey's since Harriet had brought her here for her twentieth birthday two years ago. Many locals thought it was the best restaurant in the area. The host gave them the Qunicey treatment, leading them to one of the white-linen-topped tables near the fireplace. As

Gordon pulled out her chair and helped her get comfortable, she realized several things. The arrangement of flowers on their table was larger and far more beautiful than the single cut flower on the other tables. How did that happen? And rather than choose one of the more visible tables like the three on the raised area with the lighted wall sporting the big framed paintings, Gordon had chosen a table which would not put them in the spotlight. Could this guy actually have some sensitive bones in his big broad body?

The food was extraordinarily delicious. Her branzino was the best fish she had ever had. And the chocolate raspberry cake was sublime. Gordon had clearly planned a series of questions to ask her about her life, and amazingly, when she asked him about his, he answered politely but soon turned the conversation back to hers. He wanted to know everything she had learned about the Underground Railroad. He asked about their band but wasn't pushy or nosy. He showed a lot of interest in her work at the Historical Society and was fascinated by her tale of the Arizona attorney and how she had traced the nine generations between Mr. Butler and his ancestor Johannes Gerbach who had settled near Turners Rise in 1742. "I even traced his lineage back five generations in the old country, back to the Black Forest area," she said.

Gordon kept watching her face intently. He seemed more like an old friend than a predator. But she braced herself to expect him to make an unwanted physical play before the evening was over. She had agreed to this "date" only with the condition of nothing physical. But she didn't expect him to keep his bargain. Gordon on the rebound had to be looking for a good lay, she was sure.

As they rode back to her place, she began to wonder if Gordon was playing the long game. She realized that he was trying to win her back, that he still wanted to marry her. Otherwise, how to explain this total gentleman who was reaching back into the part of her heart she thought had closed forever the night she turned down that gorgeous diamond?

He helped her out of the pickup and walked her to the porch outside her kitchen door. "I hope it wasn't a totally horrible evening for you, Christine."

She felt herself actually smiling. "I had a good time, Gordon. Thanks for a really good dinner."

He hesitated. "May I ask you a question?"

"Sure."

He hesitated again, uncharacteristically unsure of himself, then turned to go.

"What is it?" she asked.

He stopped and came back toward her. "I've thought better of it."

"No, no, ask." Are you nuts, she demanded of herself. He's leaving and you call him back?

"I'm afraid I'll offend you. And I don't want to spoil such an exquisite evening." Exquisite? Had Gordon memorized a few vocabulary words in preparation for their little dinner?

"Okay, no problem. It's your choice," she said abruptly, turning to go into the house.

"Promise not to be upset?"

"I can't promise, Gordon. Just say whatever it is that's on your mind."

"I was going to ask…." he hesitated again.

"Yes?"

"May I give you a goodnight kiss?"

She stepped back toward him. "Gordon, you have been such a gentleman, I don't see that a little kiss on my cheek would harm anything."

It was the lightest of pecks, his lips barely brushing her skin. Clearly he was trying not to cross a line.

"Goodnight, Gordon," she said. "Thanks again." And with that she went inside and waited to hear his truck pull away before she collapsed on the kitchen chair nearest the stove. Mama was still at work and Christine sat there for a full fifteen minutes in her coat, trying to figure out what had just happened.

# Forty

———

**C**hristine was surprised, almost alarmed, to find Harriet knocking on their door the next afternoon. Harriet seldom came to their house unless there was an emergency.

Christine had just come back from a hurriedly arranged meeting between Sam and their band, trying to hammer out the details of the agreement. Christine was not happy that Zach had asked his uncle Toby to review the agreement for them. She told Zach she wanted to find a different lawyer to help them with the contract. Adam clearly felt the same, and Zach quickly agreed.

She was just about to call Sharon to ask her for a recommendation when Harriet showed up. "Come in, Harriet, come in. Is something wrong?"

"Sorry to barge in."

"Not at all."

"Your mother's not here?"

"Oh, no, she's already at the diner. Did you want to talk with her?"

"No, I wanted to see you, although part of it involves Karen, too."

"May I take your coat? I'll put on some coffee."

Harriet slipped out of her coat with the dexterity of someone twenty years younger. "I'm sorry, Christine, but it'll have to be decaf since it's past noon. But if that's a problem, no worries."

"No problem. We have decaf." Christine took Harriet's coat and went to hang it up. "How's Ethan?"

"Doing better every day. He's really bouncing back."

"Oh, that's such good news. I'm so glad."

Harriet sat at the table. "Thanks for the support you gave us through the whole scary time."

"You know I love you and Ethan."

Harriet's eyes were moist now as she reached out and took Christine's hand in hers. "I can't tell you how upset I am that Betsy is trying to kick you and your mother out of this house."

"So you know?"

"Yes, I've known for some time. I wanted to let you and your mother know that Ethan and I are totally against it. But Betsy runs ahead and Bruce won't stand up to her."

"I understand."

"No, you shouldn't have to. I know I wouldn't be understanding if you were doing the same to Ethan and me, if the situation were reversed."

"Good Lord, I can't imagine me ever doing anything like that to you and Ethan."

"I know. But I need to be sure that you and Karen understand that I have nothing to do with the upheaval Betsy is causing."

"Mama and I are clear. This is Betsy's project."

"Oh, thank God. I've been worried this would fracture our relationship."

Christine poured the coffee. "Nothing could come between you and me, Harriet. You know that."

Harriet sipped her coffee. "I just can't figure out what has gotten into Betsy. They have plenty of money. Why does she want more?" They sat quietly for a moment. "I wish we had put the farm into the land preservation program before we worked out a plan for Bruce to buy it years ago. But back then Ethan said, 'Bruce would never condone development of these historic lands.' I guess we both misjudged how much havoc the loss of Nancy would bring. I try to love Betsy, I do. But deep down I know none of this would be happening if Nancy hadn't died."

"I'm sorry you and Ethan have to go through this. Your lives have been so full of thoughtfulness and generosity. It seems unfair."

"Life isn't fair, girl. I learned that a long time ago." Harriet pressed her lips together tightly. "This isn't over yet. Nothing in the Bible says Betsy's going to win this fight." She looked at Christine fiercely, then burst into one of her hearty laughs. "Listen to me, would you! 'Nothing in the Bible!' I'm sounding all whacked out."

It was amusing and poignantly sad at the same moment. But understandable with all the pressures Harriet was living with.

Harriet looked at her directly. "Ethan thinks you wrote the phrase, 'Don't rape the landscape,' that we suddenly see popping up in yard signs. Is that true?"

Christine paused, looking back at Harriet full in the face. "Is Ethan upset?"

"No, no, he's getting a kick out of it. But you didn't answer my question."

Christine paused again, trying to think what she should be careful not to say. "I knew Zach and his group were getting them produced, but I honestly haven't seen any yet."

"Zach from your band?"

"Yes, Zach Collins."

"So you did write it. Ethan was sure. We saw three of the yard signs when we went for groceries this morning."

"Yeah, I wasn't sure how much I should tell you because I didn't want to mess into your family's politics."

Harriet emitted a little snort. "Family? You're more family than Betsy ever was."

"That's kind of you to say."

"Not kind. True. 'Don't rape the landscape. Stop the Turner Estates proposal.' That should get people's attention."

"Oh, Harriet, I'm not so sure. Betsy and Bruce have a lot of powerful people on their side. I think we may end up looking foolish."

Harriet stood up and started to put on her coat. "That really touches me. You're willing to look foolish to defend our farm." She came toward Christine and gave her a big hug. "Ethan keeps saying, 'God bless Christine.' I so appreciate what you're doing. Ethan and I are trying to avoid a scandal. That's why we can't openly oppose Betsy. But to know there are people out there who are concerned really picks me up. Thanks so much from both of us."

Harriet was leaving when she turned to Christine. "I hear that Thomas has broken up with that Waldorf woman." She looked meaningfully at Christine, then turned, went to her car, and drove off, leaving Christine wondering why Harriet was telling her this news. Was that the main reason Harriet had made her unusual visit to their place?

# Forty–One

———

**With the practices for** the band's recording taking so much time, Christine called Emily to tell her she needed to take a rain check on visiting her at her home near Philly. Emily clearly was disappointed but, being the trooper she was, expressed great excitement that The Forerunners were doing a professional recording. Christine didn't breathe a word about Toyota.

She wasn't counting on any cash windfall from that car commercial wild dream, so she worked at the Society as much as she could to stockpile a bit more toward her tuition. She had sworn Sharon to secrecy when she asked her for a recommendation of an attorney to review the agreement. Sharon was totally professional but, when she was sure no one was watching, gave Christine an enthusiastic hug. "You deserve it," she whispered.

The day before New Year's Eve, Sharon convened the Society's Cemetery Records Committee. She asked Christine to attend. It opened up a new world to her. The four seasoned committee members had trekked through graveyards for years, writing down information from tombstones and entering it into their database. It made sense. People who were tracing their roots and origins needed such information.

Mitchell Roman had chaired the committee for years. Seemed like he knew every cemetery large and small throughout the whole region, including the little family plots which were preserved along fencerows here and there. "I think there are three cemeteries we haven't yet catalogued," he said. "If we get enough volunteers, we can manage these three in the coming year."

A long discussion followed. Old Hannah Price, who had arrived pushing her walker along grimly, wanted to know why these three had not been processed before.

"I guess we just never got around to it, Hannah," Mitchell said, pulling on his little beard. "Had you suggested these three before?"

"No, Mitchell, you know I didn't. I just wondered why we overlooked them."

Sharon weighed in. "I think your committee has been amazing in the number of cemeteries you have catalogued over the years. It's been a big help to researchers. I'm surprised there aren't a lot more to finish."

"Me, too. I think we've done a good job," Esther Lefler said.

"We haven't started west of the river yet," Horace Bricker noted.

"Oh, I'm not being critical, mind you," Hannah replied after a prolonged cough. "I just had a question, that's all. Whatever Mitchell wants is fine with me. Of course, I won't be able to crawl around and try to decipher the old grave markers like I used to. We'll need some younger volunteers."

"Christine, I think there are a bunch of Obers in that Northfield graveyard," Mitchell said. "Isn't that right, Sharon?"

Sharon nodded. "Have you ever checked it out, Christine?"

She felt suddenly embarrassed. With all of her interest in old things, and with helping many other people trace their family lines, she had never done her own family tree, not even her mother's.

"You'd be a great one to help with that Northfield cemetery," Hannah said, looking at her directly with those penetrating eyes.

Wasn't she even curious? Why did it feel emotionally off-limits? Are you kiddin'? With all the pain her mother carried, not to mention Uncle Jimmy, why would she want to learn more about the Obers?

"I don't know," she replied in a voice barely audible. "Maybe I should."

Sharon looked at her with a sympathetic smile. "You and I can discuss it," she said, taking Christine off the hook.

What the hell am I afraid of? Skeletons can be scary, but skeletons are dead, right? Besides, if she had decided not to pursue more information about Lenny Bryer, it might feel less painful to turn the spotlight on the Ober tree.

Christine saw everyone in the room looking at her and worried that she had spoken her thoughts out loud. Then Sharon stood up and the meeting was over.

# Forty-Two

——

**O**n the way home, as the bright red winter sunset streaked the sky and warm-lit the landscape, Christine stewed over her lack of curiosity about her own roots. Was she ashamed to be an Ober? Why had she never researched her mother's family? Was she worried it would only cause more pain?

Which made her think of Uncle Jimmy. What would he be doing on New Year's Eve? Would he sit at home alone or go to a bar?

She pulled off the road into the Wawa parking lot, called her uncle, got his voicemail, and left a message. Then she texted him. "Busy tomorrow evening? Want to do something together?"

As she pulled back onto the road and started into town, she saw Leopold, Bruce's and Betsy's younger teenage son, walking into a yard full of Christmas decorations, pulling out one of Zach's "Don't rape the landscape" yard signs, breaking it over his knee, and hurrying back to the pickup truck along the road. As she passed she saw his brother Travis at the wheel. He must have just gotten his license. At the next intersection, she saw two more of the yard signs and pulled off to the side of the road to watch in her rearview mirror as the Turner truck approached and stopped. Leopold jumped out, yanked out the two signs, and broke them over his knee, again tossing them onto the back of the pickup.

Christine picked up her phone and called Zach, telling him what she was witnessing. "That's illegal," Zach said. "I'm calling the cops. Which direction did they go?"

"They're heading toward the east end on Lost Pony Road. I'll follow them."

"I'll call you right back. Don't lose them."

She tried to stay a safe distance behind. She felt herself tensing. Goddamn, what am I getting myself into? If Betsy's boys spot me and drag me out of my car, I'll end up looking like Adam's mother after his dad beats her up in one of his drunken rages. The sun is down and it's getting dark, so I better be careful. Those boys have probably inherited the rage of their mother and the simmering anger of their father.

The pickup stopped along a triangle of open space where three small roads intersected. Leopold was pulling out three signs, one facing in each direction. She had eased onto the shoulder and dimmed her headlights so she wouldn't be detected. And just like that, a police car flew by her and pulled up behind the pickup truck, lights flashing. Travis started to pull away but, when the loud siren came on, he pulled over and stopped. A second police car came from the opposite direction and pulled in front of the pickup, lights flashing.

Zach called her back. "This is terrific for us," he raved. "It's like a gift from heaven. This will be all over the news, and people who weren't aware will suddenly be paying attention. Betsy will come off as a bully. People hate that. I'll call a reporter to make sure they're on it."

"I hope it doesn't get violent."

"Why would you say that, Christine?"

"You weren't in the car, Zach, following them in the half-dark just now. I wasn't sure the police were coming, and I didn't know what I'd do if those sizable teenagers tried to drag me out of my car."

Zach's tone changed. "Hey, would you like me to meet you? Where are you?"

"I'm okay, Zach. I'm just saying it was scary. I really hope it doesn't become violent."

"I hear you. I don't expect it to, especially since the police responded so quickly. But I'd feel better seeing you to know you're okay. How about a quick bite at Leo's?"

Christine was touched by his warmhearted response. "Okay, I'll see you there in thirty, if that suits you."

"I'll be there."

She was just pulling into Melville's parking lot to quickly buy a new lined notebook for writing first drafts of her lyrics, when Uncle Jimmy texted. "I'm free. What ya have in mind?"

"What would you like to do?" she texted back, sitting in her car.

"You chuz."

"OK, I'll let you know."

Someone rapped on her window. She looked up to see Gordon. Good God.

She rolled down her window cautiously. "Hi Gordon."

"Thanks for the other evening," he said.

She dropped her eyes purposely so he wouldn't assume she was being too friendly. When she didn't say anything, he tried to extend the moment. "You have plans for New Year's Eve?"

"Why do you ask?"

"I thought maybe I could ask you out for a proper date."

"Actually, I do have plans. I'm spending the evening with my Uncle Jimmy."

"Oh, that's nice. You've always had a good relationship with your uncle."

"You know him, Gordon?"

"I met him once or twice when I was with you. You don't remember?'

"Oh, I see what you mean." She got out of her car.

"There isn't much about you I don't know, Christine. Really. Look, if you have plans, I understand. But I'm not giving up. I'm not going to harass you, but I really want to spend time with you. And as far as I can tell, you're not dating anyone else. At least Adam said you weren't."

"You talked to Adam about me?"

"Politely. I just asked him if you're in a relationship."

"Gordon, you can't just ram into my life," she said, starting toward the store. "I have a busy life. I can't go back to high school." She could see that her words hurt him.

"Look, I'm not in college like you, I realize, and I'm not trying to turn the clock back. I offered you a diamond and you said no. That's in the past. What I'm trying to do now is—" he paused, out of words.

"Gordon, I really have to go. I'm late. Do you mind?"

He stepped aside meekly. "Please don't let me keep you." It was a different Gordon than the old super-self-confident class president she remembered. His failed marriage may have humbled him.

She started toward the store. "I don't mean to be rude, Gordon, but I am late."

He nodded solemnly and walked across the lot toward his truck.

On the way to Leo's, she talked out loud to herself. You're holding out for a guy you'll never get, stupid. And you're turning away a guy who clearly loves being with you and would support you financially and emotionally for a long time, maybe even growing old together. So why do you always hesifucktate? Hell, if you don't want Gordon, Zach would marry you. If you agreed, he would. But no, you want what you can't have. Why? Because you want to end up living alone, right? Just like your mother. Stupid, stupid, stupid.

# Forty-Three

——

It so warmed up on New Year's Eve that the predicted snow turned out to be steady rain instead. Uncle Jimmy met her at Sandy's Home Cookin' near the east end. They both ordered French onion soup and decided to split a pizza.

"What's your father like?" she asked him.

"Oh, you decided we'd have casual conversation, did you?" he laughed. She knew it was a difficult subject, but she suddenly wanted to know more about her mother's parents.

Uncle Jimmy puckered his lips and rubbed his forehead. "I suppose some in the community would say Father is a good man, reliable and steady. But he is also very difficult, has strong opinions, and can be pretty rough around the edges. Not easy."

"I don't think I ever met him," she said as their soups arrived.

Jimmy actually sounded angry. "That is such a crime. Even though Father is unpleasant, every child should know their grandparents, right? It's only natural. But what can you do about a self-righteous old grouch?"

"How did he and your mother get along?"

"He's been the cranky one, I would say. Mother has her prickly side, too. But if I had to choose one to protect me, I always chose Mother. They're both conservative, but Mother at least has a sense of humor. You wouldn't often catch Father laughing. He was strict and basically inflexible. I think when your mother was sent away and disinherited after she got pregnant, it really hurt Mother, but she had to support Father. That's just the way they've always been."

"So it makes sense that they didn't want to be with me. To them, I was the result of a terrible sin, as it was seen in those days among some, right?"

"Unfortunately, yes. And though they may have moderated a bit through the years, Father is as stubborn as they come. So no way he's going to admit he was too harsh with Karen. God bless Harriet for taking your mother in just before you were born."

The pizza arrived and they each took a slice. "What about you, Uncle Jimmy? Did your parents visit you in jail?"

He laughed that sucking sound. "That's a good question. First time I was in for six months. I was driving soused and ran off the road, I guess, and hit the corner of Fat Freddy's barn where it sits close to the road."

"Fat Freddy? The township official?"

"The very same. If you're going to hit something, Fat Freddy's barn is not the best choice."

"And your parents?"

Uncle Jimmy sat for a long moment, trying to remember. "I know my father never ever visited me. But Mother came one time, I remember, the first time I was in. She was so embarrassed, even though she's part of a prison ministry group at their church. But visiting her own son was a different matter. They had already basically kicked me out of the family because of my drinking and my dropping out of church, I guess. The thought of your own son arrested for drunk driving had to be almost unbearable for them, not to mention Fat Freddy's barn." He chuckled. "Definitely a no-no!"

It was funny the way he told it and she couldn't help chuckling. "So 'stern,' 'inflexible,' and 'humorless' would sorta sum it up?"

"You got it."

"Do you see them anymore?"

Jimmy's hand came up to his face as he looked away. "Not in years. Father's walking isn't what it used to be, I hear, and Mother's diabetes is pretty bad. I figure my showing up would only add more pain to their lives."

A dead end. She wondered if Mama would go to their funerals when they died. If Grandpa Ober died first, might Grandma reach out to her banished daughter to seek peace before the curtain falls? "You must feel lonely, Uncle Jimmy."

He tried to wave it off as though it was the lightest of burdens. But as his eyes misted over, he looked straight at her. "I've gotten used to it," he said, his voice breaking now. "That's why our friendship is a lifeline for me, Christine. I can never thank you enough."

"That's my New Year's resolution," she responded. "I want to spend more time with you in this coming year."

His smile was as true and unpretentious as a child's. "God bless my Christine."

# Forty–Four

---

She sat at her little desk trying to write some lines for the new lyrics she had promised Zach.

"We need a terrific, singable song to win people to the cause," he had said. "Something about valuing the land and the earth, saving it for future generations."

She liked the idea but always tightened up when she tried to write lines that might sound preachy. "I don't want to be too didactic," she insisted. "It has to sing itself without sermonizing."

Zach laughed. "You're such an idealist."

"No, I'm a realist."

The New Year's Day sunlight made the Turner fields outside her window, though drab with winter's brown, sparkle with a promise of new birth. Amazing how the seasons came back, year after year, fertile plants growing from the rich limestone soil, now frozen. Did Betsy care at all that these fields, tilled by nine generations of Turners, would disappear forever when she covered them with blacktop?

Christine kept writing trial lines, jotting down ideas, testing rhymes. It was midafternoon when she sent Zach an email. "Can you work with this? If we need another verse, I can add that later. Hey, maybe we could get them to record this when we're in Baltimore next week, just for the hell of it?" Then she typed in her new lines:

*What's the farmland really worth?*
*Grab the cash and lose the earth.*
*Fancy houses aren't a crop,*
*Fertile fields are not a pawnshop swap,*
*Nor can your blacktop grow a crop.*
*It's a big-time crime*
*To rape the landscape.*

# Forty-Five

—

The next day she was waiting to meet with Dr. Shriver when Zach sent her a text. "Love your lyrics. I've already written the tune. It's going to give Betsy's panties a painful twist!"

Christine winced. She was up for the battle but still hoped it wouldn't get bloody. Too much collateral damage — Mama, Harriet, Ethan, maybe even Thomas.

She realized how little she thought about Thomas these days. He was still in Connecticut on holiday break. She was actually more preoccupied with whether or not to go out with Gordon.

Dr. Shriver arrived and launched into a long list of assignments he wanted Christine to do for him. She had spent a lot of time relishing the idea of doing some actual teaching — so this was a rude shock. She had thought about the best teachers she had had, like Mr. Sterling in high school, trying to put her finger on what made them engaging. Sterling could take you back into any moment in time and dress it up, detail the setting and the stakes, and narrate the situation as though he had been part of it. That's the kind of teacher she wanted to be, if she ever had the opportunity.

But Shriver was a bore, and now Christine realized that this "special assistantship" really meant being a "personal assistant," who took all the dirty jobs and undesirable details off the plodding teacher's plate. She should have known. I'll probably have to pick up his dry cleaning, too. Looks like more of a gotcha than an honor.

She saw Adam arriving as she headed for the bus. "Hey, Zach said he really likes your lyrics, Christine," he called to her.

"Yeah, and he's written the tune already. We should find time to practice it."

"My schedule's pretty open. I'm just headed to the library to get a jump on some of the research for my presentation in Kramer's class."

"The library's closed."

"Closed?"

"Yeah, everything is. The café, too. I was just there and you can't get in."

"Oh, shit. I thought it had re-opened after New Year's." He paused. Then his face changed. "Christine, I owe you a big thank you."

"For what?"

He stepped toward her and hugged her. She was surprised.

"Whoa, what's this for?"

Adam was serious. "For whatever you said to Jenn a week or two ago. It made a huge difference."

"Oh, glad if it helped."

"She's so different. Much more relaxed. And more...." he paused with a slight blush rising in his features.

"More?"

"More romantic." Adam clearly was a happy customer. "Whatever you said, I can't thank you enough."

"Jenn and I have been friends since grade school."

"I know. She really trusts you."

"And I think she trusts you, too, Adam. I wish you both well."

For a moment she thought Adam might kiss her, his face was so happy and tender. "You're a true friend," he blurted.

Her phone rang, rescuing the moment. It was Zach, asking if they could practice the new piece right then.

"Sure, let's meet at my place," Adam suggested.

So she and Adam headed for the bus shelter together. Just as they got there, Gordon drove up in his sparkling pickup.

"Can I give you a ride?" he asked Christine through his open window.

"We can wait for the bus."

Gordon tried to figure it out. "You and Adam are going the same place?"

Adam nodded. "We're going to my place to meet Zach for a rehearsal."

"Why don't you jump in and I'll take you there. No need to wait for the bus in this weather."

Christine was flustered. "I'm used to it. No problem."

"You're refusing my offer?"

"Our practices are closed."

"Meaning?"

"Gordon, I appreciate the offer but we never permit outsiders into our rehearsals."

"Goddamn it, you two get your rear ends into my truck and I'll take you to Adam's place. I'd never interfere with your band, you know that."

So that's how they got to Adam's place, arriving just as Zach pulled up with his "Don't Rape the Landscape" bumper sticker on both his front and rear bumpers.

"Thanks for the ride," she said to Gordon, trying not to sound romantic in any way. What was her problem? Gordon could not have been more polite.

After Gordon pulled away and while Zach was still out of earshot, Adam turned to her. "Good luck with Thomas."

"Why would you say that?"

"Don't act innocent with me, Christine. I've been suffering with you for years while you wait for Thomas to make his move. I'm just saying that I hope you find what you're looking for, the way I've found Jenn, thanks in part to you."

She began to protest but realized it was silly. "Thanks, Adam," she said. "I think it's a doomed enterprise."

"Come on, guys," Zach was calling. And they followed him into Adam's basement to practice a new song that might just doom Betsy's enterprise.

# Forty-Six

—

**B**rownie greeted Christine at the front door as Ethan waved her in. She had decided to tell Ethan about the threat Arlene had received because he may have some insight. Harriet had gone shopping.

Ethan listened carefully as she told him about the note in Arlene's mailbox, rocking slowly as he pondered. "Do we know if the Wissler family or the Miller family got similar letters?"

"Not that I'm aware of, but maybe I could check that out in some way."

Ethan rubbed his left elbow which often bothered him. "That would be helpful to know. This letter was sent to Arlene, you say, before the Miller fire?"

"Yes, it said her barn would be third."

"That's scary. So, that means, if this is a serial arsonist, her barn is in real jeopardy. I'm sorry for Arlene. How are she and her girls surviving?" Brownie was nudging at Ethan's feet until Ethan picked him up, petting him as he settled into his lap.

"I think it comes and goes, but until the criminal's caught, they live in fear."

"A terrible thing."

"I wish I could help Arlene. Do you have any ideas, Ethan?"

He rocked back and forth, stroking Brownie gently, the dog's eyes closed now. "Let's put our heads together, Christine. Maybe we can think of something."

"You know both Abe Wissler and Christian Miller, right?"

"Well, yes, to a certain degree. Abe more than Christian, maybe."

"Can you think of someone who would carry a grudge against both of them?"

"Not really. But I'm not close enough to them to sort that out."

"And then there's Arlene. Is there a common enemy that all three of them share?"

Ethan started to chuckle. "I was just reading here in the paper about this 89-year-old woman in Texas who shot her gun at her 90-year-old neighbor because he refused to kiss her!"

Christine laughed. "Sounds like the Wild West. I hope you don't have any old woman trying to kiss you."

Ethan raised his hands. "Only one. And that's more than enough."

They both laughed, imagining Harriet's reaction if another woman tried to kiss Ethan. "May I get you some coffee?" he asked.

"No, I'm not staying long." They sat thinking, comfortable companions to each other. Why do I want to know more about that Lenny Bryer jerk, she thought, when I have such a fatherly friend in Ethan?

"Maybe we need to come at this backwards," he said as he rocked.

"Meaning?"

"I don't know much about computers. But is there a way you could check some common threads or links between Abe and Christian without them knowing?"

"Like what?"

"I don't know. Were they members of the same group? Or did they own a partnership together? What links exist between those two which might have created a common enemy? Did they go hunting together? And check their wives, too."

"You always wanted to be a detective, Ethan, didn't you?"

"As long as no 89-year-old flirt shoots at me."

She laughed softly. She should have thought about doing computer searches for similarities. "Ethan, that's a good idea. I'll do some online research in the next day or two and let you know."

"Good. Let's see what we learn." He started to get up, but she could see it was painful.

"Please don't get up for me. I can let myself out." She was halfway to the front door when he spoke up in that symphonic voice of his.

"Ever wonder why vengeful people burn barns instead of houses?"

"Not sure that I have."

"The barn has so many functions. Shelter for the livestock. Storage for the crops. Hub of the whole farming operation. Not to mention the beautiful structure. The barn is often more important than the house to most farm families."

She looked at him and nodded. "You might be right about that."

"Might?"

"I'm sorry. Absolutely, totally, undoubtedly correct!"

"Now we're talking, partner." She could still hear him laughing as she closed the door and ran to her car in the bracing cold.

# Forty–Seven

——

The **recording studio was** not as plush as Christine thought it might be. Even Zach seemed a bit flustered by the bare-bones facility in a ragtag part of Baltimore.

But Sam was upbeat and sounded gung-ho, floating around between them and the staff in the control room, trying not to bump her head on the low ceiling. It took forever to get the levels set to everyone's satisfaction with a thin, bespectacled tech guy named Seymour debating with Sam about every decision. It was almost lunchtime before they even laid down their first take. By then the whole thing was getting on Christine's nerves, and her voice was not as confident as usual.

"Sounds a little wobbly," Seymour intoned.

"Let's take a lunch break and then do several more takes," Sam suggested.

They crouched in a corner of the tiny studio to eat the wilted salads someone had brought in. One of the staff said it had started to snow, as forecast.

"Sam, I know I got off to a bad start with you," Christine said.

"No problem."

"Understand, I have a lot of questions about Toyota and all that. But let's just say it all works out. What comes after that? Do we do videos? Do we tour? I'm just asking."

Sam unwound her big frame and leaned toward her, grey-green eyes alert and intense. "I make no promises."

"I know. I just want to get the larger picture. For instance, I assume singing at the White House is unlikely." Christine flashed her smile so Sam knew she was joking.

Sam leaned against the wall. "So much depends on luck, to be honest. It was a little miracle of sorts that I connected with a rep for the agency that works with Toyota, just an hour after they had decided they needed a new song for a commercial they were designing. And I persuaded him to take four minutes to listen to your song right there in the hallway. It just happened to catch his imagination. He could immediately see the visuals he would put with your music. Honestly, one in a thousand chances. But it did happen. We have a concrete offer. And I think they're going to option it so they don't lose your song to another advertiser. I do. But will they ever actually use it? It's a complicated process, totally out of our control. All we can do is produce our best recording and stay in touch with them."

Christine stood up, too. "Thanks for your honesty. I'm not trying to pressure you. I just don't want us to get carried away."

"Smart attitude. It's the way this business is. A lot of hit or miss, mainly miss. All we can do is produce our best."

Zach was standing now, too. "I told Sam we have another number we'd like to do for her before we leave."

"I want to hear it." Sam took a moment to finish her salad. "If enough people like 'If You Could Only See,' that opens more doors. And being in a big car commercial doesn't hurt. Could you become well enough known that I could book you in Philly and maybe Baltimore and D. C.? It's a possibility. One step at a time. First we have to get the best take possible on this recording."

Seymour walked in, shaking snow from his coat. "We better get going. They say this fuckin' storm is turning into a blizzard."

"Yeah, and we have to drive home," Adam said. "Unless we can sleep here."

Seymour gave Adam a sharp look. Adam smiled and raised his hands. "No need to worry. We can't afford $700 an hour to sleep here!"

Seymour chuckled. "You want to pay for it, I'll be your motel for a night."

Christine felt better about her voice after lunch. And Zach kicked in that superior quality he was capable of. After three takes, Sam went back to the control room. The walls were thin, and they could hear her asking Seymour what he honestly thought. "I'd like at least two more takes," he said. "But I really think we have a cut that's good enough. They're better than I thought."

When Sam came back into the studio, they acted like they hadn't heard a thing. "What did he say?" Zach asked.

Sam was noncommittal. "He'd like a few more takes. Do you think you can reach deep inside yourselves and give me the best you got?"

"I'm sure gonna try," Zach promised.

"Yeah, me, too," Christine chimed in. "Let's do it." Is this how success happens? Cramped in a mangy, godforsaken cubbyhole as a storm bears down?

Adam grunted. "I don't think I can do better," he said with a teasing smile.

And, in fact, it felt to the three of them like they then delivered their best. Hearing that Seymour thought they were pretty good relaxed them so they were able to produce their best take.

Just before they all pushed off into the accumulating snow, they sang their new "Don't Rape the Landscape" song for Sam. She loved it. "It's catchy, it's topical, and it's edgy. That could be another song for your repertoire."

Seymour walked in. "I'll be glad to quickly record it if you can stay a few moments. I think it has possibilities. It's like a freedom song."

So they did it and nailed it the first time. A new song with the paint barely dry, and both Sam and Seymour liked it.

"I love that phrase, 'Nor can your blacktop grow a crop,'" Sam enthused. "That song could go places if we could connect to some of the large environmental organizations. Would you like me to try?"

Zach looked at Christine, then back to Sam. "Yes and no."

"We need time to sort that out," Christine explained. "We wrote this to stop a local farm, that goes back nine generations to the original settlers, from being rezoned. The current generation is trying to cash it out and populate those fertile acres with upscale housing."

Seymour grunted. "That's the kind of thing that pisses me off. No respect. Hell, I won't charge you for recording that song just now — it's my contribution to the cause."

Zach reached out and shook Seymour's hand. "Thank you, sir."

One of the assistants came in. "The snow is really piling up. I have to leave or I won't get home."

"Go, go, be safe," Seymour waved to her.

Adam wanted to hurry. "We better move if we want to get home yet today."

Their goodbyes were brief as they rushed to gather their instruments and head for the front door. "We'll stay in touch," Sam said.

The snow outside was at least six inches deep and coming down fast and heavy as they piled into Zach's car. As he tried to maneuver around the several vehicles in the parking lot, his car appeared to be stuck. The wheels were spinning as they fishtailed and almost struck a telephone pole. "Holy shit," Zach muttered. "We may not get home today at this rate."

"Shall I get out and push?" Adam asked. Just then Zach was able to pull the car out of its spin, and they lurched onto the street. They inched along, barely able to see.

"Is this the way we came?" Christine asked. "Don't remember that tall building."

"I'm sure this is right," Adam insisted. "I do remember that building. And this popcorn shop here on the right. Let's keep going. If we make it to the interstate, we can get home."

In the heavy snow, none of them could distinguish their surroundings very well. "Can we turn the radio off til we hit the interstate?" Christine suggested. "I know it sounds weird, but I can see better when there's less sound."

Adam laughed. "You sound like my mom."

"Call me old. Just remember, you're only three months younger than me, you aging rock star. Oh fuck, weren't we supposed to turn left back there, Zach?"

And so it went with them winding their way out of the city in search of the interstate. When they turned the corner at one intersection, the car got hung up in the deep snow, but Zach was able to rock it back and forth until it spun out of the little drift. Only when they finally arrived on the major highway did they relax enough to discuss the recording session with Sam and Seymour. "What do you think?" Zach asked Christine, clearly wanting to know her read on things.

"Hey, don't hit that little car there!" Adam yelled. "It must be stuck." Zach swerved and barely slid past a small car stalled in the road, almost hidden by the heavy, driving snow.

"Should we find a hotel and stay put until tomorrow morning?" Zach asked.

"Let's keep going a little," Adam suggested. "I see a snowplow up ahead. I think the road's actually a little better."

"Okay by me," Zach said. "I know you want to get home to Jenn. But if it gets much worse, let's find a place to stay. I'd hate to be out in the rural areas where there are no hotels and get stuck for the night. It's getting really cold."

"I agree," Christine said. "I'm going to try to reach my mother to make sure she made it home from the diner."

There was no answer at their house. So she called the diner. Danny answered. "Oh, we closed two hours ago. Karen was the first to leave. She should have gotten home a long time ago."

"How's the snow there? I'm calling from Baltimore."

"It's blizzard conditions here," Danny said. "Some of the roads are closed already. They're calling for as much as two feet."

Christine felt a shiver pass through her. Where was Mama? She tried the home number again, but no one answered. She dialed Mama's cell. Mama sometimes mislaid it. Rang several times and then went to voicemail. She told her mother to call her as soon as possible. But what if Mama didn't have her cell with her?

Now a small tremor of panic shot through Christine as she tried to figure out where her mother was. She couldn't think of any place Mama would stop on the way home in a snowstorm. She must be stuck on some back road. Unless she drove wrong in the blinding snow and got lost. As she made a quick mental list of anyone who might be willing and able to hunt for her mother in the storm, she realized that most of those on the list weren't available. Zach and Adam were here with her, many miles from where Mama was. Harriet and Ethan weren't up to such a strenuous task. Thomas was still in New England. And she wasn't sure Uncle Jimmy could manage it — he might get lost himself.

For a moment she considered Bruce, fully aware of the irony of having just recorded a song that would make Betsy livid — and maybe Bruce, too. But they didn't know about the song yet. Bruce was almost certainly out in the storm with one of his big tractors, snowplow attached, opening farm lanes for other farmers who paid him to keep their driveways open so large dairy trucks could get in to pick up the milk from their herds. No way would she call Betsy.

Gordon. He would gladly do it if she called him. But then she'd probably have to go out with him. So what's the problem with a little sacrifice when you're trying to find your mother, lost in this ferocious storm, stupid?

She reached Gordon, out with one of their construction vehicles, clearing roads. At first the reception was not good. But she was able to make him understand the situation.

"I can stop what I'm doing and go find her, Christine. What's the usual route she takes home from the diner to your place?" Suddenly she was much more calm. Gordon was reliable and couldn't be more motivated.

The band stopped for the night at a small motel at one of the interstate interchanges. Zach's car got stuck going up the sloping driveway, so they grabbed their stuff, left the car behind in a snowbank, and struggled up the hill to the motel. Christine wanted her own room so she could keep monitoring the search for Mama without bothering the other two during the night. They were all ravenous, but there were no restaurants in sight. So they binged on the two vending machines in the lobby, gulping down candy, chips, and soda. The balding man with the green-tinged hair on night duty just stared at them as they devoured the junk food.

"I'll call you when I know something," Gordon had told her. "But I'll call you at least once every hour with a progress report. Hopefully, it won't take more than a half hour."

An hour passed. No word. She decided she would not call Gordon and bug him. It wasn't fair. He had promised he would call.

"Would you like us to stay up with you?" Zach asked. She could see they were both completely exhausted.

"Oh, no, I'll waken you guys if I need you." Their rooms had adjoining doors, and they unlocked them so she could come over to their room without needing to go outside into the storm.

It was past eight when Gordon called. "I've driven that route two times, Christine, and I can't find your mother. She must have mistakenly turned wrong someplace. The snow is blinding."

She tried to think. If her mother was scared she couldn't make it the whole way home, where might she go? "I wonder, Gordon, with the conditions being white-out, if she might have missed the turn there near Orchard Road and continued on down to River Road."

Gordon's voice was clear and reassuring. "Good thought. I was wondering the same. And one more question, may I call the police and report your mother missing? If she drove wrong and is stuck someplace, I'm worried. It's brutally cold outside. We have to find her."

"That's fine with me. If you need me, call me back."

Suddenly she was frightfully cold. She pulled the blankets off her bed and wrapped herself in the chair by the desk, her phone beside her. Where could Mama be? What if she got stuck and had decided to try to walk home? Oh God.

She knew she'd go nuts if she kept checking the time every few seconds. So she tried to think of other things and actually started to write a lyric about being lost in a blizzard. *You don't have to be a wizard, to not get lost in a blizzard, for you think you know the road, but that plan will just explode, when the snow blinds your eyes, and you don't know...*

The ringing of her phone wakened her. She was startled—she thought she *was* awake. As she stirred, she realized Zach's arm was draped over her and the blankets as though he was trying to comfort her, asleep himself.

"Where's my damn phone?" she asked, still trying to get awake from deep sleep. He roused himself, found it on the floor, and handed it to her.

It was Gordon. His voice was troubled. "I found her car," he said. "It had rolled off the road into that ditch near River Road. But she wasn't in it. My dad and I have searched everywhere. Problem is, the snow isn't slowing down. I didn't want to alarm you, but I decided I needed to update you. The police are helping, too, but they're tied up with so many emergencies."

Christine remembered fainting only one time in her life, when she had discovered Arlene's Nathan in that horrible tractor accident on the steep ridge at the edge of the west field. Now she felt the same lightness sweeping up through her body as the energy seeped from her center. But Zach's warm cheek against her face pulled her out of the collapse.

"They can't find her," she said in a surreal voice that sounded like someone else's. "Mama is lost in this blizzard."

# Forty–Eight

——

**K**aren **Ober had stumbled** into an old barn along the creek which Pete Kleinfelter used to shelter his heifers. She'd found an old canvas in the entry to the barn and wrapped herself in it until the storm passed. It was early morning when Mr. Masterson spotted Karen when she flung open the door on the second floor of the old barn and waved for help. Christine burst into tears when Gordon called her with the news. The storm had subsided by then, and Zach and Adam had dug out Zach's car so they could crunch and plow their way back down the slope to the interstate exchange. The heater was laboring against the bitter cold, but Gordon's call warmed everything. Mama was alive!

Harriet and Uncle Jimmy were both sitting with Mama at their kitchen table when Christine came through the door. The bruises on Mama's face surprised Christine. Their hug was long and deep.

"Breathe, breathe!" Harriet laughed. "You two will hug each other to death." But Christine saw the tears in Harriet's eyes and in Uncle Jimmy's, too. So many ironies. So many memories of estrangement and pain. But a hug to live by.

After Harriet and Uncle Jimmy left, she tucked Mama into bed. "You need sleep. I talked to Danny at the diner and he said you should take a week off to recover. Said he'll even pay you for the week."

"Oh, my, I can't believe Danny said that. He's always been a penny-pincher."

"Mama, everyone is so relieved that you survived the storm. But everyone also wants you to take time to rest and rebuild your energy."

Her mother smiled from under the covers. "Thank you, Christine." And then she murmured something Christine had not heard very often in recent years. "I love you, chickadee."

"You just sleep, Mama. I love you, too. I was thinking of making some hot beef vegetable soup for supper with grilled cheese sandwiches. Would you like that?" Mama smiled faintly, but she was already breathing deeply as sleep overtook her.

Christine sat in her favorite recliner in the corner of the kitchen, debriefing the events of the past thirty hours. Sam and Seymour. Zach's car getting stuck. Deciding to call Gordon. And worry so intense she almost fainted. Now home, safe and warm, with a bruised Mama upstairs in bed. She knew she needed sleep, too.

She was wakened by Gordon calling. "Just checking in, Christine. How's your mother?"

"She'll be fine, the way it seems. She's sleeping at the moment."

He caught himself. "Sorry if I shouldn't have called."

"Call any time you wish, Gordon. Mama and I can never thank you and your dad enough. What a storm." She paused, hoping she wasn't making a mistake. "Gordon, may I take you out to dinner at Leo's or someplace to thank you?"

"I'd like that, Christine. But you don't have to. What I did for you was not more than you would do for me in a blizzard, right?"

"I hope I never need to prove you right. But I like to think that's the kind of person I am. So would Tuesday suit you to go to Leo's?"

"When should I pick you up?"

"Oh, no, this is my treat. I'll pick you up. Unless you'd rather just meet at Leo's."

As she got up to start on the beef vegetable soup, she looked in the mirror for a long moment. "Who are you?" she asked as she rubbed the freckles of the reflection peering back at her. "No, kiddo, who the hell are you? And what do you really want?"

# Forty-Nine

———

**C**hristine and Gordon were enjoying a cordial conversation over steak dinners at Leo's when Thomas Turner strode in. At first he didn't spot her. She sat back and turned her head slightly, hoping he couldn't see her. Thomas came back a few days earlier than she thought he would.

Gordon was describing in detail all the places he and his dad had searched for her mother in the ruthless blizzard. "I've never been in anything like it," he said. "Extremely cold with the snow hitting your face like little ice bullets. Basically disoriented and blind. And I was so worried that, if she had fallen along the road and was covered with snow, our big tractor would run over her." She could see the terror in his eyes. "I knew you would never forgive me and my chances would be ruined. But more than that, I was terribly worried about your mother."

For a moment, she remembered why she had been so attracted to him in high school. Basically a good person. Yeah, he used to be a bit pompous. But on the counter side, she liked his confidence, his surefootedness, his reliability.

Could they have a life together, post-Wendi? What would that be like? He still wasn't a reader, wasn't captured by ideas, and he did sorta assume his family was a stroke better than most. But he could be devoted, she knew. When he focused, he could mind every detail and tend every need. But what had happened with Wendi?

Suddenly Thomas was standing there, beaming at her. "Hey, what's up?"

She tried not to let her frustration show. "Hi, Thomas, you came back a few days early." But much as she inwardly tried to resist it, the quiet energy of his presence made it hard for her to focus on anything else. It wasn't just his talent and his good looks that she was drawn to. What she couldn't yet admit to herself was that she loved the whole of Thomas. Why should she be surprised that his showing up after so many weeks away would brighten everything?

She saw his eyes moving toward Gordon.

"Oh, this is Gordon Masterson. Do you two know each other? Gordon, this is Professor Turner, one of the music profs at Midstate."

Gordon stood up and extended his hand. "Pleased to meet you, sir. I've heard of you but don't think we've met. My dad and I might be working with your uncle and aunt on their development plans."

Christine was stunned. Gordon was involved with Turner Estates? How did she not realize?

"You and your dad found Christine's mother in the blizzard, right?" Thomas was saying.

"Yes, we did."

"My grandmother was telling me about it. That was an amazing thing you did to save her life." Thomas sounded really impressed.

Gordon blushed a bit. "In the end, she saved herself there in Pete Kleinfelter's barn. A very resourceful woman, not unlike her daughter."

Gordon's affectionate tone sent a tiny ripple of barely visible emotion across Thomas' face. Did Thomas sense that Gordon had a romantic interest? Did Thomas even care?

"Nevertheless, what you and your dad did was extraordinary. You deserve everyone's thanks."

"That's why I'm treating Gordon to a steak dinner," she explained. "Mama and I can never thank him enough."

"I didn't mean to interrupt," Thomas said, glancing around. "Nice to meet you, Gordon. And congratulations again." He paused. "Christine, are you around the next few days? I got an email from Sam, and she felt really good about your session in Baltimore."

"Sure, I'm working a good bit. But I'm around."

Thomas smiled. "I'll text you. Maybe we can find a time to catch up." And then he was gone.

Gordon seemed puzzled. "You're old friends, aren't you? I remember, back when we were dating, you used to talk with him when he visited his grandparents on the farm."

What to say? Should she signal to Gordon that he had competition? Or was that unnecessarily cruel when Gordon had risked his life to save Mama?

"Of course, we've rented our little house from the Turners all these years," she said. "So, yes, I've seen Thomas off and on since he was a kid. Looks like our house will be bulldozed if Betsy gets her way." Took him off one hook and put him on another.

Gordon winced. "Really, is that true?"

"As sure as we're sitting here. I didn't realize you were working with Betsy until just now."

"Look, it's not a sure thing that we will win the contract. Dad still has to finalize the bid on it." Pause. "I had no idea you were losing your house, Christine."

She raised her hand. "Let's not talk about that. We're here to enjoy these New York steaks and celebrate everyone being alive." She raised her wine glass. "To you and your dad."

Gordon raised his glass, too. But she could see his eyes were troubled now. Gordon's radar sensed two new obstacles in his pursuit of Christine. That Turner guy who employed a rather familiar tone when he spoke with her just now. And the prospect that Gordon was on the wrong side in the Turner Estates development.

# Fifty

———

She wanted to get to the township meeting a few minutes early, but not too early. She figured the small parking lot must be full because cars were lined on both sides of the road leading past the township building, with people walking and running toward the excitement. She hurried, worried suddenly she wouldn't even get into the building.

The bitter winter cold had taken a break, and the warmer evening made it feel like spring, though it was merely a late January forty-eight degrees. As she got out of her car, she heard the loud chant, "Don't rape the landscape." As she got closer, she could see there was a crowd of at least a hundred students outside the township building, chanting, holding signs, and occasionally singing The Forerunners' new tune,

*What's the farmland really worth? Grab the cash and lose the earth.* Zach was up on a box, leading the crowd of students in their chanting and singing, Adam and Jenn standing near Zach, pumping their fists to the rhythm.

Inside, the hearing room was already packed full. Zach's dad waved to Christine, and she pushed toward him. He had saved a seat for her beside Shirley in the second row. The room was abuzz with an atmosphere half-circus and half-lynch-mob.

Fat Freddy looked absolutely overwhelmed. Deb Brewster was standing behind the main table, hands on hips. Brewster the rooster, Christine thought. She spotted Mr. Peters, Betsy's attorney, but didn't see Bruce or Betsy anywhere. Probably waiting until the last second. Oh, over there was Toby Sickman with his distinctly droopy mustache. Eli Gibbons was in his seat behind the main table, as were the fourth and fifth members of the Zoning Board, Elmer Goodrich and Heather Miller.

Christine glanced toward the back of the room to see if either Thomas or Gordon was present. If they were, she couldn't spot them. She did notice two TV crews already recording the event.

Her heart was pounding. She never dreamed the response would be so amazing. "You and Mr. Collins really turned out a huge crowd," she said to Shirley.

Shirley smiled. "I'm startled myself. After Betsy's boys ripped the signs out of the yards, I knew we had a chance."

The chants and singing outside the building made it hard to hear inside. Christine noticed flashing lights reflected through the windows and realized someone had called the cops. Fat Freddy was trying to begin the meeting, but most people couldn't hear him. The small hearing room had no microphone because normally it wasn't needed.

Elmer Goodrich stood up, put his stubby fingers into his mouth, and emitted a loud shrill whistle. Everything grew quiet in the room, just as the students outside again swung into singing, *Nor can your blacktop grow a crop, it's a big-time crime to rape the landscape.*

Mr. Collins walked toward the back of the room, pushing through the crowd standing along the wall, and opened the door just as the students stopped singing. Zach's dad signaled to his son and everything became quiet, the police lights still flashing. Mr. Collins nodded to Fat Freddy.

"Well, well, I think we can begin," the Chair of the Zoning Board said as Betsy and Bruce slipped into their seats besides Mr. Peters. "This is a hearing for public comment about the Turner Estates proposal. My hope is that everyone who wants to speak, you know, will get an opportunity. But if things get too unruly, I will shut it down. So don't aggravate me. Does everyone understand?"

There was a murmur through the room.

Bob Collins was the first to speak. "Apart from all of the legitimate environmental and zoning issues, I want to raise a common-sense objection to this ambitious plan. Spot zoning is always a mistake. There is no residential zoning close to the Turner farm. So if the Zoning Board re-zones that ag land to residential, that's just the beginning of the dominoes, and more farms will apply for re-zoning in the years ahead. The result? This gorgeous sweep of fertile farmland will be replaced with blacktop and cookie-cutter houses. That's why we must oppose this first step."

Others jumped in, the majority agreeing with Mr. Collins. Betsy had her backers, but they became less vocal as the evening proceeded. Christine hoped Zach could keep the students quiet. A disruption by them could swing the momentum.

Bruce and Betsy never said a word but, every so often, everyone could hear one of Betsy's loud sighs. Amazingly, Deb Brewster didn't say a word either, though she smiled noticeably every time Betsy sighed.

Christine felt a tap on her shoulder. It was Zach, crouching down to whisper to her. "The TV guy wants you to come outside so he can record us singing our new song for the news later tonight. Can you come out?"

The students took their cue from Zach and remained quiet and attentive for the cameras as Zach, Adam, and she sang their new piece. It was their first public rendition of it, and Christine, seeing the glow in the students' faces, remembered Seymour's comment that it sounded like a freedom song. Which would explain why a student's recording and posting of it was all over social media, receiving an unbelievable number of likes and shares.

"They promised a second hearing soon," Bob Collins told her later, "but they may take the next one to the middle school auditorium so they have more room."

The next day Betsy posted an eviction notice on the door of the little house where she and Mama had lived since the day she was born. Just like that. Christine supposed that Betsy fancied herself charitable because they were given ninety days to get out instead of the normal thirty.

# Fifty-One

———

Christine and her mother were sitting in Gary Jenkins' insurance office, trying to get details on the insurance payment for her mother's car that was totaled when it flipped into that ditch during the blizzard. Christine's cell rang. It was Zach.

"Sam played our 'Don't rape the landscape' song for an official at the EAU, one of the big environmental groups. And can you believe it, they want us to sing it at their annual convention in Washington, D. C. in April! They'll pay us $5,000 plus expenses. Or double that if we premiere it at their convention and don't perform it any other place first."

"I can't talk now, Zach," she said. "My mom and I are at Jenkins' Insurance. I'll call you back."

Just that morning, her mother had received a check in the mail from Harriet for $4,000. "Karen, just a little something to help you get another car. So thankful things didn't turn out worse for you in the blizzard."

Karen Ober had never owned a new car. But with the insurance check and with Harriet's gift, she could afford the nicest used car she had ever bought.

Later, on her way to the Campus Café to meet Zach and Adam about the EAU convention, Christine stopped abruptly as she came to the alcove outside the blue doors. There in plain sight were Thomas and Emily, chatting and laughing in a manner that looked distinctly flirtatious to Christine. She stepped behind a partition where she could still observe without them seeing her.

"Oh, I'd love to go along," she could hear Emily saying in her most cheerful voice. "It's so kind of you to think of me, Professor Turner." Emily reached out and touched Thomas' arm in a gesture that struck Christine, hiding behind the partition, as unmistakably romantic. Did Emily have a crush on Thomas? How had she missed that? Were the two of them an item?

"When do we leave?" Emily was asking.

"Oh, about four o'clock or so, late afternoon. We should be back by midnight."

Where were they going? Was it a date? My God, when Thomas had told Christine at Leo's that he wanted to meet with her, she had thought maybe....

She sat down to catch her breath. What the hell was going on?

"So I'll pick you up at four then," Thomas was saying. And Emily, beaming her great smile, again touching him with a bit of warm intimacy, replied, "Lovely. See you then."

Christine leaned against the partition long after the two of them disappeared. She tried to restart her breathing, determined to regain her composure before she ventured through the blue doors to meet her band buddies.

Later when she got home, Gordon's big pickup was parked beside their little house. She wondered if Gordon could do anything about the eviction notice. She pulled up beside him and rolled down her window. "What's up?"

Gordon smiled. He really could look rather dashing. He seemed a bit nervous. "Why don't you park your car, and then I have a question for you."

"Okay." She pulled into her usual spot and climbed out. The cold wind was not so biting with the afternoon sun shining now.

He cleared his throat as he walked up. "Do you still like to ice skate?"

Not the question she was expecting. "I haven't for a year or two."

"I remember in high school we went skating a lot."

"Yes, I remember." She paused. "Is this a quiz?"

"No, no. Sorry." He cleared his throat again. "Ricky Bashore is throwing a skating party at their pond on Valentine's night, this Friday. Would you come with me?"

"I see." Ricky had been in their class. "Ricky still married to Daisy?"

"Does that affect your answer?"

She surprised herself by giggling. What am I now, a little girl worried she won't have a date? That's hardly fair. Gordon's being as polite as can be. What the hell, if Thomas is going out with Emily, maybe it's time for me to give Gordon a chance.

"Why not?" she said, laughing again.

Gordon looked so relieved she had to suppress an impulse to hug him. Poor guy, so in love with her, but so nervous that he would never win her heart. "It's a date then?"

"Yes, Gordon, you have that date you've been angling for. But it's one date. I don't see any way there would be another unless you turn out to be a better skater than you used to be!"

"I guess I have my work cut out for me." He laughed as he walked back to his pickup, then called back to her. "Thanks, Christine."

A new chapter? she wondered. Had the earth shifted this afternoon? Was it time to move on if Thomas was out of reach?

# Fifty–Two

—

It was a busy morning at the Historical Society. An electrical contractor from Ohio—a guy named Frank Frank—showed up, wanting to trace his family tree and its local connections. Christine suppressed her immediate urge to ask what his middle name was. Only after Mr. Frank had filled out their usual information form did she see that it was in fact Franklin. What parent would do that, she wondered. Frank Franklin Frank. His wife's name was Frances.

Uncle Jimmy showed up and sat in the reference section, waiting until she was free. She could see he was looking at a magazine so she took her time helping Mr. Frank. And just when she was about to tell Sharon that she wanted five minutes to talk with Uncle Jimmy, Mrs. Bleecher, who ran the card and gift shop next to Wolf's on Main, dropped in to ask for help on some research about the history of the local Chamber of Commerce.

When she finally sat down at Uncle Jimmy's table, she apologized.

"I can see you're busy," he said.

"What's on your mind?"

He hesitated, glancing around. "It's about your mother."

"Is something wrong?"

"No, no, it's not an emergency. I just wanted to ask you a question." He ran his fingers along the tapered edge of the table.

"Is this about that envelope full of ten-dollar bills?"

Jimmy looked stumped for a moment, then remembered. "Oh, that, no, that's something else."

"Are you ever going to explain about that envelope?"

He took a deep sigh. "Through the years, when I had a little extra to spare, I would send your mother a hundred or so—to help with the rent or whatever."

She was startled. "Really, is that what it was? Nothing questionable? Why didn't you say so?"

"Karen asked me not to tell you. I always thought she was a mite embarrassed to take money from the likes of me."

Christine's hand came up to her face as she absorbed this information. "I suppose that's why she returned the envelope the last time," he continued. "I haven't asked her."

"How often, Uncle Jimmy?"

He puckered his face and looked away. "I wasn't keeping count."

"How often? Tell me."

"I don't know," he protested. But she kept staring at him with demanding eyes. He shrugged. "Whenever I could. I just wanted to help."

"How often? I want to know."

"I honestly don't know, Christine. I suppose a few dozen times through the years."

She rubbed her face. "Are you telling me you paid Mama a few thousand dollars over the years and I never knew?"

He was getting irritated now. "It was none of your business. It was between me and my sister."

She sat for a moment, letting it sink in. "We owe you a heap of gratitude, Uncle Jimmy."

"See, that's why I didn't want you to know. It was just something I wanted to do without humiliating Karen."

She sat back and took a deep breath, looking directly at him. "Sorry if I upset you. I'm just amazed I never found out."

"No problem. I apologize if I didn't do it right."

"No, no, I apologize for questioning you. And please let me say thank you. Thank you, a thousand times."

He smiled nervously as though he was hoping it was good news. She reached across and touched his hand. "But that's not why you came, is it?"

"Like I said, it's not an emergency."

"Tell me."

"I don't know—do you think your mother's maybe different since the blizzard?"

His question surprised her. She tried to think what he might be referring to. "In what way?"

"Well, I've dropped in at the diner to get a bite a time or two, and I don't think Karen is the same Karen."

"Tell me what you mean."

Jimmy rubbed his face. "After that scary experience, I was relieved how cheerful she was—you know, in the week or two right after that storm. But now it feels like it's gone the other way. I'm worried."

Christine felt chagrined. Had Jimmy noticed something she had missed? "The other way?"

Uncle Jimmy was tapping his fingers on the tabletop now. "Maybe I'm making too much of it."

"No, tell me. What do you observe? Maybe I'm missing it."

He coughed again. "She seems down."

"Down?"

"Depressed. Haven't you noticed?

She was surprised. "How can you tell?"

"Look, maybe I'm inventing it. I don't know who I think I am to talk about such things."

"How does she seem depressed to you, Uncle Jimmy?"

"I'm probably off the beam on this one. Really, I'm sorry I bothered you." He started to stand up.

"Sit down, please," she insisted. He sat. "Now tell me what you observe. What has you so concerned?"

"I guess I think I know my sister and the way her mind works. She's going to church more, isn't she?"

"Is that bad?"

"Of course not. But when I talk with her, she seems less cheerful, more down, saying things that sound more like — what do you call it? — 'survivor's guilt' or something."

"But nobody died. Why should she feel that way?"

Christine saw Thomas walk in the front door of the Society and look around. What was he doing here?

"Karen has always felt that she didn't deserve good things in life, even though she had you, one of the best things anyone could wish for." Tears were shining in his eyes.

She reached out and took Uncle Jimmy's hand. "I'm sorry, I've been so busy, and I just haven't seen Mama much in the last while. I really appreciate your talking to me about what you're noticing."

He patted her hand. "I know Karen could slip into really deep dark valleys over the years. Maybe more than you were aware of. And I'm worried that her amazing survival in that storm may end up, over time, landing her in one of her funks. But I'm probably worrying too much."

She could see Thomas talking with Sharon at the front desk. "Three things," she said to her uncle. "First, I'm going to be more mindful of Mama. Right after her accident, I stayed pretty close. But since she went back to work and seemed okay, I've been really busy and I may have missed some things. Second, I will text you before the end of the day to set a time for us to meet and discuss all of this more. You've always had a good radar, and I respect that."

He smiled. "Thanks, Christine."

"And third, may I come over there and give you a hug?"

A blush of color rose in Jimmy's cheeks as he smiled. "Now that's something I'd never turn down," he beamed, standing as she came around the table and embraced him. The tears in his eyes were spilling over their rims now. They held on to each other for a long moment, rocking slightly as though braced against a strong wind.

"I have to go now," he said, wiping his eyes.

"I'll be in touch about getting together."

As she watched her uncle walk out to the front of the library to leave, she saw Thomas' eyes on her. Without thinking it through, she waved for him to come to where she stood. He smiled, walking toward her. Only when he was mere steps away did she realize she wanted to slap him. Right there and then. She felt betrayed and humiliated, Thomas going out with one of her best friends without so much as an invitation to her.

"Sorry to drop in on you at work," he said. "But I haven't been able to connect with you at school, and I thought maybe I could catch you here."

She didn't slap him but she couldn't have been more abrupt. "What for?"

"Could we sit for a moment?"

"I'm busy."

"Oh, sorry. Look, I'll try to call you." He turned and started to walk away.

"Thomas, since you're here, I can take a minute," she said curtly, sitting at the nearest table.

He turned and came back. Even through her anger and frustration, she could feel the beating of her heart in her ears. Something was different. Was his hair shorter on the sides? He certainly was no less good-looking than he had always been.

"Before I went home for the holidays, I said I wanted to speak with you when I returned. Do you remember that?"

She acted offhand. "Oh, that. Yeah, I guess so."

He grew quiet. "So much time has passed. So you've probably heard by now. I broke things off with Antonia."

"Antonia?" She knew she was being mean.

"Antonia Waldorf. You met her. She's the one who told you off after the madrigal holiday concert, remember?"

Christine tried to act as though it was long forgotten. "Oh, yes, that Antonia. Sure, I remember. I thought the two of you were good together."

She knew him well enough to see that he was hurt and flustered by her comment. He started to get up. "Well, I just wanted you to know. But I figured you may have heard by now."

"Yes, I think Harriet may have said something. A pity. What went wrong?"

She watched his eyes and saw his mind at work as he formulated a reply. She knew she would never love anyone as much as she loved him. But that made no difference. Thomas didn't seem to have those feelings for her. He thought of her as a sister. He was here to tell his sister about his breakup with that Ivy League snoot.

"It wasn't a good fit," he said softly. He paused. "The more I was around people like you, I realized that Antonia wasn't the future I wanted."

Whoa. What was he saying?

He started to get up. "One more thing. There's a choral convention in Philly next week, and I'm inviting some students to go along. There'll be a lecture and then a mass choir for everyone who wants to sing. I thought it might be fun. Even though you're not in any of my classes, I thought you might consider going along? Emily is. And Brian Bedford."

She didn't know what to say. So that's what he was talking to Emily about? "Let me check to see if I can get off work."

"No problem. I'd love to have you join us. We should be back by midnight or so. But I understand if you're too busy. Sam told me how excited she is about your band's prospects." He turned to go.

"I'll let you know," she said, standing.

He turned back and smiled. "You're something, aren't you, Christine? Just like Grandma says. Hot band. Assisting Dr. Shriver. Sharon says you're doing really good work here. And taking time for your Uncle Jimmy. Wow!" Again that great smile, and for a moment she thought his voice betrayed a touch of jealousy. "It's nice to see you back with Gordon." And then he was gone.

# Fifty-Three

———

"I hope no jilted 89-year-old woman is taking shots at you," she said to Ethan as she sat beside him in his rocker.

"What are you talking about, Christine?" Harriet called in from the kitchen, taking a step toward them, a strainer in her hand.

Ethan waved to his wife. "It's just an inside joke. I'll explain it later."

"Better not be any woman hanging around that I don't know about."

Christine raised her hand. "You can settle down, Harriet. It was just a joke."

"I'll expect an explanation," Harriet declared as she returned to the kitchen.

Ethan pretended to wipe his forehead. "You're getting me in trouble, Weeny Christeeny," he complained quietly with a grin. Apparently the sharp ears in the kitchen didn't hear that comment.

Christine pulled out her file and began to explain her notes. "Both Abe Wissler and Christian Miller are members of the Rotary Club. They both served on the school board for a few years, but at different terms. And both served on the County Ag Task Force, but again at different times."

"You have been busy."

"And their wives are both named Margaret, though Mrs. Miller goes by Peggy. Margaret Wissler and Peggy Miller."

Ethan chuckled. "Wouldn't that be a crazy thing if our arsonist disliked the name Margaret so much that he was burning barns to make his point!"

"Yeah, that's probably not the thing we're looking for."

"So what is? Was someone jealous of their position at Rotary? Was either of them ever president?"

"Both were, actually. But who would risk jail time and community scorn because he felt passed over in Rotary elections? I've never been there, but is it that big a deal?"

Ethan shook his head. "Oh, it's a big deal to some. But not *that* big."

Christine sighed. "Sorry I didn't find the connection. I'll keep looking."

"Oh, don't blame yourself. If it were that obvious, the police would have figured it out by now."

They sat quietly, Brownie snoring softly. "Could it be a connection through one of their children?" she asked.

"Could be. But how would you ever discover that without interviewing all of them? And if there is a suspicious link, they're not going to reveal that to a stranger in an interview."

"I agree." She packed her things and stood up. "I'll keep digging. But if there is a link, I'm not sure I'm the person to uncover it."

"Thanks for your effort, Christine. I keep worrying about Arlene." She was at the door by the time he added, "You know, I wonder if Abe and Christian ever served on any boards together—farm-related boards, business or nonprofit. Or even on boards or committees at their churches."

"I'll see if I can learn more."

"Maybe Abe and Christian were part of a board that made a decision that affected the arsonist adversely."

# Fifty–Four

—

She didn't know if Gordon had been practicing his ice-skating skills or not. But at Ricky and Daisy's Valentine skating party, Gordon was as polished as anyone there that night. He flew around the pond, cutting little figures in the ice, skating backwards faster than Christine could skate forwards. And he got everyone involved in playing Crack the Whip. Suddenly Gordon was class president again, friendly to everyone and leader of all.

She skated over to Adam and Jenn, warming themselves by the bonfire burning at the edge of the pond. They were chatting with Daisy.

"I didn't remember that you were such a good skater," Daisy said to Christine as she came gliding to a stop in a spray of ice. Daisy still sported that extraordinary chest, she noted, a feature that had fascinated all the boys in high school. Tonight she wore a tight, low-cut, bright red sweater which accented the size of her breasts, pushing them up so much that they almost spilled out of the V-neck.

"Oh, I've never been more than average, Daisy. Nice party."

Daisy grinned, tossing her long blond tresses. "Don't forget to help yourself to the hot dogs and beer," she said, skating off.

Jenn laughed quietly. "Same Daisy as in high school, right?" she said to Christine.

"I'm gonna roast a hot dog," Adam said. "You guys want one? I can do three at a time."

"I better see what Gordon wants," Christine said. "And I should get back out there to help him Crack the Whip."

"So it's a real date?" Jenn asked.

"Sure is," she replied jauntily. "After what Gordon and his father did for Mama, I figure I owe him a date or two."

Jenn came closer as Adam went to get the hot dogs. "Christine, a few weeks ago you couldn't stand him. Now you're dating him. What are you thinking? I hope you have some condoms with you."

"Hell, what's wrong with a skating party, Jenn?" She could see that Jenn was baffled and disappointed. "It's just one date," she said as she skated off to find

Gordon. He reached out, pulling her into the whipping line, twelve persons long by now. "This is fun, isn't it?" he called out to her.

She grabbed his hand. "Thanks for bringing me along, Gordon. I'm having a great time."

As they all skated away to pick up speed before Gordon stopped abruptly to swing the line in a big whipping wheel across the ice, someone started to sing the school song. Everyone joined in, singing, screaming, accelerating at unbelievably fast speeds at the outer ends of the whip, and laughing, as some lost their balance and slid across the ice on their butts. A subtle air of nostalgia gathered over the whole thing, she thought, a sense of loss, a wish for the innocence of high school when they could skate with abandon and scream their lungs out. But four years later, already weary of jobs and children and broken hearts, the skaters — most of them had not gone on to college — grabbed these moments of escape to bring back the freedom of being seventeen, in spite of its insecurities and anxieties. And though their singing was hearty and full of forced confidence, a definite pinch of sadness threaded through the tones. Had she escaped? Or would she have that same taste a year from now when she discovered that college hadn't opened doors to the promised land after all?

Later, after two hot dogs and a beer, she and Gordon were on the way back to her place. As they passed

Arlene's farm in the dim frozen stillness, the barn still in one piece, she wondered what Arlene would think if she could see her perched here in Gordon's warm, shiny pickup. Sure, Arlene and Jenn thought she could do better than Gordon. But who?

Mama was working late, and Christine could have invited Gordon in. But something in her resisted. "I'll say goodnight here," she said, her hand on the door handle, about to get out.

"Oh, I hope I didn't upset you."

"No, no. I had a fun evening. Thanks again."

"May I at least walk you to your door?"

"Sure, why not." She jumped out from her side before he could come around to open the door for her. At the porch, she turned to him. "It was nice of you to invite me."

"Was my skating good enough?"

"Oh, you're very good."

"Good enough for another date? Wasn't that the condition?"

"Let me think about it."

As he took a chance and leaned in to kiss her, ready for her to turn her face, limiting him to her cheek as she had done the last time, she put her arms around Gordon and gave him her best deep, wet kiss, catching him by surprise. She hadn't kissed a boy like that for at least two years, not since her last date with Teddy Weller. As she pulled away, she wondered why she had done it. Because he saved Mama? Because of old times? To see if she could still do it after so often feeling like a celibate nun around Thomas?

"Thanks again," she said, turning and going into the house, leaving behind a speechless Gordon who floated back to his pickup.

# SPRING

# Fifty-Five

———

**S**omething about the early signs of spring always renewed her, the first delicate crocus pushing through, the brilliant daffodils Harriet helped Mama plant along the road years ago, the breathtakingly flamboyant yellow forsythia bushes beside the porch, gardens being plowed, first plantings. Even though Betsy had made it clear that Harriet's garden was not to be planted this year, insisting that excavation of the new streets would begin well before anything Christine planted could approach any hope of harvest.

Mama was to be the invited guest at the quilting group this morning at Harriet's place. Right after Mama's accident in the blizzard, Harriet suggested they make a special quilt for Mama. She was coming today so she could see them putting in the final stiches. And Mama's daughter, one of the quilters.

Harriet seated Karen Ober to her right at the quilting frame, Christine on her left. The room buzzed with a special energy and conversation as needles flew up and down through the layers. Wanda had outdone herself, piling the table in the dining room with cookies and cake, homemade fruit salad, chocolate-dipped dried apricots, and two kinds of coffee. Of course, everyone had to wash their hands carefully after eating anything before they returned to their place at the frame so the new quilt would chronicle no telltale stains.

Her mother was visibly overwhelmed. Seldom had she been the center of so much attention. Everyone fussed about her guts, her survival skills. Christine knew from the flushed expression spreading across Mama's timid but attractive features that she was touched and honored.

"You can hold the needle like this," Harriet was telling Mama. And after a few tries, Mama was able to place three stitches into one section of the quilt's border. She had always been good at sewing. "Well done, Karen," Harriet purred. Mama beamed sheepishly with delight.

Ethan showed up with a plate of goodies and sat in the corner, munching and watching. Harriet winked at him as she deftly maneuvered her needle through the quilt. Christine surprised her mother by quilting at a decent pace, nothing like the speediest of the quilters, but better than a novice.

"Was it the scariest thing that ever happened to you, Karen?" Georgette asked. Mama hesitated, as though it was a new thought. Christine raced through her own memory archives, trying to retrieve frightening moments from her mother's life. Like when Mama's parents kicked her out and she had no place to go. Or maybe even more scary, the day Lenny Bryer broke off their engagement, days before the wedding. Or when Christine had a fever of 105 degrees the summer after first grade. There were probably other scary moments that Christine didn't know about, her relationship with her mother so stormy in recent years that she invested little time thinking about the contours of Karen Ober's life.

"I suppose it was the scariest," Mama answered Georgette now. "It was the coldest, I know that."

There was a murmur of assent around the frame, needles pausing in mid-air as the quilters all looked at Christine's mother. To most of them, Karen Ober was a stranger, someone they saw occasionally as their server at the diner, but not someone who'd ever been in their homes or they in hers. Christine they loved, partly as an extension of Harriet. But her mother was a mystery. A single mom, they knew, with some touch of tragedy about her. And probably none of them would have thought to suggest making a quilt for Karen if Harriet hadn't brought it up.

"I'm afraid I don't know what this pattern is called," Mama said to Harriet.

"Oh, we call it Bargello."

"Sorta looks like ocean waves," Mama observed. "Very beautiful."

Ethan chuckled from his corner. "Karen, do you remember when we took you and Christine down to the ocean years ago?"

Christine started to laugh. "Is that when I was such a crybaby because the wind swept my balloon away?"

Harriet let out one of her hearty laughs. "I remember that. It was in Wildwood, New Jersey. You and your mom both had new swimsuits, and Ethan bought you a big balloon on the boardwalk. You went running across the beach, out toward the ocean, and the balloon slipped out of your hand."

Christine nodded. "I was terribly upset. One of my earliest memories. I probably still owe Ethan a thank-you for that balloon."

"I thought you'd never say anything," Ethan pouted playfully.

Wanda cleared her throat to get their attention. "Don't forget all of the food in the dining room," she said. "I'm not taking it home."

The door on the far end of the room opened, and Thomas emerged, laptop and books in his hands. "Hi, Thomas," several of the women sang out.

"Hi, everybody."

Christine felt buoyed up enough by the event to call across the room, "Hey, Thomas, come over here and put in a few stitches for my mother. I'm sure you know how to quilt."

"I do not."

"Oh, yes, you do. You don't have to be perfect."

"I shouldn't be late for class."

Ethan's voice had a firmness to it. "Just a few stitches for Karen's celebration quilt, Thomas."

"OK. Grandma must show me how."

"Sit there beside Christine. She can help you."

Barbara started to hum a familiar tune and others joined her as Thomas squeezed in between Christine and her mother, his big hand taking a needle from Christine as she quietly coached him. The quilters gave them privacy with their humming and by focusing on their own stitches, with only occasional quick glances to check out the young man trying to get a handle on his tiny needle. It was the closest Mama had been to Thomas in a long time, a flushed look returning to her cheeks. The whole thing was unexpected, and Christine decided to enjoy the moment rather than overthink it. Thomas was helping with her mother's quilt. It was that simple.

# Fifty–Six

———

**C**hristine went straight to Sharon's office when she arrived for work the next morning. Sharon was buried in an old book, checking some dates. "What's up?"

"Could I talk to you about something confidential? If you have time today?"

"Absolutely. I can take time right now. Do you want to close the door?"

Christine pushed the door shut and sat down. She told Sharon about the questions she'd been asking herself in recent weeks about why she'd never done a family-tree chart for her mother. "But I've decided that must change. Do you mind if I work on that here in the library? On my own time, of course."

Sharon watched her carefully. "Of course. But may I ask a question?"

"Sure."

Sharon tried to choose her words carefully. "What are you worried about?"

"Worried?"

"Yeah, I've worked with a lot of people over the years. Researching one's family history can be worrisome, even traumatic for some folks."

Christine stood up and paced in tiny back-and-forths. "How do you mean?"

Sharon smiled. "It's a simple question. What worries you about looking into your mother's past?"

"It's my past, too."

"Of course, it is."

Christine sat back down and was surprised by the tears on her cheeks. "Sorry. Not sure why I'm crying."

"You're a really smart person, Christine. Tell me what you think. Why have you been cautious about finding out more about your past?"

She cleared her throat. "Mama has been mostly unhappy for as long as I can remember. And the only brother of hers I know, Uncle Jimmy, is pretty dysfunctional. So I figure there's a lot more hard stuff that I'll uncover if I start digging. Will discovering all that make things worse?" She wiped her eyes, blowing her nose, puzzled by her tears.

Sharon looked at her in a piercing manner that Christine had seldom seen from her. "There, you said it."

"I don't understand, Sharon."

"I think you do. You're not only head smart, you're emotionally intelligent, too. It feels to me like you're ready to learn about your past, whatever that may be." She paused, standing as she came around her desk, taking both of Christine's hands in hers. "I'll be with you all the way."

So that's how it started. Christine buried herself in the usual research on family names, historical records, and family histories, using the library and the Internet, tracing what she could of her mother's Ober heritage. She had forgotten, if she had ever known, that her mother's mother was a McWilliams, and she traced that line the whole way back to Ireland.

Over several weeks she spent evenings and week-ends glued to the project and even got behind on some of her senior projects for school. Her wish to know her roots consumed her. Why had she walled off this part of her life for so long? There weren't really any big scandals like she had somehow feared. Her great-great-great-grandfather on the McWilliams side was a Father O'Shea who had apparently impregnated one of the pretty girls in his parish and was defrocked. The resulting child, one Patrick O'Shea, was her great-great-grandfather.

She learned the Obers had been called Oberholtzers in the old country but supposedly had gotten their name shortened as they entered America. There was a famous judge in Philadelphia in the early 1800's named Jonathan Dewey Ober, she learned, presumably a distant relative. Also, she unearthed an item about a Ronald Wayne Ober who evidently went to prison for burning down the blacksmith shop of his competitor not far from Northfield.

Christine made a trip to the Northfield Cemetery and found a whole row of Ober graves, including an old small crooked stone for Ronald Wayne, her renegade ancestor.

On the way back from the Northfield Cemetery, on a whim, she decided to stop at the Ober homestead where her mother had grown up. The large farm buildings gave the place an aura of prosperity. She had often seen it from the road when she was up this way, but had never ever considered the possibility of dropping by. Her heart was beating in her neck, her throat suddenly parched as she pulled off the road into the spacious driveway leading to the farm buildings. What the hell are you doing, Christine? These people loathe you.

Several big cars were parked near the house and, as she pulled in between a BMW and a Lexus, she saw several men gathered by a grill in the side yard. It was Saturday, she remembered. Looked like a family barbecue.

One of the men came toward her as she got out of her car, and somehow she realized it must be her mother's older brother Eugene. She had seen a few family pictures that included the three older brothers, and Eugene had a distinct forehead and jaw.

"May I help you?" he asked as she walked toward him.

Christine was suddenly speechless. What right did she have to be here? What if they were as hostile as Uncle Jimmy thought they were. But wait a minute, what was the worst that could happen? Eugene wasn't carrying a gun.

"Are you Eugene?"

"Yes, I am. And you?"

Should she say it? Would Uncle Jimmy be upset if he knew she had stopped here? "I think I'm your niece."

The farmer in front of her, dressed up for a family picnic of some sort, looked genuinely perplexed. "I have four nieces, and you're not one of them." His answer was brusque though his eyes weren't yet cold.

"My mother is Karen Ober."

Eugene jerked his head up and looked at her closely. "No shit?" His two brothers, leaving the grill duties to one of their sons, were coming across the lawn now, interested in who their brother was talking to. One pushed his hands deeper into his pants pockets as they stopped a few feet away, the other with his hands on his hips.

"What's up, Gene?" the half-bald one in the plaid shirt asked. Christine figured he was Marlin. The other brother with the mustache was probably Lloyd.

"Says she's Karen's girl."

The same shocked look passed through the faces of Marlin and Lloyd. "Holy shit," Marlin said. "You mean our sister Karen? I thought she was dead."

Suddenly she wanted to get back to her car. She wasn't wanted here, she could tell. What had she expected?

Lloyd seemed to have the better manners. "What's your name?" he asked.

"I'm Christine Ober," she said, extending her hand to him. "You must be Lloyd."

Lloyd stepped toward her and shook her hand. His clothes and manners seemed more refined. "Christine, is it? I never had the privilege. You look a lot like your mother. Don't you think so, Gene?"

Eugene grunted. "I wouldn't have the slightest." Marlin cleared his throat and spit on the ground the way some farmers do. For a moment all three stared at her. She saw some women and young adults come out of the big house. Must be her aunts and cousins.

"What's your business?" Eugene asked gruffly, his eyes frosty now.

"Oh, no, I'm not in business. I'm just finishing college."

Lloyd smiled. "I think Gene means to ask what brings you here today."

"Oh, sorry. I'm working on my family's history and I was just at Northfield Cemetery, checking out all of those Ober gravestones."

"You were?"

She nodded. "And as I was coming down here past the homeplace where my mother grew up, I thought I'd take a chance and drop in. Sorry, I didn't mean to interrupt your barbecue."

"Yeah, we should eat soon," Eugene said in his blunt, unfriendly tone.

"Hey, do you want to join us?" Lloyd asked.

"She wouldn't know anyone, would she?" Marlin inserted in the same "you're-not-getting-into-our-family" tone Eugene had used.

She knew she needed to get out of here before they escorted her off the premises. Clearly, everyone but Lloyd was upset that she had dared to show up. Probably assumed that she was going to ask for money. "Oh, no, I can't stay. I need to get to work. I just had never stopped before."

Marlin did some more spitting while Eugene mainly glared. But Lloyd followed her to her car. As she was about to open the door, he said, "I can't tell you how wonderful it is to meet you, Christine."

She paused. "Thanks. You know, you look a lot like Uncle Jimmy."

"You know Jimmy?"

"Yeah, sure do. I see him all the time."

"So he's out of prison now?"

"Yes, he is. He works at the poultry plant east of town." She smiled as she opened the car door. "Uncle Jimmy's really sweet to me and Mama."

She saw something pass through Lloyd's kind face as though he suddenly realized there was a whole other Ober family that got together and had good times without anyone who was here at this picnic today.

"Lloyd, you comin'?" Marlin was yelling.

Lloyd turned and signaled to his brother, then turned back to Christine. "And your mother — how's Karen?"

"She's good. She works at Danny's Diner. She almost died a few months ago — she got lost in that terrible blizzard, but she's really bounced back."

"So she's okay?"

Christine could see what he was asking, and she wanted to tell him he had no right to ask that. But Lloyd seemed genuine to her, so she answered. "My mother's life has basically been overwhelmed with sadness and depression," she said.

Marlin called for Lloyd again, almost as though Lloyd was speaking with the enemy. But Lloyd didn't respond, just kept looking at Christine. "Is there any way I can be in touch with you, if you're willing?"

"Sure, I'll give you my cell number."

So that's how Uncle Lloyd got her phone number. She didn't hear from him that day or the next day or the next week. But as she headed back to the Historical Society to her job and to her own research, she felt less lonesome than she had in some time. Her family tree wasn't all dead people. Some were alive.

# Fifty-Seven

———

That Thursday was the first time Shriver asked her to teach. The second half of the period as a trial run. It was the moment she had waited for since the beginning of the semester, but it couldn't have come at a worse time. She felt overwhelmed with school work and, with Toyota probably exercising their option and Sam urging them to set up a legal entity for their venture, Sharon needing her to plan the Spring Festival at the Society, while trying to figure out all of her own feelings about her mother's family, she didn't get to prepare as much as she wanted. But she was actually looking forward to it.

They were in the Reconstruction Period after the Civil War, and she had really studied it. So she was caught by surprise when Shriver interrupted her after she had spoken a mere three sentences. "Well, Miss Ober, I'm not sure you have your facts right," he said.

She could feel her face getting red as the under-class students looked from her to Dr. Shriver and back again. "I think it actually happened first in 1869," she said, trying to recover. "Sorry if I misspoke."

"Oh, I think that's what you said," the professor said. "But I believe you're wrong."

Christine knew she was right. She had the ability to recall dates without even trying. So what was happening? Was Shriver bent on bringing her down a peg? But why? She had slaved for that man the last two months, doing a lot of his dirty work well outside the parameters of the job. Now when she was finally trying her hand at teaching, he was making life miserable for her.

Shriver took over. "Tell you what, we can just leave things there for today. Class dismissed."

As the students drifted out of the classroom a half hour before the normal end of the period, Christine let her emotions boil over in a manner she seldom permitted. When the room was empty, she demanded, "What was that all about?"

Shriver was surprised by her outburst but he appeared unfazed. "You have to prepare. You have to know your stuff."

"I did. You were wrong. I must have offended you in some other way. What did I do that upset you?"

Dr. Shriver pretended that his comments were only for her good, but his tone betrayed him. "A lot of students think teaching's an effortless piece of cake until they have to do it themselves. Sometimes they get a bit of icing on their faces." Damn, did this guy have a self-esteem problem or what?

Christine somehow was able to clamp down on the tempest inside herself, gathered up her materials, and walked out. "Better luck next time," Shriver called after her.

"Fuck you, Shriver," Christine was yelling inside her head. But to the best of her recollection later, she didn't say another word out loud as she headed for the student center, passing two students who had been in the class and who observed her now with stares of pity as she swept by.

# Fifty-Eight

———

**G**ordon asked her to go to D.C. to see the cherry blossoms. She would have loved the break, but she was simply too busy. Gordon kept trying to find ways to spend time with her, but it often didn't suit her. They had gone to the Spring Fair near Turners Rise one Saturday afternoon, and a week later dropped in on the big annual community sale for the fire company below the forge. Technically not dates, more like outings. No more deep kisses.

Gordon clearly wanted more outings, but when she wasn't ready or available, he demonstrated more patience than she thought him capable of. "I know you have all of these projects to finish before you graduate," he said. "I can wait. Hopefully this summer we can spend more time together."

But Christine did get to see the cherry blossoms in full bloom after all. Just not with Gordon. The Forerunners were appearing at the EAU convention as planned. Zach was really jacked, but for some reason Christine was having a nervous breakdown about it. For the first time it felt like they were on the cusp of a huge breakthrough as a band.

But did she want to be on the road to B-list cities and towns the next ten years, performing in front of crowds who wanted to think of their humble trio as big-time stars? Zach might like groupies from time to time, but she found the whole fan-club adulation thing suffocating and degrading. A decade of her life for that? Was this to be her career? Not that she had a lot of alternatives. Her flop at teaching had bewildered her. Was she as good as she thought she was or as bad as Shriver made it seem?

She and Sam had gotten into a throw-down drag-out fight about changing the name of their band. Sam wanted something more snappy and edgy. "Even if you just drop the 'Fore,' that would be stronger."

"You mean 'Runners'?" Christine shot back. "What the hell does 'Runners' mean? That sounds silly and contrived. I'm against it."

Zach and Adam had the good sense to steer clear of their fight, though Zach did counter with the suggestion of simply going with the name "Fore." Sam wasn't impressed. "What does 'Fore' fuckin' mean, Zach?"

"If you don't get it, forget it." Zach seemed resigned to letting Christine be their last line of defense against Sam's intense arguments.

In the end, they kept their name. "I've always liked it," Adam grunted. "Couldn't understand why Sam wanted to change it."

The day before they left for the EAU convention in Washington, Christine was shopping for a few things at Roger's Supermarket when suddenly, smack there in front of her stood her old friend and competitor Wendi. Still attractive but looking a few years older. As painted and glossy as ever.

"Oh, hi, Wendi. Didn't see you. Sorry if my cart bumped you."

"Oh, no, it didn't," Wendi replied, her eyes narrowing. "I hear you're fucking my husband."

"I am not!" Her voice was louder than she expected and hoped other shoppers didn't hear. She saw Zach's dad talking with a customer at the other end of the aisle.

"Fuck him all you want," Wendi responded gaily. "I knew he could never get you out of his silly little head. But hey, I'm not complaining. I'm divorcing his ass and making off with a nice slice of the Masterson fortune." And with that, Wendi blew her a kiss and headed for the check-out lanes.

My God, what was that all about?

Mr. Collins saw her and came over to say hello. "I hope your trip goes well. Shirley and I had planned to come hear you perform at the convention but my assistant has a really sick child and is off for several days. I'm working double duty."

"Sorry to hear that."

"Zach says he thinks you guys are prepared for the big event. But he leans on you for steadiness. How are you feeling?"

She wanted to say she was unsteady and frustrated, worried about the bright lights and pretentious stardom. But she simply smiled. "We'll be fine. Zach's terrific."

"You'll still say hello to me after you're a big star?" She could see he was half-joking but equally serious.

"Absolutely. It ain't gonna happen, but if it does, it's not gonna change who I am. As you know, it's all a circus. No point in getting dizzy on the merry-go-round."

Mr. Collins took her hand and kissed her fingers. The look on his face a second later indicated that he was as surprised by his deed as she was. "That's my Christine," he said in a near-whisper. "Everyone counts on you being grounded."

As she left Roger's, she got a text from Thomas, asking if they could meet briefly. They arranged to huddle at the Historical Society since she was headed there for work. He was waiting in the parking lot when she pulled in. Something in his smart appearance captivated her. Again. She would reason with herself that she could easily wipe him from her mind. He clearly had his faults — he wasn't perfect. He was just another guy, right. Until she saw him in person again — and his thoughtful conversations, his elegance, his kindness sparked a heat that would spread through her body from her temples to her toes. But why?

"Would you be upset if I came to hear your band tomorrow afternoon?"

"In D.C.?"

"Yeah, Sam told me about it. I have a class in the morning but, if I left promptly, I figure I can be there in time to hear you."

"It's only four minutes. One number."

"Yes, I know. 'Don't rape the landscape.' If Grandpa was in better health, he and Grandma would like to be there."

"They know about it?"

"I told them. They're so excited for you. They hope that song can stop Betsy in her tracks." He paused. "Maybe afterwards you might drive back with me? We could take a detour to see the cherry blossoms and the monuments if you have time."

Before she could stop herself, she blurted it out. "Would I be your half-sister or your date?"

He seemed stumped for a moment. "I was thinking 'friend,' I guess."

Did he know how she felt? Was he playing with her? Had he decided that their backgrounds made them an unlikely pair? Or was he just plain clueless?

"Sure," she smiled. "I'd love to drive back with you."

# Fifty-Nine

———

It was not a concert crowd. Three thousand in attendance at this high-profile get-together of environmental activists, a panel of three senators to be the main event later. The Forerunners were squeezed in between two early afternoon business sessions.

"Now to perform publicly for the first time their new song, 'Don't rape the landscape,' I bring you a small band who wrote the song to try to stop a beautiful spread of prime historic farmland from being bulldozed and blacktopped to build upper-class homes for the wealthy—please welcome The Forerunners."

The conversation among delegates was louder than the applause. Tough audience. We're just filler, she realized. We're elevator music. Not performers. Welcome to half-famous.

But something inside Christine stirred her to seize the moment. She grabbed the mike and raised her voice. "Hey, people, are you in favor of raping the landscape?" The audience quieted down a bit and some answered with a muted "No."

Christine plowed ahead. "I ask you again, are you going to destroy the fields and crops?" The crowd was much louder this time. "No."

"I'll give you one more chance — do you think we should rape the landscape?"

Now the crowd roared a resounding "No!"

Zach hit the opening chords and launched into their little song, Christine harmonizing with him, Adam on the drums. *What's the farmland really worth? Grab the cash and lose the earth.*

As they came to the end of their freedom song, the huge crowd was on its feet, thunderous applause coming back to them on the stage like so many sonic waves. They had been told to clear the stage quickly and they did, but the audience wanted more. "Just a quick bow, don't milk it," she said as the three ran back on stage. Wow. She could see in the eyes of the audience that their song had connected.

Sam was ecstatic as they came backstage. "Holy crap, you guys really nailed it! We gotta capitalize on this ASAP."

The convention leaders moved on to the next agenda item. Adam and Christine drifted out into the lobby area carrying some of the drum set, while Zach and Sam stayed behind to visit briefly with a few of the activists who wanted to immediately book The Forerunners for other events. There was a dizzy titillation about it all, but Christine also felt a tiny sour sadness creeping in. Until she spotted Thomas by the big purple pillar.

"Congratulations," he beamed as he walked toward her. "You were amazing the way you took control of that crowd. And they loved your song!"

She had told Adam that she might go back home with Thomas if he showed up. "See you later," Adam said now, giving her a gentle nudge. "I can manage."

"You're sure?"

"Absolutely. Get out of here."

She turned to Thomas. "Were you still thinking—?"

"If it's okay with you."

The photos she had seen through the years did not prepare her for the breathtaking grandeur and grace of the real thing. Cluster after cluster of the Japanese cherry trees burst with millions of pink blossoms. As Thomas followed the slow traffic around the Tidal Basin, Christine was transfixed by the overwhelming magic of the scene. "I've never seen anything like it," she whispered. "If there's a heaven, this is what it must be like."

Thomas reached over and took her hand. "I guess we're in heaven then. Permit me to welcome you."

They came around a corner, and there on a stretch of grass were children and adults of every shape and color, flying kites, a splash of radiant hues caught in the breeze, dancing in the luminous day.

Unknown to her, Thomas had reserved a paddle boat for them to use, floating their way around the basin, paddling as close to the Jefferson Memorial as she had ever been, the cherry blossoms flaunting their stunning loveliness at every turn.

She had thought that standing in Harriet's garden on a brilliant autumn morning couldn't be beat when she could see the whole way to the river, the fertile fields, abundant color with a sense of place and history. But in the little paddle boat with Thomas, gliding along under the canopy of a thousand thousand intricate blossoms, music from an orchestra waltzing across the water toward them, Christine was simply swept away.

"Thank you for this gift," she said to him, knowing her eyes were shining, her voice still a whisper.

"Oh, no, thank you," he whispered back.

It was dusk by the time they caught some food and headed home. She was surprised that her mother came out on the porch as they pulled up. She never did that. Christine jumped out of the car and ran to her. "What's wrong?"

Mama's face was colorless and taut, her eyes averted. At first she said nothing. Then she burst into tears. "Uncle Jimmy's dead. He was in an accident this evening. The police just left."

# Sixty

—

**All through the night** she could hear Mama sobbing in her room down the hall, a sound she had almost forgotten in the past year. She remembered one time long ago when she was in grade school she had asked Jenn as they walked in the little woods behind the basketball courts whether she heard her mom crying at night, too.

"My mom doesn't cry," Jenn had said flatly, looking at her quizzically.

Now she wondered how she had escaped this house and her mother's dark moods. How had she become so fierce at combating the demons? Without a father and trapped with a fragile mother, how had she survived?

But had she? She was still cooped up in this small, snug room in the same little tenant house, mere weeks from eviction, miles from the house up the hill where a grandson slept, dreaming who knows what. He treated her like a friend, but that didn't mean she could ever be part of his world, right? Could she be anything more than "poor Karen's illegitimate girl"?

An unusually loud sob snapped her back into the moment. Should she go and try to comfort her mother again?

Uncle Jimmy was dead. So sudden and unfair. And final. She felt the hot tears on her cheeks and hugged herself tightly to control the convulsing of her own sobs. Such a kind and innocent man, the only uncle she had ever known. Gone. A traffic accident just up the road from the poultry plant. Head on into a truck, apparently. The police were still investigating.

She saw Uncle Jimmy's speckled eyes looking at her now. "You're a light in my life, Christine." Those bad teeth, that sucking sound.

She could see how the meager foundations in Mama's troubled life would be swept away by this tragedy. Mama could get so mad at Jimmy. But since Christmas, Mama and he had become more reliable siblings than she could ever remember. Now this.

She got up before the sun and made coffee. Mama must have fallen asleep. Christine started to make a short list of her questions.

Who would bury Uncle Jimmy? He had no children as far as she knew, and both his wives had long ago disappeared from his life. Should she and Mama take leadership in planning his funeral?

But what about his long-estranged parents, her grandparents? Someone should tell them, right? And what about the three uncles she had met at the homeplace on her trip back from the Ober graves? They should know, right? At least Uncle Lloyd should.

Suddenly she wanted to talk with Harriet and Ethan. They knew her best. They always had good advice. Maybe later after breakfast time. Thomas might even be there. Were those cherry trees even real, or did she dream that?

She knew Uncle Lloyd owned Ober's Home & Garden Store in the small hamlet of Northfield. She'd call him after the store opened.

Her eyes partly swollen, Mama came down the steps in her housecoat. Christine went to get her coffee and brought it to her at the table. "What are you writing?" Mama asked.

Christine wasn't sure she wanted to discuss the questions she had jotted down. "Did you get some good sleep, Mama?"

"No, I don't think so." She took a deep drink of coffee. "What are we going to do?"

"How do you mean?"

"Without Jimmy?" For a moment Mama looked like she would start sobbing again, but her tears must have spent themselves. "For so many years, you and I have had almost no family, with Jimmy unreliable and in and out of prison. But these last few months were the best family feeling I've had, certainly since I was a girl at home."

"I'm sorry, Mama, I really am. It did feel like Uncle Jimmy had come home."

"Who's going to plan the funeral? I can't afford it, that's for sure."

Christine looked at her. "I don't know. Harriet might help."

"Maybe I could sell that new used car I bought last month."

"No, no, don't do that."

"But I can't take charity from Harriet all the time."

"What about Jimmy's family?"

"What family? He had no children, and his wives left him years ago. Each time he got into trouble and went back to jail, he lost another wife or girlfriend."

Christine knew she was risking her mother's anger. "What about Jimmy's parents?"

"He doesn't have parents." Her answer was quick and final, leaving no room for discussion.

"But he does. They should be told."

Her mother's face grew red and tense. "After all these years and the way they've treated Jimmy and me, you want to give them the satisfaction of knowing they won?"

"I didn't say anything about 'winning,' Mama."

"For the past twenty-some years, they have treated both Jimmy and me as though we were dead. No communication. No connection. Only hate."

"Hate's a strong word."

Mama's voice went up several decibels. "Why are you taking their damn side?"

"I don't mean to be." Mama seldom cursed. Christine walked to the window. "I understand how unforgivingly mean they have been. And I'm not excusing that. It's been terrible. All I'm asking is how you would feel if—" she paused, then decided to go on—"if your parents or brothers died and no one told you. Purposely decided not to—so you couldn't show up at the funeral? How would that feel?"

"As far as I'm concerned, they're already dead."

She came and sat beside Mama, trying to find a way to calm things. "We can talk about it later."

"You need to say you're sorry."

"Pardon?"

"Sometimes you get too big for your britches. And this is one of those times. I will not condone your taking the side of my hateful family. You think you're more intelligent, but you're acting ignorant. Say you're sorry."

"Mama, I don't think—"

"Say you're sorry."

"I'm sorry if I upset you, Mama."

"That doesn't count."

"Mama, can you stop for one goddamn minute?"

"Did you just swear at me?" Mama's face tensed. "You've crossed a line, Christine Lynette Ober!"

She knew it was getting out of control. Whenever her mother used her middle name, things were about to blow. "Mama, Mama."

"Don't 'Mama, Mama' me. Say you're sorry."

Christine hesitated but knew she had to say it. "I'd like to be in touch with Uncle Lloyd."

Her mother's eyes flew open, then narrowed. "Did you say Lloyd?"

"Yes, I did."

"What do you know about Lloyd?"

"He's your brother, right? And I think he should know about Jimmy's death. He may want to help plan the funeral."

"Do you know Lloyd?"

"I met him a few weeks ago at the homeplace. I never got a chance to tell Uncle Jimmy."

It was more than Karen Ober could absorb, especially in such an emotional state. All she could utter was, "That can't be."

"Mama, I don't want to rush you. But there is planning to be done. My hope is that we can do it in such a way that we honor Uncle Jimmy."

Mama's jaw was set. "You think we can't handle it."

"I want you to be at the center of the planning. We need a funeral home. But do we want the funeral to take place in a church? If so, which church? Do we want to plan for a small meal after the service? So many decisions. And you and I can go ahead, Mama. I'd just feel better if we'd give Jimmy's family an opportunity to be involved — if they want to be."

In the end, Mama agreed. Reluctantly. "It's going to be weird if they decide to come. What would Jimmy say?"

"I'm sure he'd be pleased."

She was able to reach Uncle Lloyd at his store by mid-morning. The phone was quiet for a long time. Then she could hear Lloyd's voice, almost a murmur. "Jimmy's dead?" After several moments more she asked Lloyd if he'd be interested in attending Jimmy's funeral. His voice was firmer now. "Absolutely. I'll be there. And I'll tell Marlin and Eugene. And our parents. Not sure they'll come but I'll let them know."

Mama and Christine met Uncle Lloyd at the funeral home that afternoon. There were so many decisions to make, but Lloyd must have done it before. He seemed like a pro.

When Lloyd first saw Karen as he entered the lobby of the building, he put his hand to his mouth and appeared to flinch slightly. It worried Christine — was it too big a leap back into history?

But then Lloyd relaxed and lit up a smile. "Karen, Karen, it's been so long," he said, crossing to grasp his sister's hands in his. "Thank God for your daughter. She's a bridge-builder." And then as Lloyd hugged Karen, they both broke into tears. It had been a long time. A very long time.

# Sixty-One

———

**S**he **tried to cancel** or delay as much of her schedule as she could. Sharon was very understanding. And Zach and Adam postponed a practice session they had scheduled at Sam's request.

But she decided she couldn't ask Shriver to be excused from the class she was supposed to teach the next day. I'm not ready to concede defeat to that mediocre know-it-all. I still think I can maybe be a good teacher.

She dropped by to see Harriet and Ethan. He opened the door and, in his compassionate way, extended his arms to her. "I heard about your uncle," he said. "I'm so sorry, Christine." They hugged a long time as she fought tears. "Harriet's not here at the moment, but please come in. I want to visit with you for a little."

Ethan's walking seemed a bit better than it had been over the winter. "How about a cookie?"

"Sure." She sat in the friendly stuffed chair next to Ethan's rocker.

"How are you holding up?" he asked gently, handing her a plate with two cookies. "Iced tea?"

"Thanks, Ethan." She waited while he poured two glasses of tea and came to sit beside her, rocking quietly for a moment. Silence had never intimidated Ethan.

"I think it's the closest that death has come to me," she said. "I didn't realize how final it would feel."

"No going back."

"Jimmy was not the usual uncle, I guess. We had some great times when I was growing up, but then he was in and out of trouble and prison. Now in the last half-year or so, he and Mama and I had become really good friends."

"I'm glad that happened. Your mother needed that." Again Ethan rocked, totally comfortable with her silence. As he finished his cookie, he asked, "Will you and your mother be okay?"

"Complicated question, isn't it?"

"Sorry, I don't mean to pry."

"I think I'll be okay. Not so sure about Mama. In recent weeks Uncle Jimmy was worried that Mama was slipping back into one of her melancholy moods, sort of a survivor's guilt ever since she outwitted that blizzard. A big high followed by a gradually descending low."

"I wondered about that. Harriet was glad to see Karen at church more than sometimes in the past. But I was a little worried about why she was coming more. Sounds pathetic on my part, but I was a bit afraid that it might signal something deeper."

Christine reached over and laid her hand on Ethan's as it rested on the rocker's arm. His skin felt a little scratchy between the deep wrinkles and the purple veins. "What about you?" she asked.

"Me? What about me?"

"Do you sometimes think about death?"

He smiled as he continued rocking, her hand going back and forth as she continued to hold his hand. "At my age, you can't avoid it. Hardly a week passes that the obituaries don't feature someone I know. Sometimes several days in a row. It's the natural order, isn't it?"

"Forgive me if my question is out of line."

"No, no, Christine, it wasn't. I recognize that I may not be here tomorrow or next week or next year."

"Oh, I don't want to even think about that." She hesitated. "Does it scare you?"

"Not really. I've had a good life, and I won the lottery when Harriet agreed to marry me. Thing is, we're all going to die sooner or later. Pretending that we're the exception is a little ridiculous and a waste of time."

She fell silent, still holding his hand as he rocked. "It's the separation that hurts, isn't it? Sure, I realized that probably Jimmy wouldn't live forever. But I'm really going to miss him. The sorrow is in the parting."

"Oh, yes, the parting. No denying that pain."

She took her hand away as she reached up to wipe her tears. "I should be going."

"No need to rush on my account. My secretary says she cleared my calendar." That warm chuckle.

She got up to leave. "You asked about Mama, and I answered. But I've always wondered, Ethan — what do you really think of my mother?"

He looked at her directly then, pausing in his rocking, scanning her face for clues. "How do you mean?"

"Just be honest."

"Well, well. I don't think you ever asked me that before!"

"If you'd rather not — "

He raised his hand. "No, it's okay." He rocked for a moment, deep in thought. "I want to be fair to you and fair to your mother." Again he paused. She knew waiting was the appropriate response, so she said nothing, slipping back into the stuffed chair. "Harriet and I have often talked about endurance, you know. Why do certain events crush some folks and strengthen others? It's a mystery, isn't it?" Ethan continued to rock as he pondered, almost as though he were alone.

"And?"

"Oh, yes. When I first became aware of your mother as a teenager, she was energetic and sociable, easy to visit with, dependable and talented. And good-looking. I was a little surprised that she fell so hard for that Bryer fella from across the river."

"Why?"

"He seemed a bit shallow to me, maybe a little immature, if I'm honest. But then I was always cautious about that family. Karen knew him better than I did, that's for sure. She appeared to be in the clouds over him. She never saw it coming—well, honestly, who would? So it was humiliating, to say the least, when her fiancé backed out just days before the wedding. I was shocked. That just about never happened back then. But I thought, hey, Karen is a can-do, attractive young woman. It'll all work out."

He rubbed his face, remembering.

"Two things I hadn't counted on. One was that she was pregnant. That certainly complicated things. And second, I never guessed how much this sequence of events would crush her spirit. Then her parents kicked her out on top of everything else. Amazing turn of events.

"I knew Oscar Ober fairly well, and he could be an unpleasant grouch, even a bit mean. But expelling his own daughter was extreme. Your mother went from heaven to hell in a short period of time. It crushed her, it really did. She was never the same, not even close.

Even as you were born and grew into such a wonderful young woman, the cloud of darkness that hung over Karen seldom lifted. It broke my heart."

Ethan paused again, lost in memories. "Truthfully, when she survived that blizzard, I told Harriet, 'That's the old fighter. Reminds me of the fearless teenager Karen used to be.' And Jimmy's return and friendship seemed to energize her." He coughed. "And now Jimmy's gone."

She walked to the window and studied the innumerable shades of green across the lawn, trees, and the fields beyond. Life had come back. "Am I doomed to be like Mama?"

Ethan snorted. "I don't want to hear you say that again, young lady. Never."

"Why not? I'm asking honestly, Ethan."

"You know why not. You're a smart one, Christine. You are talented and strong, partly fearless and yet extra patient somehow. Amazing qualities in anyone, let alone someone who's so young."

"I wasn't asking for praise."

"I know you weren't. And I wasn't trying to pile it on. I was just telling you the truth as I see it. Growing up in the home you did, with all its melancholy and pessimism — it's amazing how you've turned out."

"Wouldn't have happened without you and Harriet. I can never thank you two enough."

Ethan brushed it off. "It was all you, Christine, not us."

"You know that's not true. I would never have survived if you two hadn't been there for me every step along the way."

Again he shrugged, but this time he conceded. "Glad we could help."

As she gave him a hug and moved toward the door, his voice brightened. "Thomas says you were a hit at the convention in D.C."

"Our song seemed to connect with people."

"I'm sorry I wasn't feeling well enough to make the trip." He stood now and followed her to the door.

"Thomas thinks you can stop Betsy." His eyes had that twinkle.

"Oh, I don't know. She and Bruce have so many connections throughout the township. I wouldn't bet against her."

"My money's on you."

Christine stopped and looked at him. "I've been trying to help Mama pack up our stuff so we can vacate. With Jimmy's passing, I'm not sure we'll meet the deadline."

"Oh, don't worry about that. I meant to tell you."

"Meaning?"

"I spoke to Bruce yesterday in a way I should have years ago. I told him your house was not coming down before he had a permit to wreck it. And if he or Betsy tried to kick you out before that, he would have to deal with me. I'll come down there and be a squatter in your house. If you'll have me, that is."

"My God!"

"So you can take time to bury your uncle. And don't worry about moving out for the time being. We'll see what happens at the township meeting next week."

As she drove to the university, past Arlene's and on through the covered bridge, she tried to take stock. Ethan certainly was a great gift to her life.

Shriver never interrupted her a single time as Christine lectured about the confusion that follows a devastating war, and the class had a lively discussion about how society tries to rebuild from a world in ruins. Several students stayed afterwards to ask questions, and Shriver didn't say a word but packed up his things and wandered off into the hallway. Christine wasn't sure what to make of it.

# Sixty–Two

___

**G**ordon saw the news story about the huge poultry truck hitting Uncle Jimmy's car head on as he came around that sharp corner, the truck flipping on its side with wheels spinning and chickens flopping helter-skelter across the landscape as they fled.

"Is there anything I can do?" Gordon asked, his voice full of concern.

Honestly, was she going to marry this guy? Why was she encouraging him? Hey, don't get emotional. This is the wrong time to decide anything, in spite of that paddle boat under dazzling cherry blossoms.

"Thanks for calling, Gordon. It's a tough time. And very busy. I'll let you know if you can help." Uncle Jimmy's face popped into her mind again.

"I don't want to intrude. I just want you to know I am ready to do anything you need."

"Thanks, Gordon. I understand. And I do appreciate it."

Dicey time. There had to be a limit to how much polite rebuff Gordon would accept. He seemed a changed guy, true, more mellow, less selfish. But for weeks she had begged off from so many of his attentions and invitations that she sensed his patience wearing thin. When would her delays and brush-offs morph into rejection in Gordon's heart?

Zach texted her as she was returning home for the meeting with the funeral director. "I know you have a funeral but we urgently need to meet. Toyota wants to exercise their option. Sam has a stack of invitations from our performance at the EAU thing." More pressure.

Uncle Lloyd was just arriving as she got there. It was the first time he had visited their modest little home. Christine could see he was surprised by its sparseness and smallness. But he simply smiled, "So this is where you live."

"Not for long," his sister shot back in a bitter tone. "We're being evicted so they can bulldoze this house, and Betsy can build fancy houses here." Christine hadn't had time to tell Mama what Ethan had explained to her earlier.

Lloyd looked at Christine for confirmation. "Unfortunately, it's true," she nodded. "I've never lived anywhere else." Standing there by the table, with the light touching him, Uncle Lloyd strikingly resembled Uncle Jimmy. Jimmy had been thinner and more worn down and damaged by life. But Lloyd had a similar nose and face and used his hands the same way.

Uncle Jimmy's dead. Holy Jesus. She fought back her tears as she went to answer the door. It was Harriet. The woman who had been her real mother reached out and clasped Christine in her arms. "I'm sorry, Christine, I know it hurts." Then Harriet turned and hugged Karen.

Mama cleared her throat. "I asked Harriet to join us for this meeting. I thought her experience could be helpful." Christine was startled by Mama's initiative.

The funeral director arrived at the same moment, and they all sat down to plan final details. Lloyd could not have been more courteous. Until the question came up about where Jimmy should be buried.

"I personally would not oppose it," Lloyd said, a bit of a flush rising in his face. "But—" he paused, raising his hands in exasperation—"the rest of the family won't hear of it."

"I knew it," Mama moaned wearily. "They're all haters. Do you believe me now, Christine?"

Harriet interrupted. "Lloyd, are you saying your brothers and your parents won't let Jimmy be buried in the Ober section there in the Northfield Cemetery?"

"That's what they're saying. I couldn't get to first base with them."

"But is it their decision to make?" Harriet pressed on. "Your family disowned Jimmy a long time ago, so they gave up their right to decide where he should be buried. If Ethan and I buy a burial lot there for Jimmy, who can stop us?"

The whipsaw clearly surprised Lloyd. "Father's on the cemetery committee." Lloyd's tone had taken on an edge of combativeness.

"Lloyd, I wish you no disrespect," Harriet continued. "But Ephraim Conoy is chair of that committee, and he said Ethan and I can buy a lot for Jimmy if we want to."

"You've spoken with Ephraim?"

"I have."

A long pause. The funeral director coughed. "Shall we discuss the details of the service?"

# Sixty-Three

---

**A** **numbness settled over her** after being battered by so many raw emotions. Uncle Jimmy's death. Hostility from Mama's family, in spite of Uncle Lloyd's warmth. Shriver's behavior. Their rousing success at the convention in Washington. The paddle boat ride under the Japanese trees. Uncertainty about how many more nights she'd sleep in the cozy room that had always been hers.

Sam stretched out her long legs across a chair in Adam's basement and outlined three solid invitations she'd received from EAU-related groups. The first came from California, somewhere near San Francisco. Another from Minneapolis. And the third from a retreat center near Orlando. None offered major bucks, and none paid travel or expenses.

"We could lose money on this," Christine observed. "And it'll take a lot of time traveling all over the country."

Sam frowned. "That's rather negative."

"But it's true, right?" Christine persisted.

Sam stood up. "Look, there are a few rules in the music industry. You can't become well known without developing a following. And you can't gain a following without traveling and performing all over the place. Your opportunity at the convention in D. C. was one in a million. And you nailed it. But if you don't build on that and the interest it generated, you might as well forget it."

Zach came and sat beside Christine, saying nothing at first. Everyone waited. Then he put his arm around her, like an old friend. "I know it's a tough time. So we can put this off if you'd like. It's just that when Sam said she was coming through here on the way back from her meeting in New York, we said it would be fine to meet. But your instincts are always good. I believe in your gut feelings about these things."

"I agree," Adam added, a new confidence in his manner. This all probably thrilled Adam, she realized. He had always wanted to be part of a band that was taken seriously.

"You'd like to go the whole way, Adam, right?"

"I don't know about 'the whole way.' But I've always dreamed of the kind of good luck we're suddenly having. Hey, I know your Uncle Jimmy just died. That's a blow. I was concerned this might be the wrong time to meet with Sam. It's too big a decision to make under pressure."

Christine reached over and patted Adam's hand. "Thanks, buddy." She rubbed her face and flicked her long hair. "What's the latest with Toyota?"

"They've exercised their option on the song. They can now use it in commercials, per our agreement. And they'll pay us for every use."

"So we don't have to do anything else related to that deal?"

"All you have to do is cash your checks." Sam unveiled one of her rare smiles.

"Pay dirt," Zach said, trying to suppress his enthusiasm.

"So the Toyota agreement is an isolated deal, right?" Christine said. "It'll be what it'll be. The big decision we face is whether we want to write another batch of songs so we have enough for a complete gig—and whether we're ready to give up the next few years of our lives, touring hither and yon."

Zach nodded, visibly restraining himself. Sam walked over to the corner, also clearly determined to say nothing.

"Tell you what. First of all, Sam, we owe you a great deal of gratitude. I don't know how you did it, but you did it. Thank you, sincerely."

Sam was caught off guard by her flat-out compliment. Braced for a debate, she could hardly switch gears fast enough. "Thank you, Christine," she gulped, a slight blush spreading across her face.

"Tell me, Sam, will these three offers disappear during the next week? Or will they still be viable a week from now?"

"We have at least a week in every case."

Christine let out a long, weary sigh. "I have an uncle to bury. Let's talk about this next week." She stood up, gave them a polite wave, and walked out into the balmy April afternoon, sensing the sadness mingling with the seductively warm air, the wash of the fresh greens, and the brilliant light of the day. An uncle to bury.

# Sixty-Four

———

**Meeting one's cousin for** the first time at a funeral was a bit strange. Laura was Lloyd's youngest, sitting next to Mama and Christine on the second bench at St. Mark's as the organ music swelled. Uncle Lloyd and Aunt Audrey sat next to Laura. The rest of the bench and the two benches behind them reserved for family were empty. No one else from Jimmy's family had showed up.

"I love your music," Laura whispered, brushing back her long dark hair as she smiled nervously.

"Really?"

"Yeah, my friend Starla goes to Midstate, and she took me to one of your concerts at the Root Cellar. I didn't even realize we were cousins until later. That's why I came today—so I could meet you."

Awkward. Uncle's Jimmy's being buried, and the only niece who showed up for his funeral beside Christine is a fan of The Forerunners. Sorry, Uncle Jimmy.

Christine was totally surprised to see Thomas and both Zach and Adam walk in with the choir as the service began. She wondered how that had happened. Harriet, her usual dignified self as she stood in the front row of the choir loft, probably had a hand in it. *Amazing grace, how sweet the sound.*

Christine glanced toward the back of the sanctuary and was surprised to see that it was more than half-full. Jimmy had always been adept at making friends, and a remarkable number of them had come to say goodbye. She noticed Gordon on the aisle partway back.

She took Mama's hand and squeezed it, holding it tight through the whole service until Mama started sobbing and freed her hand to wipe her tears. Rev. Kellerman said some worthwhile things, probably, but Christine was far away, caught up in memories of some of those good times with Uncle Jimmy. A life cut short, a life so freckled with false starts and misplaced finishes. His tough but innocent countenance smiling at her now, "You're like a light in my life."

Had she failed Jimmy, so caught up in her deadlines and work? Had she been too selfish?

Before they headed out for the burial service in Northfield, Aunt Audrey made an effort to visit with her. "I hear you're a senior at Midstate. What will you be doing after graduation next month?"

"Good question. Not sure."

"I thought maybe show business. I know Laura thinks you're very talented."

"Oh, I don't know about that."

She noticed Laura talking with Zach near the front of the sanctuary. Thomas walked up and gave Mama a hug and then cautiously embraced Christine. "My condolences," he said, almost formally.

"Thank you, Thomas. Do you often sing in the choir?"

"No, Grandma invited me since they were a little shorthanded. And Zach and Adam. When a funeral's during the week, some of the regulars can't get off work."

Zach took her hands and gave her a long hug. "I don't know what to say. But if you want to talk, I'm always available."

"You're the best, Zach. Thanks."

Then Adam and Jenn both hugged her. "Did you take off work?" she asked Jenn.

"Of course. I knew it was important to you."

She looked around for Mama and saw Harriet by her side. God bless Harriet and Ethan, paying for the burial plot as well as the entire funeral. When they saw a need, they quietly took care of it.

Thomas came toward her again. "I'm sorry I can't stay, Christine. I need to get back for classes. Maybe we can catch coffee sometime soon and I can hear your memories of Jimmy."

"That would be nice. I do thank you for coming."

The day was too resplendent, too shining, too full of possibilities for the unpleasant task of putting a friend in the ground. Forever. As they drove toward Northfield, she mused about how quickly someone can disappear. *You slipped away with no goodbye, and left me here to wonder "Why?" But on this day I promise you, I'll not forget the friend I knew.*

She stared at the row of lilac bushes, almost like a fencerow standing at attention, along the south edge of the cemetery near the entrance. She'd always liked their beauty and enticing fragrance.

Zach and his parents and Adam and Jenn stood close behind them at the graveside. The lot Harriet had secured for Jimmy was only one row over from the other Ober graves. *Ashes to ashes, dust to dust, the dead shall rise.* Rev. Kellerman's voice was perfect for the setting, she thought. Did he know something she didn't?

As they were about to lower the casket, she glanced back and was surprised to see how many had come to the cemetery. Nice weather, for sure, but another sign that Uncle Jimmy had a lot of friends.

The second time she looked back, she saw an old woman in a wheelchair sitting at a distance under the big maple, a younger woman assisting her. Christine took a longer look, wondering if that could possibly be Jimmy's mother, her own Grandmother Ober, sneaking here to watch her youngest boy be put in the ground, hoping her mean old grouchy husband wouldn't find out. She glanced at Uncle Lloyd and raised her eyebrows. He nodded imperceptibly and looked away.

# Sixty-Five

——

**S**am kept stressing that national attention to the Turner Estates controversy and to the role of their song could catapult The Forerunners onto a coveted platform. Zach and Adam agreed. Only Christine was worried about dragging the national press into their neck of the woods.

"But why?" Zach kept asking. "What's to lose?"

Christine wasn't in a mood to debate. She was tired of being the wet blanket as each new brainstorm emerged. "Fine, go for it. But if this all ends up embarrassing Harriet and Ethan, I'll never forgive you."

The hearing had been moved to the middle school auditorium from the small township hearing room. Christine assumed that no more than fifty or a hundred locals would show up. So she was both surprised and worried when she spotted lots of out-of-state license plates on the cars packing the school parking lot when she got there a half-hour early. What did it mean that people had driven from Maryland, Delaware, New Jersey, and even New York? She worried it could backfire. Fat Freddy and the rest of the Zoning Board did not want to be pushed around by outsiders. Too much publicity could end up making Betsy seem like a victim.

Fat Freddy looked lost on the big stage, even though they had drawn the main curtain closed to make the stage less cavernous. She noticed he was holding a gavel. Wonder where they found that. *The meeting could unravel without a proper gavel.*

The auditorium was already nearly filled. She noticed several national TV crews in place. Wow. Zach and Sam had gotten the word out. Hope it doesn't blow up.

Before she could spot Mr. Collins, who had promised to save a seat for her, a young man with short red hair rushed up. "You're Christine Ober, right?"

Something made her cautious. "Who's asking?"

He extended his hand. "Jeremiah Tumbleweed, *Philadelphia Ledger.*"

She shook his hand quickly and started to look for Mr. Collins again.

"Do you have a minute for a question?"

"I'm not speaking with reporters at the moment."

"Actually, you are," the young man persisted, rubbing his slight goatee.

"Look, I don't mean to be rude —"

"Then don't be."

She turned and looked at him again. "Is your name really Tumbleweed?"

"As sure as yours is Ober." He reached inside his jacket pocket. "Here's my card. I've underlined my cell number." For the first time, he smiled, exhibiting dimples in each of his cheeks. Sorta cute. "You have a story to tell, Christine. I'd like to be the one who helps you tell it."

She took his card. "Never heard of the *Ledger*."

"Oh, see, now you're trying to hurt me. We're a well-known cultural online site. You must have heard of us."

"Sorry." Again she turned.

"May I talk with you after the hearing later?"

"I said I'm not speaking with reporters."

His voice had a firmness now. "You do want to speak with me."

"And why would that be?"

"You're an amazing woman. I've been researching you." Again those dimples.

Zach walked up and rescued her. "My dad's saving you a seat in the fifth row on the aisle."

"Thanks, Zach." She started down the wide aisle, glancing back to see that Tumbleweed redhead smiling at her. Damn. He was either a breath of fresh air — or a menace.

The hearing quickly became contentious. Fat Freddy asked Attorney Peters several questions about the revised plan that Betsy and Bruce had submitted. Peters could not have been more courteous, answering step by step in a clear voice. At one point Betsy jumped in with a correction and the lawyer repeated her comment. "This revised plan is environmentally very sensitive," he concluded.

"That's a lie!" someone shouted from the back of the auditorium. Several others joined in. Freddy took the gavel and rather awkwardly tried to pound it. Less than effective.

Deb Brewster leaned into the mike on the table in front of her. "Mr. Chairman, perhaps we should open the floor for public comment?"

Freddy never lost control, but voices were raised, a lot of emotional allegations were made, and audience members constantly shouted out disagreement. Christine had never attended a meeting like it. She was glad Harriet and Ethan weren't there.

Eli Gibbons finally got the floor, and he leaned into his mike so his voice boomed through the place. "Mr. Chairman, may I propose that we restrict all comments to persons who are residents of our township. We appreciate the visit of out-of-state and out-of-township friends, but I believe local matters should be settled by the elected representatives of the local people. And this is a local matter."

The crowd grew quiet. "Mr. Gibbons raises a good point," Freddy pronounced calmly. "For the rest of the evening, we will reserve the time for local residents to speak. Please give your name and address before you share your comments so we know that you do live in the township."

For the next few minutes the momentum seemed to swing in Betsy's direction. Two women gave testimonials about "what fine people the Turners are." Another man from the far end of the township asked what right out-of-town people had to come and stir things up. "I'm a farmer, too, and I worked hard to pay for my land. I don't need big city liberals trying to tell me what to do with my property. I'm not driving to *their* zoning board to tell them what to do with their properties." This brought a round of loud applause from frustrated local folk.

Then Bob Collins took the floor and in a respectful, almost subdued tone faced the large audience. "Sometimes in our individual lives, we reach a turning point, a moment of truth. I believe this decision is a turning point for our community. If this prime historic farmland is rezoned to permit asphalt streets and expensive houses to replace the crops, there's no turning back. And if this farm is rezoned, how can this zoning board refuse to rezone other farms? It's true, we need a plan for orderly growth. And we probably do need new homes to be built from time to time. But on the edge of town is better than in the middle of an isolated stretch of historic farmland. I'm for preserving our precious farmland rather than destroying it, just so a few people can get much richer."

The applause was deafening as Mr. Collins came back to his seat. Christine turned and gave him a thumbs-up. The tide had turned. When the applause died down, Freddy was trying again to pound his gavel and Christine thought she heard a loud sigh from Betsy.

In the end, the board voted to postpone the decision while they received more information. But being officials who responded to the desires of the local electorate, it appeared the handwriting was on the wall.

Afterwards, the press crowded around Mr. Collins to ask him lots of questions for their broadcasts and write-ups. Christine put her arm around Zach and whispered in his ear, "How does it feel to have a dad who's more popular with the media than you are, Zachery Thackery?"

Zach smiled broadly. "I couldn't be more proud." And she knew he meant it.

She turned to see Betsy glaring at her as she and Bruce left the auditorium, Bruce looking a little beaten down. She noticed the Tumbleweed fella standing beside Bob Collins taking notes. I guess he is a real reporter. Just then he looked up and came walking toward her. "Would you have a minute now, Ms. Ober?"

"I'm not the story."

"You are for me. My readers would really like to meet you."

She laughed. "I'm really not interested."

"Please call me. I'm not giving up." And with that he was gone.

# Sixty–Six

—

**C**hristine called Ethan the next morning to say that she may have found a clue about the arsonist. Abe Wissler served on the board of Farmers United Bank for many years. And it appears that Christian Miller also served on that same board for a time, she said. Could one of the actions of that bank board be at the center of the grievance or grudge, if that's what it was?

Ethan was intrigued. "There should be a way to find out who else was on that board over the last twenty years. You may be on to something."

"How do you mean?"

Ethan lowered his voice. "If that bank board called in a loan, for instance, in a way that seemed unfair, and it ruined someone's business, that could really enrage a certain type of person."

"And they'd burn down barns of board members in revenge?"

"It sounds a bit farfetched. But let's see who else was on that board."

Christine was tantalized. "I never would have thought of that. I'm crazy busy, but I'll try to find out soon." She was sure Arlene had never been on that bank board.

When she got to work, Sharon asked to meet with her. She said she loved having Christine on the staff, but she had to acknowledge that The Forerunners' sudden popularity made things more complicated at the Historical Society. "You'll soon need a personal secretary," she laughed. "Someone must have published an item saying that you work here. Everyone and his wife's uncle are calling here to connect with you."

"I'm sorry, Sharon. I've tried to discourage it."

"I know you have. Here are two calls that came in yesterday. One from a guy who insists his real name is Tumbleweed. And another who claims to be your cousin."

It was going to be a tough few weeks until graduation. Research paper deadlines. Sharon needing her on several important projects. The band trying to chart its future. Gordon becoming impatient. Mama struggling to find positive things about life.

She texted Jeremiah Tumbleweed and said she couldn't do an interview. Jobs that needed to be completed before grad left no spare time. He responded that his deadline was in ten days. "Please call me. I promise to take very little of your time."

"My answer's still the same," she shot back.

"You have to eat. Let me buy you some food (your choice) and I'll keep the interview short."

"Not interested. Sorry."

"Why have you decided to get me fired?"

She laughed out loud, sitting right there at the Society's front desk. That redhead was certainly funny and persistent. "I'll get back to you by noon tomorrow," she responded. "No promises."

After work, on her way to the university library to check out several more details for her Africa history paper, she decided to quickly return the call from her newly-discovered cousin. "Laura, this is Christine."

"Thanks for calling back."

"Sure. What's up?"

"I know you're busy. But I wondered if we could meet for coffee sometime soon."

Christine paused. For the first time in her life she was struggling with being sorta famous. Here she was, screening each contact in a newly skeptical way. What were the real motives and intentions of everybody who suddenly wanted to meet with her or even exchange emails or texts? "I'm sorry to say this, Laura, but I'm terribly swamped this month with grad and all."

"Okay, I understand. I just thought you might like to meet your grandmother."

Christine pulled off the road, afraid to breathe. "What did you say?"

"I told Grandma I had talked with you, and she insists she would like to meet you. She's been rather sick. So we shouldn't put it off too long if you're interested at all."

Sitting there at the side of the road as farmers planted crops, the early corn already pushing through like irrepressible little shoots of childhood, Christine tried to breathe. What should she say?

"Could we meet at that old Becker's Joint on the west end?"

"I can meet any day after five."

"How about Thursday at 5:30?"

"I'll be there. Thanks, cuz."

As Laura hung up, Christine wanted to cry. It was too much, too much pressure, too much emotion. All at once. Too many festering wounds nearly forgotten, now freshly resurrected, aching with no prospect of resolution.

# Sixty-Seven

———

**E**than **asked Christine to** go along to visit Abe Wissler. Because Ethan had given up driving, it was the first time he'd been in her rickety car. "I hope Abe won't refuse to talk with us if we arrive in such an embarrassing vehicle," she said.

Ethan chuckled. "Abe's not that kind of guy."

When they explained the reason for their visit, Abe was surprised. "You think it's a serial arsonist?"

"We don't know what to think," Ethan responded. "Christine here enjoys researching, and we got to talking about it, and one thing led to another." He paused. "Abe, would it be possible that, while you and Christian were both on the bank board, you called in a loan on a business that caused it to collapse?"

Abe stroked his chin for a long moment, thinking. "Things like that are always possible with lending institutions, I suppose." He paused, still searching his memory. "Did you have someone in mind?"

"Oh, no, Abe, the records are confidential, of course, so we don't know what loans were called."

"I see."

Christine cleared her throat. "And one other question we had, if that's okay—?"

"Absolutely, young lady."

"If there's a chance that this is what's happening, we were wondering if there's someone else who served on that bank board with you who might own a barn. I have a list here."

Abe was impressed. "You've done your homework." He looked at the list. "You mean you think this crazy barn-burner may still be targeting someone else?"

"We don't know what to think." She and Ethan had decided ahead of time to not mention Arlene's situation.

Abe studied the list. "No, not John Henry. Not Harry. And I don't think Madeline owns a farm. Who else?" He kept looking at the sheet of paper. "Ah, maybe Stevie Adams. I think his son owns a sizeable farm. Have you touched base with Stevie?"

"No, we haven't," Ethan said. "But back to our first question—do you remember any contentiousness around the calling of a loan when you and Christian were on the bank board together?"

Abe's forehead wrinkled as he tried to remember. "In truth, I can't recall details. I left that board several years ago. Of course, every customer is upset when we call their loan. But I can't think of the type of episode you're asking about."

They chatted on, and Ethan and Abe recalled some stories from their farming years. Ethan mentioned that Christine had included the Wissler barn in her high school study of outstanding barns. Abe's face grew sad as he talked about that beautiful barn, now gone.

As they were leaving, Abe had a thought. "You know, it just comes back to me that there was one really ugly incident when we called in the loan on Homer Winters' big hardware complex and businesses, and he had to close his operations. He took it very hard."

"I remember when that happened. I used to shop there sometimes."

Abe continued, "Homer had a temper, that's true. But I can't see him burning barns to get even."

On their way home, Christine asked Ethan what he really thought about Homer Winters. "He could lose his temper some. One time I was in his store and he yelled at a customer for handling a piece of equipment incorrectly or something. Can't believe it helped his business. But he did keep expanding and expanding."

"You think he's vindictive enough to burn barns?"

"I would hope not, Christine. But I guess none of us ever really knows about people."

She looked at Ethan as she drove. "Do you think we should warn Stevie Adams? Or is that really unfair, when we have no evidence?"

Ethan was quiet for a while. "Maybe we should wait on that. But I've known Sheriff Springer fairly well through the years. I may say something to him, off the record, so to speak."

# Sixty–Eight

———

**S**he **found herself enchanted** by his graceful hands as he led them, keeping the group in perfect rhythm if amateurs were capable of such a feat. Why had she always been so mesmerized by madrigals? So beautiful yet dissonant. Stray fragments floating unconnected from so many threads of human hopes, spun in the evening air about them into six distinct but blended tones, reflecting the unresolved harmonies of her young life. She should have skipped the practice, but she wanted to see him.

"Let's try it again," he said.

She wasn't so fixated on Thomas that she wasn't aware of the fifteen other singers in Arlene's big farm-house kitchen. But having Harriet mention that her grandson may be leaving for most of the summer had set off a panic of sorts inside her. In a few weeks, he could be gone. What if he didn't come back to Midstate? She had imagined a hundred conversations she would have with him when she got through school, but she hadn't stopped to realize he might move away.

She noticed Emily with her regal bearing, great neck, healthy chest, twisting her nostrils ever so faintly as she sniffed a touch of unpleasantness in the air. Must be the cow barns. The windows in Arlene's kitchen were open to receive whatever fragrance came floating in on the warm evening breeze. What a polite Main Line sniff. Little did Emily or the others guess what tragedy may await Arlene's big barn.

"Do you have any suggestions?" Thomas asked Arlene.

"Since it's our last program of the season, I hope we can all be sharp. But it sounds good, don't you think, John Jr.?" John Jr. simply nodded.

As Thomas gave them their pitches and his confident fingers swept them back into the compatibly disagreeable tones of the old, old music, she imagined him reaching out to her, taking her hand as they drifted together into the evening sky, out over the farms, past the university, crossing the river, and then to Europe to sample the music of Vienna and the magic of Paris. How soon was he leaving?

John Jr. coughed. Hard. So hard that Thomas waved for them to pause. Arlene rushed to get him some water, and John Jr. slipped into the family room to get control, still heaving his ample frame. A great tenor he was. She wondered if it might have been a naughty bug on twilight adventure, swarming John Jr.'s throat on one of those vulnerable high notes.

Arlene was pouring her great lemonade into mugs as Thomas led them through their final number, the trance long gone, the vivid outdoor colors a mere memory. Through the open window she heard a cow calling to its ambitious calf. Remember who you are, little one. Remember.

# Sixty-Nine

——

**A**fter the madrigal practice, Arlene asked Christine if she could drop around for a few minutes the next morning. When she arrived, the three girls were sitting with their mother, all in a row, with a rather formal demeanor. Christine was surprised.

"We're sorry to have drawn you into all of this drama," Arlene said after an awkward pause.

"No, no, it's no bother. I've been worried about you."

Arlene raised her hand. "That's what we're trying to explain."

"Oh, okay…"

"Turns out it was a prank."

"A prank?"

"Ill advised, for sure. Almost stupid."

Christine, now puzzled, waited for her to go on. Arlene was clearly embarrassed. "Love is a funny thing, isn't it?"

Christine looked from face to face. Ellen jumped in. "My Floyd was just trying to get my attention. He didn't realize how it would upset us."

Christine was confused. "I'm lost."

Arlene got up and walked toward Christine. "Floyd Hooper is a little wacky, some would say, but he loves my Ellen, and it seems she has feelings for him, too."

"Are you saying he sent that threatening letter?"

Ellen's voice was firm. "He didn't mean it. I should have realized it was one of his pranks. But when he came to see if we could get back together, and I let it slip about how upset we were by that pasted-up letter, he actually broke into tears, took responsibility, and asked us to forgive him. And we did. He promised never to do anything like that again."

"Like I said," Arlene added, "love is a funny thing."

It made Christine furious but she knew she had to be very careful. "Are you saying that it was a prank that got out of control because Floyd wanted to get back together with you, Ellen?"

"He didn't mean it," Ellen repeated. "He knows now it was really immature of him."

"And the police?"

"Oh, we never told the cops about Floyd," Becca said.

"Wow, the whole thing's a bit random, isn't it?" Christine said, trying to absorb it all. Who the heck are these people? She thought she knew them really well.

"Ellen and Floyd are engaged now," Susie volunteered sweetly.

Christine couldn't believe it. "Really?"

Arlene was laughing, as though acknowledging the wild improbabilities of the whole sequence of events. Then she grew serious. "Christine, we wanted to explain to you in person and apologize for involving you in this weird drama. Will you forgive us?"

Can love be that simple, she wondered. Or that dangerous? Had she misjudged Arlene and her girls? "Oh, sure," she murmured. "No problem. And I guess congratulations are in order for you, Ellen."

Ellen twisted in her awkward way and blushed. "Thanks, Christine," she purred in a smitten tone.

Christine was so exasperated when she left Arlene's place that she drove back home instead of going on to the Historical Society and work. She needed time to think. This whole thing was crazy Floyd's attempt to win back Ellen? After all this worry and fear? She should just call the police and tell them about Floyd. Ellen wouldn't be a very happy blushing farm girl after that, would she?

Christine sat staring at herself in the mirror and then started laughing uncontrollably, rolling across her bed as her body convulsed. "What the hell kind of marriage is that going to be?" she shouted to the empty house. "What will Floyd threaten to do the next time?"

Over the next hour as she calmed down, her emotions seesawed between giddiness and sadness. If love was that simple and easy, maybe she should just start making crazy threats and demands of Thomas. Would that work? Then the sad giddiness overwhelmed her again and she lay there rocking with laughter.

# Seventy

———

"**I'm the youngest,**" **Laura** was saying, running her hand through her long black hair.

"You work at your dad's store?"

"Yeah, I have for the past year since I'm out of high school. I've been thinking of maybe taking some business classes part-time. Do you like college?"

Laura's face had a pleasantness about it, good looks edged with uncertainty. Pretty but a bit nervous. Christine liked her immediately. Almost like an instant younger sister. "Oh, yes, for the most part, I've loved college. You should try it."

"Uncle Gene says the Obers are a business family, not a college one."

"Is that like a rule?"

Laura relaxed a bit and smiled. "I didn't know you existed until I tried to figure out who this singer-writer named Ober was in The Forerunners. I had always been told that Jimmy was a jailbird and your mother was dead." Laura's eyes widened as her voice intensified. "Can you believe that?"

"Actually, I can."

"I'm sorry, I really am."

"It's not your fault."

"I want to do something about it, though, unless you don't." She paused to sip her coffee. "You should know that you and your mom and Uncle Jimmy are not the only recipients of Grandpa's anger and meanness. For as long as I can remember, Grandpa has openly complained that he thinks my daddy could have married a better woman. I love my mom. And so does Daddy. But Grandpa just always picks on my mom. 'Lloyd could have married quality but he settled for that O'Malley woman.' It's been hard on Mom."

"Whoa... I'm sorry to hear that, Laura. If Oscar Ober is picking on your mother's Irish background, he should know that his own wife has Irish background. I was just researching that."

"Really?"

"Yes, our great-great-grandfather was an O'Shea, the child of a defrocked priest and a pretty parish girl named Malinda. Lots of interesting history."

"How did I never know about you, Christine? Don't take this the wrong way, but I think you're a lot more interesting than my other cousins."

Christine smiled. "I suppose I should say thanks, but I don't want to be criticizing anyone if I do."

They talked on about lots of things, so many blanks to fill in, numerous untruths to undo. Finally Laura grew serious and cleared her throat. "I mentioned perhaps meeting Grandma. I maybe was premature."

"I see."

"Well, when Mom learned what I was planning, she became concerned that Grandpa would find out and try to stop it."

"Stop what?"

"The idea was to invite Grandma to our place to have lunch with Mom and me. It's a way to get her out of the house and to give her a break. We've done that a few times in the past year. So it shouldn't raise any concerns for Grandpa. But since she's in a wheelchair now, she normally has an aide assist her if she goes out, unless one of the family can help. When Daddy found out what we were trying to plan, he said he'd help with Grandma's transportation." She paused. "And, of course, the idea is to invite you to come, if you're game."

"What's Grandma like, Laura?"

"She's a bit gruff. But I've always liked her. She's had a hard life with Grandpa being so difficult. She told me recently about how angry she was when Grandpa kicked your mother out after she got pregnant. She got tears in her eyes. 'I lost a daughter because of that horrid old man, and I've never met that granddaughter of mine. Before I die, I'd like to make peace with both Karen and her daughter.'"

"My God."

"Yeah, isn't that something? Grandma said she'd like to meet you as soon as possible after I told her you existed and that you were so nice to me. She'd like to meet your mother, too, but my dad thinks it's best to go one step at a time."

"I understand. Not sure what my mother will say. She's been very angry. Do you have a date in mind?"

"Tuesdays are usually the best day. I guess the first Tuesday that suits you."

So Tuesday it was. Sarah Ober was actually a few years younger than Harriet, Christine realized, but she looked and acted older as she sat at the table in her wheelchair. Her face had seen a thousand troubles.

"I'm delighted to meet you, Grandma," Christine said after she had been introduced.

The old woman's response surprised her, a deep guttural scrape of a voice, coming from the cavern of her chest. "The pleasure is mine, Christine. I've waited a long time for this day."

"Christine," Laura interjected, "please sit down here beside Grandma so you can speak more freely."

Aunt Audrey was smiling broadly as she placed the plates of quiche and fresh fruit in front of them.

"Do you mind if I say grace?" Grandma Sarah asked her daughter-in-law.

"Please do," Audrey said, sitting now, too.

Again that surprisingly deep voice. "Dear God in heaven, thank you for giving me the strength to live long enough to meet my long-lost granddaughter. Bless Christine and her mother. And all of the rest of us. Amen."

They all sat in silence, taking a first bite of the food. What should she say? Really, she should wait to see what Grandma wanted to talk about. But after a rather long silence, she smiled at her grandmother and ventured, "You're a descendant of the McWilliams family, aren't you?" What made you say that, dummy? Maybe she hated her parents.

Grandma turned to look at her with those piercing dark brown eyes. "How did you know that?"

"I've been working on my family history and I learned that."

"You like genealogy?"

"Some. Not sure why. I never paid attention to mine until recently. But I do like history."

Grandma studied her face for a moment. "You look a lot like your mother."

"People say that."

"How is Karen?"

MERLE GOOD

Christine had realized that such a question would likely come up but when it did she was unexpectedly shaken. What should she say? She didn't want to anger her ailing grandmother. But now that this moment had arrived, Christine figured that truth was the only option. "I hope Mama gets to meet you, Grandma," she said.

Grandma was seized by a long fit of coughing, her eyes watering from the considerable effort. "Think maybe it's too late?"

What a question. So much pain etched into her gravelly voice, her hand shaking visibly now. Christine reached out and took her grandmother's hand. "It's never too late, is it, Grandma? Look at us, sitting here, side by side. Who would have guessed this was possible just a month ago?"

Laura was caught up in the moment. "See, Mom, I told you she's a kind person."

The penetrating eyes were still fixed on her. "I'm going to ask you again, Granddaughter, and I want a straight answer. How is my daughter Karen? Lloyd says that maybe the next time we meet, Karen can join us."

"I'm hoping so." An impatient tear pushed itself from the corner of Christine's eye as she sat up straight in her chair, rolling her head back as she did sometimes to clarify her thoughts. She glanced at Laura and Aunt Audrey, sensing they were encouraging her, so she turned and looked Sarah Ober full in the face. "I'll try to be honest."

"That's what I want."

"It may be painful."

"Can't be worse than what I've been through."

Christine hesitated again. Remember your biggest weakness is saying things you later regret, stupid. Be careful. "Mama's had a hard life, I would say. Very hard. I hope you can imagine how much she might despise her family after the way she's been treated."

"Oh, yes, I can. But I never wanted it that way, please understand."

Christine raised her hand. "You asked me to be honest. It may be true that you never wanted things to happen the way they did these past twenty years. But for Mama, that's hard to believe. She was on the receiving end of what seemed like downright meanness, hostility, and shame. It crushed her. She's lived a sad broken life. All because she gave birth to me."

"Now wait a minute," Grandma snapped in that rasping tone. "It was not because you were born. No one had anything against you. You must never think that. It was because of what preceded that. I was against how your mother was treated."

"Then why is this the first time we are meeting?" Christine shot back.

"I didn't know you were alive. I didn't even know if Karen was still alive." Grandma's voice was filled with pleading. "I didn't know. Please forgive—"

Abruptly Sarah Ober's features froze. She didn't move, frozen in mid-sentence, her hand half raised. It shocked Christine. Had her grandmother died in front of her? Was this a heart attack or a stroke or something else? A hot panic surged through her as her grandmother stared at her, apparently alive but frozen in place.

"Don't worry," Laura said. "It's a mini-stroke. She has them every so often."

And just like that, Grandma's color returned and she was moving as before. "What was I saying?" she asked Audrey.

Audrey's manner impressed Christine. If she was as abused verbally by her father-in-law as Laura had implied, she certainly did not seem bitter. Audrey reached out and took Sarah Ober's hand. "I think you were asking Christine to forgive you."

"Which one is Christine?" Grandma asked, glancing around a bit vacantly.

Aunt Audrey smiled again. "Mother Ober, this is Christine, sitting next to you."

"Oh, hello," the old woman said, managing a half-smile as she pushed her fork toward a piece of her quiche.

# Seventy-One

––––

**S**he needed to speak with Thomas. Heart to heart. And she didn't want to wait for some moment to develop. Normally when she felt this heavy and needed to unburden, she'd seek out Harriet. But today she needed Thomas.

He agreed to meet at the old Coffee Drip just off campus. He seemed a bit nervous as he slid into the booth, those eyes she could barely look away from scanning her face, examining it for clues.

"Thanks for coming, Thomas. I know it's a busy time for you."

His smile was tentative. "Is something wrong?"

"No, no." She studied two robins on a railing outside the window. "I've never had a parent to share things with the way most people seem to. Your grandma's been there for me, though, for as long as I can remember. She's great. But today I had this need to confide in you."

The color in his face deepened slightly, his eyelids flickering. "I'm complimented, Christine."

She stared at him intensely then, her tone all business. "How do I know what I'm supposed to do with my life?"

She could see he was surprised. "Tell me what you mean."

Christine told him about how the prospect of the Toyota commercial made her feel mercenary, about meeting her gravelly-voiced grandmother and the strange mini-stroke experience, about her mother's growing depression, and about the strain and paradox of Uncle Jimmy's death.

"But more than any of that is the identity crisis I've been struggling with. Most of the time I refuse to think about it. It's like I've always assumed I could not fly. And now, more and more, when I open my eyes, it appears that I'm actually flying. In the same instant, however, I'm overwhelmed by the belief that I'm going to fall, to crash, to end up in pieces. I honestly never thought I'd go to college. Mama always scolded me for dreaming. But here I am, about to graduate. Who am I? It's like I should be starting a career but I haven't properly prepared because I was always braced for disaster. So Mama was probably right. I wasn't born to fly."

Thomas just sat there, staring at his coffee cup, his sporty tie loose around his collar. Then he looked at her. "What about you—what do you want to do with your life?"

"See, that's the point. I don't know."

Thomas nodded. "I understand. But let me ask you this. If you could lay aside your mother's warnings for a moment, and if money weren't a concern, what would you really like to do? Be a lyricist and music performer? Be a college prof? Be a leader at a historical organization? Own a restaurant?"

"A restaurant?"

"Yeah—if you could do or be anything—what would you like?"

"It's not that easy."

"Let's for a moment pretend that it is. What's your answer?"

This wasn't going quite as she thought it might. He couldn't understand. He'd always lived in a world of privilege. He couldn't conceive of always being braced for failure.

"You may not be as solitary as you think," he said softly, running his fingers through his hair.

"Solitary?"

"Alone. Unique."

"Yeah, I know what solitary means. But what's your point?"

"You don't think I worry about failure? Everybody does. Nothing is guaranteed for any of us in life, is it? Look at my parents. Best schools. Prestigious jobs. Finest social circles and neighborhoods. Global travels. Several houses around the world. And tons of money. But—" Thomas raised his hand as high as he could and brought it down swiftly— "No happiness, zero contentment. Observers think my parents have everything. But in truth, they have nothing. That's why I'm asking—what do *you* want, Christine?"

The intensity of his response surprised her. "I know I have to earn enough to pay the rent, wherever I end up living. And I do enjoy—" She caught herself.

"What?"

"See, I'm not comfortable saying it out loud. It feels like I might stir up the curse."

Thomas leaned toward her. "What the hell are you talking about?"

"Unless you've lived under a suffocating cloud of self-doubt, you wouldn't understand. Sorry."

"Hold it. How did we get from 'I do enjoy' to 'stirring up the curse'?"

Christine closed her eyes. She was not going to cry in front of Thomas. How could she explain it better? "Am I going to be Harriet or will I be Karen, my mother? I fear to imagine how my life would have turned out without Harriet and Ethan. I love them. But it's still a fact that my identity, even as confident as I can be, suffers from a serious undertow of foreboding, expecting the worst, assuming failure and disaster. To say I can just take a magic tonic and wave farewell to the emotional inheritance I received from my mother is unrealistic."

"I never said that. But let me emphasize as strongly as I can—I don't think you're Karen or Harriet—you are Christine."

"Great."

"I'm serious. I think you're wonderful."

"Thanks. But that's not what I was asking for. Look, maybe I'm just wasting your time."

Thomas frowned. "It's hard for you to accept compliments, isn't it?"

Christine sat there staring at the man she believed she might love, trying to figure out if he could ever be happy with her. He probably thought she was a nut case, unable to handle either failure or success. Had she misjudged him?

"You know the identity questions you're having are typical, right?"

"Yes, I know I'm typical."

He looked frustrated. "Look, Christine, I was taking you seriously. But when things get close to the bone, you like to play games, don't you?"

Was he angry? What had she missed? "Sorry, Thomas."

"Don't be sorry, be honest." He *was* angry. "Christine, you're very bright, and you're good at protecting yourself. We all are. But sometimes you avoid direct conversations by playing words games when things get serious."

"Are you mad at me?"

"No." Thomas paused and wiped his forehead with the back of his hand. "Christine, I apologize. You honored me by sharing your inner anxieties with me."

"Can you tell me what upset you?"

Thomas took another sip of coffee, looking out the window. "I like you a lot, and I guess I get upset when I think you're selling yourself short.

Christine let out a deep sigh. "Are you going to call me two-faced again?"

"That's not fair."

"I maybe made a mistake in the way I framed our discussion. I don't believe I'm all that unique, but I do think I may have a harder time believing I can be successful than some other students do. That's all I was trying to say."

"I understand. Maybe I was too abrupt."

They sat there in the Coffee Drip, talking for another hour, Thomas displaying more vulnerability than he usually did and Christine slowly beginning to believe that the risk of asking him to meet with her was maybe not a bad idea. He seemed to know her better than she realized.

# Seventy–Two

—

**W**hen she got to her desk the next morning, she saw the Toyota commercial with their song as its theme for the first time. Sam had sent a link. "It starts airing nationally next week." Watching the ad was both exhilarating and a bit underwhelming for her. It was a commercial to sell cars, for heaven's sake. The wistfulness of her words, written in her longing for attention from Thomas, was now, through clever camera shots, directed toward various Toyota models! Why the hell did I permit my tender lyrics, which always brought audiences to their feet, flush with desire and hope—why did I let those words be used to encourage people to buy pretty cars?

Okay, it wasn't Toyota's fault. That was the deal. In fact, Zach, Adam, and she had just received checks for another $10,000 each as part of the roll-out of the ad campaign. A lot of money. So why this sour-ish feeling in her gut?

Sharon heard the music and came to see. "Is it on the air already?"

"Next week."

Sharon was euphoric. "It's unbelievable. Our very own Christine has made the big time!" Then she noticed. "Oh, sorry, maybe you're not overjoyed by it."

"I have mixed feelings."

"I think they use the song well. Or maybe you think they muffed it somehow?"

"It's an adjustment." Christine raised her eyebrows. "I didn't write the song to romanticize cars."

"But it doesn't take anything away from your song. This exposure will only add to its popularity, don't you think?" Sharon pulled up a chair beside her and spoke freely, the library having no visitors at that moment. "And you and your mother can use the money, right?"

Christine shook off her trance of disappointment. "Of course, we can. It's such a blessing. We're really lucky." She paused and looked deep into Sharon's eyes. "I guess I hadn't stopped to realize how it would feel."

Sharon hugged her. "I understand. And I'm with you the whole way, whatever happens."

Everywhere she went on campus people raved about the Toyota commercial and their song. *Why can't you feel my eyes on you?* Emily gave her an enormous hug when they passed each other near the library entrance. "I always knew you'd make it to the big time," she whispered as she kissed her cheek.

"It's just a car commercial," Christine protested demurely.

"Zach's really pumped," Emily was laughing. "He's so excited." Emily lowered her voice. "We spent the night together last night, and I don't think he slept a wink."

Damn. Emily and Zach. That was news.

Social media danced in celebration, the local TV station did a story on the success of the little hometown band, and her cousin Laura left three messages congratulating her. Tim Schmidt, a classmate from high school, sent her an email about investing in a new company he was forming. Christine Ober an investor? She laughed out loud when she read his message. Every "Tim," Dick, and Harry would be asking her for money. What a drag.

Mama's reaction was unanticipated. Everyone at the diner was buzzing about The Forerunners' success and teasing Karen about how she'd soon be so rich she'd never work another day in her life. Christine had purposely not told Mama anything about the Toyota deal because she honestly thought it was a pipe dream, even after Toyota exercised their option. But she had not expected her mother would find out at the diner before she had a chance to tell her. She should have planned better, she saw that now.

Mama seemed depressed and angry about the situation. "It was really embarrassing, all of them teasing me, and I'm in the dark," she snapped.

"I'm sorry, Mama. I meant to tell you."

"You never tell me anything. I'm always the last to find out."

"Honestly, I didn't think it was real. These fairy-tale things always have a way of falling through."

"So what's the truth—is it real?"

She sat down at the table, motioning for her mother to sit across from her. What should she say? Would her mini-success now convince Mama that she was wrong with her endless predictions that Christine would live a life of regret on the margins, just as she had? Could Christine possibly make her good fortune, such as it was, a source of good news and uplift for her mother, too? Could they become a team in her mother's mind, rather than some kind of rivals?

"Mama, I'll tell you the whole thing. But I need two promises from you. First, don't tell anyone else the details I share with you, especially about the money. It's none of their business. Okay?"

"I never blab."

"I know that. But people suddenly know about this because of the stories in the press, so they have no filters about asking anything and everything."

"Oh, I see. So you've been dealing with this?"

"As a band, we have known this could happen for quite a while. Months. But we agreed to keep it confidential, partly because we'd look foolish if we announced it and it didn't work out. Plus I was especially skeptical that it would ever happen. And now, after months of being very tight-lipped, suddenly everyone knows. Everyone. I have a reporter from Philly who's hounding me for an interview."

Her mother reached out and took her hands. "You poor dear. I'm sorry I haven't been there for you."

"No, no, it's my fault, not yours."

Mama eyed her for a long moment, then rubbed her face. "You mentioned two promises."

"Yes, I did."

"So what's the second? I promise not to tell anyone your confidential stuff. What else?"

Christine bowed her head as she tried to think of what to say to her mother. "I wish we could be a team."

"A team? In what way?"

"Please don't get mad at me. Just hear what I'm trying to express."

"I'll try, chickadee, I will."

So Christine launched into a quiet exposition about her experience as Karen Ober's daughter. Each good moment through the years had almost always been summed up with a warning from Mama to lower her sights, to not expect much from life. Sometimes it felt like Mama saw it as a competition, that Mama would be disappointed if anything worked out better for Christine than it had for her. "Mama, I know you've lived through very hard times. But I have, too. And I'm determined not to be defeated by them."

Tears glistened in Mama's eyes. "I never meant it to be a competition. I just didn't want you to be disappointed and crushed like I was. But I never wished anything bad for you, honey."

"I believe you, Mama. But there are two sides to the experience. There's how it feels to you. And that may not be the same as how I experience it."

"Of course, of course."

"Just as your experience was different than your own mother's experience probably was."

"What made you say that?"

Oh, God, now she had stepped in it. "The question is whether we can move on from the past and set a new tone for our future together. Can we be a team that wants to celebrate positive things that happen instead of fearing the worst?"

"I think I can promise I want to do that—if that's what you're asking."

Christine slipped her arm around Mama. "What I'm going to tell you is confidential. Toyota is paying us to use our song. It's like royalties, depending on how often they use it. So if the commercial doesn't perform with viewers the way they hope, this is the end of the road. But if it does meet expectations, they may pay more royalties."

"I think I understand."

Christine walked to the window. "To date, my share of the proceeds comes out to a little more than $13,000. That could be it. Or there may be a lot more."

Mama's face showed true surprise. "That's a lot of money."

"For me, it is, yes. I got the most recent check for $10,000 only a few days ago, and I really couldn't believe it was true. I didn't tell anyone, and I wanted to make sure it cleared before I decided it was real. This morning I checked my account and the money's there."

"So it's real?"

"Yes, Mama. Even if there are no more royalty payments, it's a nice little kitty."

Mama got up now, too, and started to pace. Finally she smiled. "You did it, didn't you!"

Christine walked across and hugged her mother. "I suppose I did, with the help of Zach and Adam. And Sam, our agent. And Thomas, who made the connection. I owe thanks to a lot of people."

"So you want me to promise to be more optimistic and to be happy, right?"

"Mama, we're a team. We should both be glad when good things happen for either of us. We're in this together. I'm your daughter, and you deserve part of the credit for this, too, for the way you raised me. Please own that."

"Oh, no, I don't deserve any credit for this."

"See what I mean. That's the second promise I need from you. Don't be so down on yourself. Be happy when good things happen. Don't be so sure that moments of success will turn to trouble. Celebrate the good wherever we find it, especially in each other. We can do it. Just look at that new quilt on your bed. So many people are happy that you survived that blizzard. It's a happy quilt!"

Karen Ober started laughing and crying at the same moment. "A happy quilt! You've always been like an angel to me, sweetheart. Why do I forget that?"

In spite of the warmth and nearly giddy buoyancy of the atmosphere, Christine decided not to tell her mother that her secret hope was that the Toyota royalties would increase to the extent where she could afford to buy a nice little house for her mother, all paid and debt-free.

But hey, that would mean her lyrics, written about Harriet's elusive grandson, would have to entice lots of materialistic TV viewers to go out and buy more gas-guzzling vehicles.

# Seventy–Three

———

Thomas was waiting for her when she got to the Society. The May morning's magnificent light on the blooming, greening landscape had already made her resent that she'd work indoors all day. She couldn't wait for grad and all of its related deadlines to be over.

"What's up, Thomas?'

He seemed surprised by her abrupt tone. "I can come back if it's not a good time."

"Oh, no, sorry. The day's so gorgeous, I guess it makes me grouchy about all of my deadlines and needing to work inside."

He smiled. "So you do get grouchy?"

"Don't act as though you haven't catalogued my many faults."

He stood beside his sporty convertible, looking at her intently. "I was thinking about your graduation."

"You think I may not make the grade?"

He laughed. "I wanted to discuss your graduation gift."

"I'm not expecting any gifts." She hadn't even thought about it.

"There's a show of antique quilts at a small museum near Philly. I wondered if I could take you to see that exhibit, catch a nice dinner, and then go to a concert nearby."

She was startled. She figured that after grad Gordon would be suggesting ways they could be together. But this was unexpected.

"Wow, aren't you the planner, Thomas!"

"If these ideas don't interest you, I have some other ideas we could talk about. And I know you're terribly busy. I'm fine with doing this the week after grad if that works better for you."

She walked closer to him and gave him her best smile. "Sounds lovely, Thomas. Thank you so much."

"So that's a yes?"

"Maybe I should check the date to make sure the band's not scheduled —"

"I've already checked with Zach."

She was impressed. Clearly this was important to Thomas. Then she heard herself giggle. "Is it black tie? Do I need a special dress?"

He laughed again. "You can wear anything you like. It'll just be you and me. I wanted to do something special to let you know I admire the way you've lived your life so well in so many ways."

Oh, so it wasn't a date? She caught herself before she blurted the thought out loud.

"And I'd like to buy you some jewelry as a special gift, but I need your help to pick it out. Would that be okay?"

The morning was enchanting and, with Thomas looking at her so intensely, she was overwhelmed with a romantic hope that maybe, maybe, *maybe* this was the real thing. "I'd love to," she said.

Thomas beamed, clearly pleased and relieved. He reached out, took her hand, and raised it to his lips, kissing it gently. "You just made me really happy. Thank you, Christine." And before she could say another word, he slipped into his car and purred out of the parking lot, leaving her to wonder if any of it had actually happened.

# Seventy–Four

———

**The Forerunners played a** gig in a club just west of Philly, and it didn't go well. Adam was having a spat with Jenn, and Zach was so infatuated with Emily that he seemed distracted and a little off. Emily had invited them all to her home for a party afterwards.

Not that Christine had been so great either. Her voice was giving her trouble, and she felt tired to the bone, resenting having to do this concert when deadlines loomed on every side.

Sam, full of disappointment and fury, laid into them backstage as soon as they closed their final number. "I got some important people here tonight to hear you guys, and you sounded like a bunch of fucking amateurs."

Emily's mother and her new man Theodore were nowhere to be seen as Emily welcomed them into the spacious Main Line mansion where she had grown up. Nor was her unpleasant sister Tammy around. So they had the place to themselves. Emily had invited Sam, too, but she had backed out in a huff after their bad performance.

Emily tried to pick up their spirits by putting on some lively music and laying out a great spread of delicious food and drinks for them. But no one felt like dancing, and Adam had foresworn alcohol since his dad's last drunken beating of his mother. He knew Jenn was worried about whether it was a genetic thing. Christine decided to limit herself to one small glass of wine.

"I'm ready to head home any time," Adam said. Emily was clearly disappointed, but she was a grown-up. "Maybe I can invite you all here some beautiful day after grad."

The next morning was Christine's last time to teach a class for Dr. Shriver. Things had gotten better as students responded well to her teaching, inspired by her love of how things were connected through the decades. Shriver had even warmed up as mysteriously as he had turned mean a month earlier. Christine was packing up her materials from the class when Shriver waddled over from his desk and stood beside her. First, he sighed. Then he said, "I wasn't wrong about you.

You could be a decent teacher someday." Not a flat-out compliment or a thank-you for all the dirty work she had done for the professor. But I'll take it, Christine decided. I'm too tired to quibble.

Gordon insisted that she permit him to treat her to a quick dinner at Leo's that weekend. Christine knew if she put him off again, Gordon wouldn't be so understanding. She ordered the crab cake special with some carrots and sat looking at Gordon. "How are you?" she asked.

Gordon did not answer in his usual upbeat tone. "I'm worried."

"About—"

"You."

"You shouldn't worry about me."

"It feels like you're busy 24/7."

"In two weeks, with grad over, I'll be a new person—cheerful, carefree, stress-free, and partly bored."

Gordon chuckled in spite of his deep concern. "That I want to see!"

"How's your life, Gordon? How's your work going?"

"That's one reason I wanted to talk with you." He looked at her intently now, laying down his fork and sneaking a sip of coffee. "I'm worried that I got myself crosswise with you about the Turner Estates project. And I wish we could clear the air."

"I'm listening."

Gordon launched into a long description of how his dad had gotten involved with Betsy and Bruce through the years, first as investors in some of their Masterson development projects and, more recently, in helping the Turners think through how best to maximize the value of their farm. Gordon explained that he had never seriously stopped to question any of the ethical questions some liberals have about building lots of homes on open land. "It's been done since the first settlers," he said. "If we don't do it, someone else will." But he went on to say that her lyrics and Zach's dad's comments at the meetings had really gotten him to think about this in a new way. He hadn't sorted it out yet, but he was clearly struggling with it. "And Christine, if you're willing to build a life with me, I'm willing to consider leaving the construction business."

Shock! Had anyone ever offered to give up so much for her? She struggled to catch her breath. "It's too much for me to deal with right now, Gordon," she whispered. "But you are very sweet."

# Seventy-Five

———

**P**ersuading her mother to meet with Grandma was less difficult than Christine had expected. Perhaps their little talk about being more open to good things made a difference in how Mama felt about the mother she so despised.

Laura had let her know that Grandma had slipped some. "One day her thinking will be clear. The next day she's all confused. But it probably won't get any better, so why don't we try it and pray that it's a good day for Grandma's mind."

Aunt Audrey had enlisted Uncle Lloyd to join them, so Mama would have a shield of sorts if Grandma lost her cool. Christine was learning to appreciate Uncle Lloyd more all the time.

But it was still awkward. Audrey tried to get everyone relaxed as she served a wonderful lunch she called "French Chicken Bake," coupled with a salad using lettuce just cut from her garden.

Grandma kept looking back and forth between Christine and Mama as though she was trying to place them. Finally she fixed on Mama. "Which one are you?" she demanded.

Mama took it in stride, a bit nervous but realizing her mother's mind was maybe somewhat muddled. "I'm Karen," she said. "I'm your only daughter."

"You remember Karen, don't you, Mom?" Lloyd chimed in.

"Karen's dead," Sarah Ober said, then took another bite.

Lloyd tried to reassure Mama with a quick glance and then explained, "No, Mom, Karen's alive. And she's sitting right here beside you."

Grandma turned to look at Mama and then Christine. Suddenly a light passed through her eyes, and she spoke in a more normal voice. "This one I remember," she said, indicating Christine. "She says she's Karen's girl."

"Yes, she is, Mother Ober," Audrey tried to explain. "Christine is Karen's daughter."

"Holy smokes," Grandma sputtered, peering sharply at Christine. "Did you ever forgive me? I can't remember."

Mama looked at Christine with startled eyes. Probably the last thing she had expected to hear. Uncle Lloyd touched his mother's hand, trying to get her to focus. "Mom, can you look at Karen, your daughter, here beside you?"

Sarah Ober turned slowly and looked at Karen with fresh eyes and an unclouded mind. "Oh, Karen, where'd you come from? They said you were—"

"I'm alive, Mom. I'm glad to see you."

Grandma's voice became emotional. "I've asked God all these years to let me live long enough to see you again. Oh my, I can't believe it. It's really you."

"Yes, Mom, it's me." And Karen began to choke up, too.

Laura reached over and squeezed Christine's hand, Laura's eyes shining and bursting with what could only be called joy. Even Uncle Lloyd was wiping tears.

"Sometimes my mind is not so clear," Grandma was saying. "But I'm sure I know what I'm saying. Karen, please forgive me for the terrible things your father did to you. I was totally opposed. But I didn't stop him, did I? And that has brought me much grief and torment. So I'm pleading with you, Karen, before I die, please forgive me for all that I did not do. For ruining your life. I'm so sorry." Grandma was sobbing now.

Before Mama could answer, the outside door tore open and Oscar Ober burst into Audrey's kitchen. When he saw what was happening, his face turned blood-red with anger, his eyes taking an exaggerated shape in his rage. "There's going to be hell to pay for this, Sarah," he yelled. "And you, too, Lloyd. Hell and damnation."

# Seventy–Six

---

**G**raduation **was a bit** ho-hum. Christine nearly fell asleep during the ceremony, she was so exhausted. Mama had gotten off work to attend, sitting beside Harriet and Ethan, all three clapping loudly and proudly when Christine walked up to get her diploma. Thomas was sitting in the fifth row of the faculty section, but she couldn't see him from where she was.

Emily and Jenn both wanted a photo of Zach and Adam with Christine. Was this the end or the beginning?

After it was all over, Christine skipped the two parties she had been invited to, jumped into her old Ford, and just drove. She wasn't even thinking about where she was going.

At one point she overlooked the Jagged Valley and its beautiful quilt of fertile fields, just as it began to mist a light rain. She drove nearer to the gorge and the ancient rushing river.

What do I want? Where am I going? Turners Rise lay in the distance, but she headed north toward the mountain range instead.

Why don't I just keep driving? I'm free now. What's out there for me? I can go anywhere the road takes me.

# SUMMER

# Seventy–Seven

———

**She and Mama were** just leaving the pharmacy when it happened. After the realtor had shown them the duplex along the west edge of the park, Mama wanted to pick up a few things at the drugstore. It was the first that Christine had been a passenger in Mama's new car, and she was both surprised and entertained by the confident way in which her mother handled the bigger car. She had never thought about whether Mama could be a truck driver, but hey, she probably could. They had one more appointment on their house-hunting morning together, a cute cottage just a block from the diner.

As they were coming out of the store's main entrance toward the parking lot, a middle-aged man of medium height and dark hair—nicely put together—came walking toward them on his way into the store. As he removed his sunglasses, Christine saw he was looking intently at Mama. Just as they passed, he gave Mama a slight bow with a big smile, greeting her in a sweet tenorish voice, "Good morning, Karen." She saw her mother blush a bit as they continued on to the car.

"What was that?"

"What?" Mama acted like she was clueless.

"Do you have an admirer?"

"Oh, you know how it is. If you're lucky enough to keep yourself half attractive, people are always flirting."

An unusual comment from Mama, to say the least. She studied her mother's face. "You know him, don't you?"

"Of course, that's Richie Adler." They got into the car.

"How do you know him?"

"We went to high school together. I must have mentioned him to you before."

"Were the two of you an item?"

"I guess you could say that. Before I met—" her lips hit the brakes with a sort of involuntary pucker. Mama could not bring herself to utter Lenny Bryer's name.

"Who'd he marry?"

"Who?"

"That Adler guy."

"Oh, Richie. He never married." As Mama started the car and headed back to the street, it came to

Christine with a shock. Mama had broken Richie's heart just as sure as Lenny had crushed Mama's.

The small cottage was charming, really. It even had a basement and an attic. Christine knew they could afford the down-payment, but were they able to swing the monthly payments, especially if she went on to grad school? There were two bedrooms, so she could stay with Mama if that's what she wanted. Decisions, decisions.

"Mama, may I treat you to lunch at Leo's?"

"Oh, the diner's cheaper."

"You're there all the time. I'd like to treat you to something different."

"I know the diner's not good enough for you young people."

"You know that's not true."

Leo's was pretty empty, and they found a booth in the corner. "Order anything you want, Mama. I'm paying."

Karen Ober actually giggled. Maybe the prospect of a new home and the treat at Leo's paid for by her daughter lifted her spirits. And perhaps the attention from Richie Adler.

They ordered and talked about the various living spaces they had visited. Clearly Mama liked the cottage but was worried they couldn't afford it. Then Christine changed the subject.

"Has Richie Adler asked you out in recent years?"

Color rose through Mama's pretty face. At first she acted like she didn't understand, muttering something about audacity.

"Mama, has he?"

"Has he what, for heaven's sake?"

Christine smiled. "I'm serious. I want to know."

There was a long pause while Mama worked on her crab and linguine dish. "It's none of your business, Christine."

"Maybe it's not, maybe it is."

Mama glanced around to make sure they weren't being overheard. "He has asked me a few times."

"Recently?"

"Well, yeah, I guess you could say that."

"Last week?"

"No, no."

"Last month?"

"Okay, yes, I guess."

"And you said....?"

"No, of course. I'm too old to be dating."

It was one of those moments. Here was her mother, early forties, still quite pretty, especially when she was relaxed, having decided she's too old to be happy. Ridiculous. Why do half the people in the world swim in a pool of regret because they never became part of the relationship they most wanted?

"Would Richie like the cottage we just looked at?"

"Why would you ask something so stupid?"

"You'd have to live someplace if you got married."

"Now, Christine, stop this idiotic drivel." Mama looked perturbed but still flushed. "Besides, Richie has a nice house of his own."

"You've been there?"

"One time for a Christmas event."

Christine couldn't help herself. "Do you find him distasteful?"

"Who, Richie?"

Christine just waited, still smiling at her mother. How did she never know this stuff? "Well?"

"He's nice enough."

"What's his job?"

"Oh, I'm not sure. I think he and his brother operate a business related to building supplies."

"So what would one date hurt?"

Mama almost choked on her pasta. "You're being asinine. Now stop it!"

"I'm just being realistic. Do you really want to be alone the rest of your life?"

"But I have you to take care of. And I can hardly make ends meet."

"That could all change." She reached over to touch her mother's arm. "I'm being honest, Mama. Would you like me to be in touch with Mr. Adler?"

Mama almost exploded. "Don't you dare! And don't you ever mention this to anyone. Never. I promised not to blab your details and information about the band. I need the same promise from you."

Christine sobered. "You have my promise, Mama. But only if you promise me you'll think about maybe having at least one date with Richie."

Mama's face was resolute, but, around the corners of her mouth, Christine could detect a faint smile.

# Seventy-Eight

———

**T**homas **texted details about** their date for Saturday. They would visit the exhibit of antique quilts near Philly, catch dinner at a nice spot he'd reserved, and then go to the concert. She sensed unmistakable excitement in his tone. She still wasn't sure how much of the summer he would be around.

Which made her remember Gordon. She knew she couldn't put him off much longer. Graduation was over so she didn't have school deadlines to blame for not doing things with him. Gordon was not casual. He wanted to marry her. As soon as possible.

Driving past the university campus these days felt surreal. For years she had hoped she could find the money to go to college. Then she got accepted and discovered she was good at it. Then continuing to fall in love with history, trying her hand at teaching Shriver's class, experiencing the weird, wild adventure of their band's moment in the sun. The campus empty now before summer classes would begin, she knew she no longer belonged there. Seventeen years stretching from kindergarten to college graduation — and now, a stranger. She'd always thought of alums as has-beens who came back to campus to try to persuade her and others that they had once been hip, too. Now she was an alum. How had she gotten old so fast?

She checked the messages on her phone as she parked behind their house, leaving the car's partly dented door stand open as she skimmed, fresh air brushing her face and lifting her hair. She had no deadlines, no concerts, no meetings. She'd even asked Sharon for a week off to go to the shore with Emily and Jenn, but that had fallen through at the last minute, so she could just sit here now in this old car until the cows came home. *My car's my friend, don't mind the rust, relax and mend, no jobs, no must....*

She spotted an email from Tumbleweed. His feature story had just posted on their website. "Caught between Fame and Authenticity" the headline blared above a close-up of Christine. She was shocked by the intimacy of the photo and story. It felt like Tumbleweed had crawled inside her life and exposed her inner conflicts and musings. Sitting there in the warm breeze behind their little house, her face took on a frozen blend of horrified grimace and pleased smile. No hiding from this.

Sam had said exposure would come with the territory. Too much exposure, maybe. Privacy tossed to the winds. Not that the story was inaccurate. It was amazingly meticulous and on the nose. In great detail. But the comprehensive scope of the *Ledger* piece sorta rocked her. She had never been profiled so extensively and publicly before. The tone of the feature was discovery — discovery of a treasure, a soon-to-be-star. "Will her modesty undercut her potential?" screamed one blurb in big print.

Her first concern was Harriet. Would she disapprove? And what about Thomas? This was a little-known Philadelphia online site, so most locals would never see it. But what if they did? Would Zach be upset? He and Adam had met Tumbleweed and knew he was an eccentric. Until a piece is published, one can easily discount someone like Tumbleweed as a second-rate wannabe. But a published story rivets the mind. For whatever reason, this reporter believed he had discovered the next big star.

Did she believe it? And if she did, did she want it?

She felt a tear slipping down her cheek as she struggled to understand the many forces yanking at her heart. Her first real date with Thomas. School over. No more homework and paper-writing deadlines. A sense of meaning by maybe stopping the Turner

Estates project. What to do about Gordon? And the rest of her life — what did she want to do the next five years? Be on the road with the band? Go to grad school and teach? Would Mama be okay without her? And who was this Richie Adler, anyway?

Tumbleweed was right that she didn't want to be famous. Celebrity always resides on the false confidence of a fragile sinkhole cover. Being well-known might be okay — but was there a difference?

A loud sound wakened her. Must have been the horn of a truck out on the road. She didn't realize she had drifted asleep. Her alarms went off — what was she late for? Then she realized she could sit in her friendly car all day long and not be late for anything.

In a few days, she'd be back at the Historical Society, trying to figure out the future. But here now, on this beautiful, peerless day, she would soak up the warmth and the gentle massage of the light breeze, hidden from the world.

# Seventy-Nine

———

**C**hristine **was alone at** home when she picked up her phone and dialed the California number. Now that she knew more about her mother's family, she decided to reach out to her father. What could go wrong?

"Bryer Real Estate," a pleasant young female voice answered. Okay, it was real. Should she hang up?

"Is Mr. Lenny Bryer there?"

"May I tell him who's calling?"

Christine had secretly rehearsed this moment in her mind for years. But now she felt rattled. Stumped. What should she say?

"Tell him I'm Karen Ober's daughter. He'll know."

"Just a moment, please."

The background music came on as she was put on hold. Christine felt panic sweep across her, more fear suddenly than anticipation. Was she actually willing to travel to California if Lenny was interested in meeting her?

The pleasant voice came back on the line. "I'm sorry, miss. Mr. Bryer is not available."

"May I ask when he might be?"

The voice was less pleasant now. "Oh, I'm sorry. He has no interest in speaking with you. Thank you for calling."

Click.

# Eighty

———

Christine was stunned. The old but magnificent quilts were mounted and lighted so dramatically that they appeared to float in a rarefied space separate from the museum's surroundings.

A young girl, barely ten, stood in front of one of the classic Log Cabin textile masterpieces and asked her companion, "Grandpa, why do I like this one so much?"

"You tell me, Olivia, why do you?"

"I like the colors, of course. So many colors. But that's obvious, isn't it?" she said, lifting her finger to her lips. "You know, Grandpa, what I like is the feeling I get that a long time ago, before I was born and maybe even before you were born, some women—and maybe a man—gave their love and their very best to making this spectacular quilt. It's a work of art, don't you think?"

"Yes. And thanks for thinking of the man that helped, Olivia."

As the young girl and her grandfather walked on to the next room of the museum, Thomas slipped his arm around Christine and whispered, "Do you agree with the precocious Olivia?"

Christine smiled and leaned into him, gazing at the masterpiece hovering in front of them. "I'm a novice, of course. But I find the way the different colors and shapes lie next to each other breathtaking."

"Then you're precocious, too." They stood there for at least two minutes, just feeling each other's shape and warmth. She was so moved by the visual quickening from the exhibit that an intense energy and exhilaration flowed through her body, not unlike what she sometimes experienced with a great piece of music. Let's make love, her body cried out. Right here, right now. She glanced at Thomas to make sure she hadn't said it out loud and saw in his eyes a fevered intensity. Before she could react, he bent and kissed her, his lips massaging hers in a sublime moment as she felt her legs grow a bit limp. My God! Thomas had kissed her. She grabbed him and pulled their bodies together for a long moment there in front of that Log Cabin jewel as they kissed again.

An hour later, as they were finishing their meals at the first-class restaurant he had booked, their conversation turned to the future. Thomas said he was splitting the summer between Connecticut and being close to his grandparents. "I'd love to take a trip to Europe, maybe Italy, just clear out the cobwebs," he said. "But I'm not sure that'll work out."

He asked about her plans. "I hope to go to grad school sometime, but I'm sure it won't be this fall. And the band's future is up in the air."

He nodded. "I have a personal question." He looked across the room, suddenly unsure of himself. "How do I get to know you better, Christine? I really like you. But I'm not sure I have a chance."

She thought the moment would never come. But wait, what exactly was this moment? "Sorry, Thomas, not sure I follow."

"I know you've been seeing Gordon some. I don't mean to put you on the spot."

She looked at him carefully. "What are you asking?"

He took a sip of wine, trying to fashion his response. "I guess I was — if I stayed around some this summer, hoping to spend more time with you — would that be okay?"

Her heart sank. Does he still prefer her to be his half-sister or a buddy — and nothing more? He waited while she wondered what to say. Christine, this is not the time to speak off the cuff. "May I go to the restroom?"

"Absolutely, please." He stood with a well-bred flourish.

When she came back to the table, she sat for a long moment as he nervously waited. "May I be honest?" she asked.

"I've always liked that about you."

She smiled. "I would enjoy spending more time with you, Thomas. But you always confuse me about the nature of our relationship."

"I see."

She sighed. "You just gave me one of the best kisses I've had in my whole life. So for a moment I could imagine that you might have romantic feelings toward me. On the other hand, ever since you came here last fall to teach, I haven't been able to tell whether your now-and-then interest in me is mainly as a friend, or some kind of half-sibling, or maybe eventually as a partner." She paused. "There, for better or worse, I said it."

"I understand."

"You do?"

"It's my fault," he continued. "You have every right to be upset."

"Oh, I'm not upset. I'm just confused."

"I apologize."

"I'm not asking for that. I just want to understand. My mother, as you know, has told me not to reach too high. So I've always assumed you were out of reach. And I can try to make peace with that—what I feel and wish for may not be realistic." Her voice broke.

"It's the opposite of what you think, Christine."

She raised her hand. "Thomas, I need you to be straight with me."

"Let me try." The suave, white-haired man who was serving them interrupted to ask about dessert. Thomas told him to check back later. "My worry, Christine, is that I'm not good enough for you."

She was stunned. "Not good enough? Is this a joke?"

He reached over now and took her hand. "I keep telling Grandma that I'm afraid you'll be disappointed in me if you learn to know me better."

She pulled her hand away from him and pushed her chair back a bit, fiddling with the edge of the white tablecloth. Her eyes narrowed and she could feel her face getting red. "If you're making fun of me, Thomas Turner, I will never forgive you."

He reacted with alarm. "No, no, I'm totally serious. Please listen to me. The school's policy about faculty not dating students was a factor, of course, but we both know there are plenty examples of that happening. The main thing that stopped me every time I wanted to be closer to you was that."

"What?"

"I respect you so much that it would break my heart if I knew you were disappointed in me, if you rejected me." Now his voice broke.

"You're talking crazy. You're in a different class than I am, everyone knows that."

"You're referring to money?"

"Money, education, manners, life experience. I grew up on the bottom rung and you on the top rung."

"It hurts me if you think that money is so important to me."

Something inside her persuaded her to pause, to think carefully, to give him the benefit of the doubt. What if he was serious? What if he really was worried that he would disappoint her? What didn't she know? She still found it unbelievable.

"Thomas, let's start again. What do you want to ask me?"

He sat back and clasped his hands, looking at her intently. "Are you open to the two of us spending more time together, learning to know each other, seeing if you could ever come to love me?"

She couldn't stop herself. "I've always loved you, Thomas. I just assumed you were out of reach."

"And I assumed that I would not measure up to you, Christine, that over time you would be disappointed in me."

"Wow, that's a surprise."

The waiter came with the dessert tray. When they'd made their selections, Thomas went on. "Sounds like we're both worried we won't measure up."

She stared at him, and it came to her that he was dead serious, that he wasn't being held back by reservations about her but by reservations about himself. Before she could stop, her eyes filled with tears. "I'm sorry if I've been unfair to you."

"God, no, you haven't."

"So the answer's yes, I'd love to spend more time with you. But I'd like to say two things. I had planned to break things off with Gordon — and I will. And second, I want to spend more time trying to understand why you worry you might disappoint me. Okay?"

"Perfect." Thomas let out a big sigh, followed by a poignant silence. And then — "I'm so happy."

# Eighty-One

———

Laura called to say that Grandma Ober was in the hospital. It was a major stroke this time. She just thought Christine might like to know.

"Is there anything I can do, Laura?"

"Not really. She's pretty incapacitated. Thought we should tell you and your mother. Plus, I wanted to hear your voice again."

"Thanks for calling. Let's get together sometime soon."

She sat at the kitchen table watching the straight rows of corn in Bruce's fields. Teenagers, she thought. Those stalks are just about to pass me by in the cycle of growing things. They'll be middle-aged before I even figure out what's going on. Did they know?

Zach was trying to set a meeting with her to talk about the next township meeting. She knew he would use the occasion to try to persuade her to let Sam nail down a two-week tour for them before the summer was over. But hey, she was on relax. She didn't want to be bothered by either Betsy or Sam.

"I may not have gone to the shore, Zach. But I'm on vacation for two more days. And you should be, too."

"Actually, I'm getting ready for Saturday's marathon across the river."

"Oh, good luck with that."

"You want to come? Emily is."

"I'm on vacation, remember?"

"Yes, madam."

"Don't you 'madam' me, old man." They both laughed.

"I haven't heard you be so relaxed in a long time, Christine. Is this the new you?"

"I doubt it. But get off the phone so I can enjoy my vacation."

That evening as she binged lazily on old movies, her mother came home from work in an upbeat mood. There was a lot of that lately. She buzzed around the house checking things, making food for herself, humming as she went. Christine roused herself from her slumped indifference and stepped into the kitchen.

"Something happen?"

Her mother's face looked more awake than usual. "What do you mean, chickadee?"

Christine leaned against the doorway and was surprised to hear herself chortling. "Is there news about Richie?"

"None of your business."

"Okay, be that way. I'm not interested." She started back to her movie.

"Next Friday. I got the night off. He wants to go to that Tractor Pull thing on the north side."

"How are you feeling?"

"Absolutely frightened." Mama paused. "But a bit—I don't know—"

"What?"

"Excited." Mama looked at her with a shy smile. "Is that bad? Will I regret it?"

# Eighty–Two

---

$S$he learned from Ethan that the police had caught Sonny Winters trespassing and snooping around the Stevie Adams barn. "They also arrested Sonny for burning down both the Wissler and the Miller barns. A terrible pity." Christine knew the Winters family because Sonny's mother Edith came to the Historical Society occasionally to research her family's history, the Tucker side.

"Homer and Edith have tried to work with their son Sonny through the years, with his emotional imbalance and all," Ethan continued. "Sonny probably heard his dad rage about the various bank board members. I expect he was trying to be a hero to his tough-to-please dad. Sounds like an old story, only ratcheted up a good bit." Ethan sighed audibly over the phone. "So that terror is finally over. Thanks in no small part to your good research."

"Oh, no, I didn't connect the dots. You did that, Ethan. Plus your tip to the sheriff."

"Well, we're a good team, Christine. Maybe we should start a detective agency."

She laughed. "I'm just relieved it's over." She still hadn't found the right time to update Ethan on the situation with Arlene's place and Ellen's crazy Floyd.

It was a perfect June day, and she knew she couldn't stay in the house much longer, prolonging her hibernating vacation. Tomorrow Sharon was expecting her back at work. And she'd finally promised to meet Zach this afternoon at Leo's.

She had hardly slipped into her seat when Zach blurted out, "If you really want to deep-six The Forerunners, I'd like to go to grad school. I was accepted, as you know, and had delayed it. I think I can still get in."

"Drop the band for good?"

"If that's what you want."

"But I never said that, did I?"

Zach's face was tight. "I've always loved you, Christine darling. But I couldn't bear to see you drag around hither and yon with our band, just to be nice to Adam and me. These should be the best years of your life. I mean it."

She took his hand and rubbed his fingers affectionately. "Zach 'darling,' you've always been a good friend to me, a true comrade. I can't begin to say how much I would miss you if you went off to grad school halfway across the country."

"Same here." She could see in his eyes that he was frustrated and sad as he said it.

"Zach, tell me honestly what you want to do about the band."

He picked at his pecan strawberry salad and rubbed his blond spikes. "If you were on board, I would say let's give it everything we can for the next year or two, see what doors open, can we climb the so-called ladder, can we make some money. Millions would give an arm and a leg to be poised where we are at the moment."

"Sorry, fame doesn't interest me."

"You've made that damn clear. That Tumbleweed piece really highlighted that."

"Oh, sorry, Zach, about that article. I had no idea he was going to make such a big thing of it. I thought of him as mainly a nuisance. I apologize that it all centered on me and barely mentioned you and Adam."

"No, no, you deserved it, Christine."

"No, I did not. And you know I didn't." She suddenly realized that Zach was maybe hurt and a bit depressed about that article, more than she realized. He was used to being the star with young females adoring him. Tumbleweed had upended that balance a little. "For some reason that guy got obsessed with me. You and Adam and I have always been a team. Somehow Tumbleweed missed that."

"He saw you as a rising star. And he was right."

"What a bunch of shit. I am a fatherless, poor-white-trash nobody, living one step off the farm. And that's the truth. Forget the 'star' crap."

Zach reached across the table and took both of her hands in his, his eyes now totally focused on hers. "I don't want to ever hear you say that again, Christine. Not ever!" He squeezed her hands hard, then pulled his away. She was startled by his intensity.

"I'm sorry if I upset you, Zach."

"You're a treasure, don't you see that? You've survived so much. You have such strength and guts." He paused. "I worry that your demons will win, that you'll pull back and settle. Just settle. God, it hurts me. I would love to give the band our very best for the next two years and see how far we can go. But not if your heart's not in it."

She didn't know why she did it, but Christine got right up from her veggie sandwich and walked straight out of Leo's. She could hear Zach calling after her, but she just kept going, the bright sun making her squint as she reached the sidewalk.

# Eighty-Three

---

**Zach asked to meet** with her two days later, just to clear the air. "I don't know why I walked out on you at Leo's," she said. "That was rude."

"Do you maybe think after all these years that sometimes I might understand you, Christine, maybe a smidge better than you understand yourself?"

"Is 'smidge' a proper word?"

"Oh, shut up, you know what I'm saying."

She surprised herself by spitting on the ground, the way farmers like Becca do.

Zach laughed. "Did you just spit?"

"Only a smidge."

Zach grew serious. "I think you're pinching yourself, Christine. You've lived in a cage of sorts, hemmed in by limits and schedules and deadlines.

And suddenly you see no limits — and everything in you is suspicious of that sense of freedom. You're sure it's a trap, a deception that's gonna undo who you want to be."

"That was a smidge profound."

"Are you going to spit again?"

Christine walked several strides away from him and then came back. "We can agree to small steps with the band, but small steps so easily become larger and larger. And then we wake up and we're thirty or forty years ancient."

"I understand, I really do."

They agreed to do several concerts during the summer before deciding about signing on to a longer tour in the fall. Step by step.

The Gordon decision hung over her like dense humidity just before a heavy storm. How would he take it? Did he really think she was going to say yes?

She debated about how to handle the conversation. It had to be in person, she was sure of that. But just meeting with him and dropping it on the guy was scary. On the other hand, going out with him and then unloading at the end of the evening felt unscrupulous and a bit ruthless.

She had no one to help her sort it out. Certainly not Mama. Not Emily. Not Jenn. Not even Harriet. *Tell me how to be serene and then act mean in an audacious but gracious way, oh please....*

Turned out she bumped into Gordon in the parking lot outside Roger's Market the very day she'd planned to call him. He was his charming best. "Can I carry something for you, Christine?"

"I was going to call you."

He smiled. "I'm right here, but if you'd prefer to talk with me without seeing me, you can call me later." He laughed and she did, too.

It was really hot. "Can we climb into your truck for a minute?"

"Absolutely. I'll start it up so it begins to cool down." She could see by the set of his jaw that he was worried.

They sat in silence for a moment, listening to the cooling fan, watching Adam's mother push a cart piled with bags of groceries across the lot in front of Gordon's truck, bending to scratch her leg without a clue that they were watching her. A large delivery truck wheeled through on its way to the dock area.

"Why don't you want to marry me? I've tried to be patient through all your senior papers and endless deadlines."

"Gordon, you've been a real gentleman. I appreciate that."

"I think we'd be happy together."

She covered her eyes for a moment. "I can't prove we wouldn't be."

"So let's get married. If it doesn't work out...." his voice trailed off. She wondered if Masterson men ever cried in front of women.

She turned in the seat now, looking at him directly. "Gordon, I've finally had time to clear my head since graduation. And I've decided it's totally unfair to string you along when I'm really not sure this is what I want."

"I've become a patient man, Christine. I believe I love you more than anyone ever could."

I'm not going to cry, she insisted to herself. And I don't want to drag it out. I promised Thomas.

She saw Zach's dad coming back from his late lunch break, striding into the supermarket. A fine man. He had supported her on the Turner Estates episode every step of the way. Zach was such a balanced person in spite of his occasional flirtations with the many groupies who flocked to him like good-looking flies on a sex reconnaissance. Undoubtedly, Zach's parents had given him common sense and rootedness, along with a lot of talent and flair.

Gordon cleared his throat. They continued to sit in silence. A motorcycle came roaring past on its way to the market's pharmacy. Two seniors in their sixties or seventies who seemed hopelessly in love.

"Gordon, I can't lie to you. I don't think you want me to."

"No, absolutely not."

"I wish there were a way to do this that wouldn't feel to you like a betrayal. I wish we could remain friends.

"No problem."

She sighed deeply. "I just don't think we have a future together. You're a great guy. But I think we should end it now."

Gordon's face got quite red but he did not cry. "I knew it was a stretch. I respect you a whole lot, Christine. And you're breaking my heart. Again. I'll let you get out now."

Surprised by his abruptness, she climbed down out of the truck. Gordon stepped on the gas and peeled away with such force that his tires left distinct laments on the asphalt.

# Eighty–Four

—

**C**hristine **was distressed by** the news of Sharon's miscarriage. Poor woman. Years of planning and trying, about to abandon hope when, like a miracle, she conceived. Choosing names, preparing the nursery though it was still many months away, cuddling with Bradley as they sang soft lullabies to the family member growing inside her. Now gone. Sharon was devastated. She asked Christine to help cover the schedule at the Society, saying she didn't know if she would ever come back to work, she was so lost in deep depression.

Christine didn't often feel totally clueless. But Sharon's grief unnerved her. She had never thought about having a baby, not seriously. She always assumed she could conceive if and when she decided to. She had let the idea of having children drift to the back of her mind. Off limits. Not that she had sworn to never have children. But observing others had made her cautious. Besides, she had plenty of time to figure it out.

What should she do for Sharon? She didn't know what to say. It would be phony to act as though she understood what Sharon was going through. Not just phony, but absurdly unkind.

She called Harriet to ask her opinion. Not surprisingly, Harriet had already heard. "Let's go visit her," Harriet said. "I'll bake a pie."

The light summer rain had stopped by the time she picked up Harriet and her apple pie, the sky clearing dramatically with huge clouds charging toward the horizon as though under the control of a master stage manager. The wet was evaporating off the cornstalks and the trees, the road gleaming brightly.

"How's Ethan?"

"Pretty good these days. I'm so thankful that his mind is remarkably clear."

They rode in silence for a bit. "I feel ill-equipped," Christine said. "I really have no idea how Sharon must be feeling—or what I should say."

Harriet nodded. "I understand. But don't worry. I've always thought that showing up is what matters most. Silence is okay. Too many words at a time like this can injure, especially those in grief."

"Thanks, Harriet. I'll do my best."

"You'll be fine."

Sharon did look like a very different person, dark pouches below her eyes, her hair unwashed, her spirit distraught, a vacancy in her face. Harriet hugged her and took her by the hand, leading her toward the back of the house. "Would it be okay to sit on the back porch, Sharon?"

Sharon pulled back. "I don't think so."

"Just for two minutes. Then we'll come back in."

The three of them sat on the back porch for a few minutes, looking out across the back yard, Sharon's garden, and the little shed which Bradley had recently built. There was nothing to say. Nothing at all. Just letting you know we're here for you, Sharon, at this time of crushing loss when you feel betrayed by your body, and maybe by God.

It's strange, Christine thought, how all over the world, people happy with good results, others weeping because of loss or of being left behind, while the sun keeps shining behind the clouds or around them. And each of us thinking mainly about ourselves. Billions of people, and each of us thinking primarily about "me." A bit strange. A bit sad.

"Shall we go back in?" Harriet asked.

Sharon stayed put. "Let's rest here a bit longer."

A squirrel scurried down the trunk of the larger maple and sat in the grass, studying the three of them. Christine moved her arm abruptly and the squirrel took off toward the fence separating Sharon's place from the family next door.

Sharon hugged them as they left. "It was so kind of you to visit me," she murmured. "Christine, I'm afraid I've left you in a lurch at work."

"Don't you worry for one second. Everyone's pulling together and we'll be fine. We all are hurting for you and Bradley."

Sharon started to cry then, a startling low moan beneath her tears. Harriet walked back and took her in her arms. "I know the pain must be raw, like you're bleeding inside. I had a miscarriage myself years ago. Men have no idea how it makes us women feel—like a failure, not good enough, not normal."

"I wish I could die."

"Oh, Sharon, don't say that. Please don't say that to Bradley. Things will get better, I promise you. And I'll pray for you every day."

As they headed back, Harriet was unusually quiet. Christine wondered if long-ago memories had caught up with her. She realized how little she knew about the world of adult women, all their worries, secret pain, unknown sorrows.

As they drove through the covered bridge across the West Branch Creek, Harriet cleared her throat. "Would you mind if we stopped for a few minutes at the park along the creek?"

Christine was surprised. "No, that's fine."

"I'd like to talk a little."

As Christine steered her car out of the bridge, she took the little side road that led to the park's entrance. What was so important that Harriet wanted to stop here?

The West Branch Park was not a favorite like some of the other small parks around. But if privacy was on Harriet's mind, this was a perfect setting. No one was in sight except a young woman playing near the swings with two children. Harriet walked to a picnic table near the creek.

"What do you think of Thomas?" Harriet began as the two of them sat down.

"Thomas?"

"Yes. Do you like him?"

"Of course, he's very likeable."

Harriet paused, peering at her with her irresistible eyes. "Would you like to marry him?"

Christine gulped and could feel the color rising in her face. "What's this all about, Harriet? Have I upset you?"

"No, I'm not upset. But you didn't answer my question."

"Harriet, I love you, you know that. But I'm not sure what you're getting at."

"I just want to know. Would you marry Thomas if he were interested?"

They were seated so close to each other on opposite sides of the picnic table that Christine could see every wrinkle in Harriet's attractively seasoned face. What the heck was going on? Christine felt a sweaty sense of jeopardy creeping up her back as though, right here right now, some important decision was being made. But what? And why?

"Harriet, you have the advantage on me. I'm afraid I don't understand what you're asking or why."

"See, that's what Thomas always says."

"I'm lost. I really am."

Harriet reached across the table and tapped the tabletop. "Forgive me. I'm being unfair."

Fuck yes, she wanted to respond. But she decided to just sit and wait. Was Thomas' grandmother trying to get her to back off?

"You and I have been pretty close, wouldn't you say?"

"Very. You've been like a mother to me."

"And have I ever told you who to date and who not to?"

"Not in so many words. You have a good way of asking pointed questions at crucial moments."

Harriet let go one of her heartfelt laughs. "Good answer." Then she rubbed her face and sighed. "My goodness, I'm getting all nervous about this."

Christine stood up and walked to the creek's edge, watching the sunlight play across the ripples. Harriet came up beside her, standing there for a long moment.

"Are you trying to tell me to give up on Thomas?" she blurted.

Harriet groaned. "Just the opposite."

"Can you just say it in plain English?"

Harriet sighed again. She bent down to pick up a small flat stone, pulled back her arm and, with a quickness that startled Christine, threw the stone at a flat angle toward the creek, the small stone skipping in neat little hops to the other bank. "I think you've had your eye on Thomas, off and on, through the years, would that be right?"

Was this a trap? Should she tell the truth? "I guess you could sorta say that."

"Yes or no?" Harriet couldn't have been more serious.

Christine paused, totally perplexed. "Yes," she answered in a voice barely audible above the sound of the rushing stream.

"But you're hesitant, aren't you?"

"I've always assumed I'm not good enough. He comes from a different class."

"I see. But you think he's good enough?"

"For what?"

"For you, Christine, for you."

"Harriet, you're really confusing me. Can we just drop it?"

Harriet snorted. "So that's your response when the questions get difficult? I thought you were tougher than that."

It had been years since Christine had gotten really angry with Harriet, but she suddenly wondered if that was about to happen. Would she lose her cool with Harriet and ruin everything?

"Honestly, Harriet, I don't know what you're asking."

Harriet picked up another flat stone and skipped it across the creek in perfect little arcs, like the twelve-year-old girl she used to be. "If Thomas would be willing to marry you, would you marry him?"

"Would we have your blessing?"

"Absolutely, if you both are willing."

Christine let out an exasperated heavy groan. "Why does it feel like you're trying to discourage me?"

"Really?"

"Are you?"

Harriet came and put her arm around Christine. "I'm not trying to be unfair. I just needed to hear your answer." She sat down at the table again as though their discussion had sapped her energy. "See, I've noticed for a long time that Thomas had his eye on you. But I love and admire you so much that I knew I could not bear to see my grandson ruin your life, especially if you thought you were lucky to have him. If you were to enter a marriage with Thomas, thinking of yourself as lucky rather than equal, that's a formula for failure. And Thomas, to his credit, has increasingly come to see himself as lucky if he were to wed you. In fact, he's worried he's not good enough for you."

Christine looked at Harriet, trying to make sense of it all.

Harriet stood up. "Okay, we can go now."

"That's it?"

"Did you want to discuss something else?"

"No, I guess not. So where does that leave Thomas and me?"

"That's for the two of you to figure out." Harriet laughed. "I'm not a matchmaker, am I?"

"So what was this all about?"

"I love you like a daughter. You're a wonderful young woman. And it's my job to make sure that no one ruins your life—not Zach, not Gordon, and especially not my grandson."

When she dropped Harriet back at her place, Ethan was sitting on the porch reading. He looked up, beamed, and waved. Christine waved back.

Just as she was about to pull away, Harriet turned and came back to the car. "Oh, and one more thing. If you ever break Thomas' heart, I'll never forgive you."

# Eighty-Five

Fat Freddy came across as definitely grouchy, cutting people off if he thought they went a half-sentence too long, seeming peeved that he needed to chair one more contentious meeting about the Turner Estates proposal. The meeting room at the Township building was packed, and the air conditioner was either set too high or wasn't calibrated to remove so much summer warmth, body heat, and spirited discussion at the same time.

Mr. Peters, the attorney for Betsy and Bruce, was missing for some reason. His associate excelled at being so timid that Betsy needed to interrupt him during every other sentence, much to the obvious delight of Deb Brewster, sitting with the other Zoning Board members behind the big table.

No TV crews had shown up and only one news reporter. Only township residents were permitted to speak, and Fat Freddy restricted the time for comments to a total of thirty minutes. Zach's dad gave a summary of his earlier speeches, and several others weighed in. Surprisingly, only two persons spoke in favor of the Turner proposal itself.

And then the Board voted. In less than a minute, the proposal was defeated 4 to 0. For some unexplained reason, Eli Gibbons abstained.

Christine watched Betsy as the vote was taken. Had she still hoped to win approval? If she, like everyone else, expected a negative vote, why had she even shown up? Betsy was not a sympathetic figure, but Christine wondered what she must be feeling as her ideas and hopes for a financial windfall went up in flames. So publicly. No way to spin it, really. And Betsy's own young sons' brash destruction of the yard signs may have been the turning point. That, and maybe Christine's catchy lyric.

Would Betsy ask her to revive Harriet's garden? Would she remove the eviction notice from their little home? Would Mama want to stay put instead of buying that cottage near the diner?

Fat Freddy came up beside her. "Hello, Christine," he said. She had no idea that he knew her name. "Sometimes young people do things that renew my faith, you know—like that song you wrote—it made a big difference." His manner was friendly, his smile genuine.

"Thank you, sir." She consciously tried to avoid his nickname for fear of offending him. "Zach Collins wrote the music. I just wrote the words."

His eyes twinkled. "The words are what people remember." She felt herself blushing a bit, the compliment so unexpected. Did he know, she suddenly wondered, that it was her Uncle Jimmy who had driven a car into his barn all those years ago? If he did, he gave no indication but simply patted her gently on the shoulder as he turned to go.

# Eighty-Six

———

Thomas' voice sounded more raw and stressed than usual. "I have bad news, Christine."

"Oh?"

"Grandma died in her sleep last night."

"Is this a joke?"

"Grandpa found her this morning." Thomas' voice broke.

Christine was silent a long time. "How can that be? I was just with her yesterday."

"It's a terrible shock. Grandpa asked me to call you."

Christine knew her systems normally delayed her responses to big news, whether good news or bad. Sometimes several days passed before she could feel the full emotions. But today was different. She was in tears before the phone call ended, sobbing as her face contorted into a pained grimace of anguish and disbelief. Harriet gone? Impossible. Her anchor, her friend, her wise parent.

"It can't be, Thomas. It can't be."

They were both quiet for a prolonged moment, lost in incredulity. The earth stood still.

At long last, Christine stirred, phone still in hand. "How's Ethan?"

"Tough and matter-of-fact, the way he always is. I think he's still in shock."

"I should probably go up to see him."

Thomas was silent. Then, his voice breaking, "If you think you're up to it. Please don't push yourself unnecessarily. I'm leaving here shortly to drive to Pennsylvania. I should be there by early afternoon."

Another long silence. Then she found her voice. "Thomas, how are you?"

"Don't know yet." His voice broke again. "I wish I were there now. I suddenly miss you so much."

"Then hurry up!" she said between tears.

"I will."

"But drive safely, Thomas."

"I will. I wanted to also tell you that Grandpa asked if you and I would help him with the funeral planning."

She wasn't sure what to say. "I'm not family."

"Grandma always said you were the closest thing to a daughter she ever had."

Christine now realized that she had slowly dropped to her knees as she absorbed the disturbing news of Harriet's passing. Kneeling there beside her little desk, ready for work, orphaned, and miserable. Did Harriet have a premonition yesterday that she was about to slip away? Did that explain those frank words in the park beside the creek?

Thomas was blowing his nose and clearing his throat. "I'll see you soon."

She sat back against the side of the bed, feeling the braided rug on the floor against her bottom. "I'll be here when you get here."

# Eighty-Seven

———

**B**ruce and Betsy were with Ethan when Christine got there. And Reverend Kellerman. Ethan took her in his arms and they embraced in a long sob of mutual condolence. "We lost her, Christine," Ethan managed to say.

"I can't believe it."

Ethan was amazingly composed. "Like we were saying recently, it's the parting that hurts so. We're living it now."

She gave him another hug. "Tell me what I can do."

By the time Thomas arrived after lunch, Ethan had gone to bed and was having a long nap. Christine burst into tears when Thomas came through the door. Romance seemed far away. All she could feel was the loss of Harriet. Standing there in her kitchen with the dishes, the photos, the little reminders — a spirit bigger than life, now silenced.

They sat on the porch without talking. Just looking at nothing. An hour passed. What was there to say? It was like the sky had disappeared and all growing things had dried up. Light extinguished. Harriet gone. Oh, God.

Ethan showed up after his nap with a paper in hand, Brownie sniffing, sniffing.

"What's that, Grandpa?"

"Harriet's plan for our funerals."

"Really?"

"Yeah, she started on it when I turned sixty. Why let others plan our funerals? she said. And every so often she would haul out this paper and make a change."

Thomas took the sheet from Ethan, studied it, and then handed it over to Christine, sitting nearby on one of the rockers. "She chose the hymns, the way it looks. And the scriptures."

Ethan chuckled. "'Why should we let other people mess up our funerals with the wrong selections, when we know what would be best?' she'd say." His voice broke. "My gal's up there in heaven right now, chuckling about the whole thing."

Thomas was back to studying the paper with Harriet's outline and notes. "It says 'Madrigal' here. What does that mean?"

Ethan nodded. "Yeah, Harriet always said that was her dream."

"What was?"

"She thought her ideal funeral would include her favorite hymns and one or two of her favorites from our madrigal group." He smiled. "That's my Harriet. She was one of the founders, you know, assuming that's not too pretentious a word." A happy grin spread across his features, not unlike the delighted smile that had often lighted his face as he watched the love of his life walk in from her garden.

"You were a founder, too, right?" she asked.

"Well, I guess so, along with Arlene and John Jr. The four of us sang as a quartet years ago. And then Harriet and I heard a madrigal group — in Williamsburg, Virginia, or someplace — and we both thought it would be fun to try."

Thomas looked at Christine with concern in his face. "Not sure I'm up to leading our group at my own grandma's funeral."

Ethan came to sit beside him. "It's your decision, of course, Thomas. I'm not saying it's easy. But Christine will be there to support you, right?"

Christine realized that a certain giddiness was mingled in the shock that Ethan was experiencing. He had expected to go first, and, now that Harriet had, he was already looking forward to joining her on the other side. The sorrow for him would be shorter than for Christine because Ethan was counting on a reunion with his beloved Harriet. Soon. Not morbid, really. Finespun happiness through tears, perhaps. Whereas Christine had a whole life ahead of her to mourn the loss of her surrogate mother.

Toward evening she and Thomas took a walk down to Whisper Run, going the back way below the west field. She hadn't been back there since the surreptitious trek to meet Arlene and Becca, worried about a barn fire. Thomas seemed to be catching his second wind, though he would pause mid-sentence from time to time and wipe his eyes. So many memories of an extraordinary grandmother.

"Something I've been thinking about," she said.

Thomas stopped, blew his nose, and looked at her. "Tell me."

"It's probably crazy. But Harriet loved quilts and her quilters group so much—shouldn't we find a way to include that in the service?"

"Quilts?"

"We have music for the ears, and Wanda's coordinating a special meal for us to taste after the funeral. But why not have something visual? Could we track down some of the quilts that Harriet made over the years and include them somehow?"

"Let's suggest it to Grandpa. Good idea."

# Eighty–Eight

—

**S**he was awake before dawn, lost in a fog of half-sleep, dreams, and grief. Her cheek was wet when she touched it. Had she been crying aloud in her sleep like her mother used to?

She turned on a light and sat up in bed. What day was it? Oh yes, *that* day. The day to say goodbye. She sat there staring at the stack of boxes in the corner, all prepared for their move weeks ago, still mostly empty. Maybe this house wouldn't be bulldozed after all, though she'd heard that Betsy planned to make a second run at getting her plans approved.

There was a light tap on her door. After a moment, Mama pushed open the door and stood staring at her with sympathetic eyes. "Can't sleep?"

Christine quickly wiped her eyes and sniffed. "I guess not. You?"

Mama came and sat beside her. "I know Harriet was so very special to you, honey. But she was like a mother to me, too. My parents kicked me out and Harriet saved me." Mama was wiping her eyes now. "I don't think I could have survived with a baby without Harriet. She was such a good person."

They sat there, huddled in silence and the light of early dawn. Then Mama slipped her arm around her only daughter, pulling their bodies close together. Christine hugged Mama in an embrace more mutual than usual. They were orphans together now.

# Eighty–Nine

———

**S**t. Mark's was packed. The sanctuary was full to overflowing, and Thomas said ushers were setting up extra chairs in the church hall to accommodate the crowd.

Ethan had insisted that Thomas and Christine sit with him on the front bench. "It's not a day for Betsy to merit the front pew," he whispered. Christine obliged but wondered what criticism she may invite by doing so.

Ethan seemed almost upbeat. "Let's give my gal a proper celebration," he said to Thomas and her. "Grief can come later. Let's give Harriet a send-off worthy of the wonderful life she lived."

Sharon came early to find Christine. They hugged. "I'm better now," she said, and she did look more like herself again. "I'm back at work. You can take off as much time as you wish. I know losing Harriet is a major blow."

In observing the crowd from a side view before they went in with the family procession, Christine noticed a lot of the quilters group, Farm Women folks, local politicians and Township officials, relatives, neighbors, and so many persons she'd never seen before. "The largest funeral in years," the funeral director said to no one in particular. Harriet and Ethan were beloved, a sort of local royalty, cherished for their interesting lives, their impeccable integrity, and the innumerable good deeds they had done for countless others.

The choir rose to the occasion, singing beyond themselves, missing their most senior member. *In heavenly love abiding.* Zach and Adam were helping again, as was Emily. Bless them. Reverend Kellerman's voice filled the church with a joy and assurance about lives well lived — and selflessly. Then came their madrigal group. She squeezed Thomas' hand before they rose to sing, hoping both of them would have the strength to get through. And they did. Both Arlene and John Jr. were fighting tears, but the ancient chords swept over the crowd like an intricately complex comfort, Ethan beaming the whole time.

Then Reverend Kellerman made an announcement. "Before the service draws to a close," he said, "we're going to be treated, at the request of the family, to a 'visual feast,' celebrating the life of Harriet Turner. As most of you know, Mrs. Turner was an avid quilter. Family members have selected seven quilts which Harriet made or helped to make over the years, all gifts to family and friends. They will be held up now for us to enjoy in a moment of silence."

Christine hadn't been sure how well the idea would actually pan out when she suggested it. But the crowd grew hushed as members of her quilting group held up the seven gorgeous pieces of handiwork, stretched taut, side by side like a seamless wall of lovely artistry. Across the entire front, the width of the sanctuary, a silent display, floating in front of the massive crowd, no motion, no words, like a testament to contrast and beauty, with Mama's Bargello in the middle. It created an energy in that place that Harriet would have loved. She reached up to wipe a tear and saw both Thomas and Ethan do the same. It was a beautiful goodbye. But final, nonetheless. Gone forever.

As they stood for the final hymn, Christine felt a tap on her shoulder. It was Betsy, standing in the row behind her. "That was really stunning, Christine," Betsy said in a low voice. "Thanks for making that happen."

# Ninety

———

Long after the burial service, complete with brass band, and the tasty meal served by Wanda and her helpers, Christine and Thomas were back on the little porch outside Harriet's kitchen, Ethan safely in bed for his afternoon rest. The humidity had lifted, and the clear air soothed the two of them. She wondered if they would both fall asleep, too, weary from several days of intense events and emotions.

"Christine, how would you like to get out of here?"

She looked at Thomas, waiting for him to say more.

"How long would it take you to pack a few overnight things? We could just drive wherever you wish."

She was surprised. "Just go?"

"Yeah, why not? I cleared it with Grandpa. He'll be fine."

She sensed her body smiling all over as she stood up. "I'll be back in twenty minutes."

And even before she reached her car to run home and pack her stuff, she could feel the page turning.

# About the Author

---

Merle Good's books have sold nearly a million copies. His Op-Ed essays have appeared in *The New York Times*, *Washington Post*, and *Los Angeles Times*. His play, *The Preacher and the Shrink*, opened Off-Broadway in New York in 2013. Academy-Award-winning actress Geraldine Page starred in the movie Good helped to produce, titled *Hazel's People*, which was based on Good's first novel, *Happy as the Grass Was Green*.

In addition to his continued work in book publishing, Good is at work on two new plays and a new novel.

Good has been married to *New York Times* bestselling author, Phyllis Good, for more than 52 years. They live in Lancaster, PA, and have two adult daughters, a son-in-law, and two grandsons.